The Trip

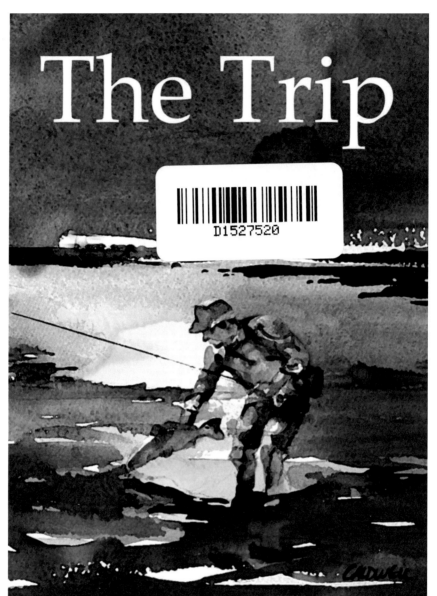

Caldwell

We never dream what is;
we dream what was,
what might have been,
what could be.

This is for old friends,
new friends,
and friends I haven't met

The Trip

Seven outdoorsmen journey to the hunting of South Texas and the fabled beaches of Mexico.

Six return.

Ben Kocian

Illustrations for chapter heads include art by Ben Kocian, Herb Booth, Al Barnes and Sam Caldwell.

The Trip: **Author John Graves:** "At long last (and with further apologies) I reached a lull in my erratic activities that let me read *The Trip.* I liked it, especially its subject matter and tone... the art has a hell of a lot of emotional content."

Texas Sporting Journal commissioned two excerpts from The Trip: **One Helluva Buck** *and* **El Tigre.** *Both won First Place Outdoor Feature awards from the Texas Outdoor Writer's Association (TOWA).*

Other work by Sam Caldwell

Not That Serious Collected: Twenty years of award-winning stories by Sam Caldwell, paired with illustrations by Ben Kocian.

John Graves: "Tough, funny stories and illustrations...hard-edged, as most real humor is. Ben Kocian's fine action paintings catch the mood of Caldwell's tales and anecdotes perfectly, and furthermore, constitute high comedy all by themselves. It is a delight to see these columns brought together in book form."

Artist Jack Cowan: "Thanks, Sam and Ben, for so much fun...for making us roll in the sand, doubled up with belly laughs."

Author-fisherman Lefty Kreh: "There's not enough humor and fun in outdoor writing. This book is a successful attempt to just amuse and pleasure you. Sit down, open it and start reading—your day will seem brighter."

Herb Booth

Change of Tides: A Historical Narrative of the Coastal Conservation Association By Sam Caldwell and Fred Carr. Named **"Best Outdoor Book of 2000"** *by the Texas Outdoor Writers Association (TOWA).*

Perry R. Bass: "Your book is great...Thanks to you, we have gone down in history as people who put the resource in the forefront of any personal desires."

Al Barnes

Sam Caldwell was named Texas State Artist for 2004 and Ducks Unlimited State Artist for 2015. The Dallas CCA named him Conservationist of the Year for 2015. Caldwell was elected to the Perry R. Bass Wall of Fame in 2016. His paintings are in collections across America and Great Britain.

A 40-year member of the Coastal Conservation Association, Caldwell is Editor of CCA's Texas Currents Newsletter. Sam and wife Vizi live in Kingwood, Texas.

"As you go through Matamoras or anywhere in Mexico, you should remember that you are guests in a fine country and that Mexicans are some of the best people on earth, if you don't rub'em the wrong way. But, being Texans, you'll probably forget that.

*Vaya con Dios and Buena Suerte. I've got a feeling this group is gonna need a little help from Dios, and a lot of Suerte before you get back to Houston. "–***Rancher Jack Voss**

*Fishing is not the most important thing in life. It's more serious than that. –**Anon***

Hill Country Stream   Sam Caldwell

One morning

His mother is crying.

Momma?

Go on back to sleep, Lee. She is huddled in the front seat of the car. He works out of the covers in the back seat, leans over and hugs her. She smiles at him, then wipes tears from her cheeks with the backs of her hands and laughs at herself in that way she has. I was just crying at the sunrise how pretty it is this morning.

He touches one of her tears and tastes it. The teardrop is salty like his, but smells like perfume, and her.

His dog is not here, and neither is his daddy. Lee knuckles the sandman's gravel from his eyes. Where's Will T?

Honey, don't rub your eyes. Your daddy is still out looking for that old dog.

You said Lefty would be back this morning.

I was wishing, honey.

Is Daddy coming back to us?

You'll have to be a big boy for me, Lee. We're going to wait here and think really good things, and they'll come true. She pushes the seat forward, so he can clamber out. While it's cool, we'll make a trip down to the creek and take our bath and pick some flowers.

What if Lefty comes back to the car, or Daddy?

That old dog can trail us down to the water, and Will T will honk the car horn.

The horn won't make any noise because the battery's dead.

His mother turns away from him. Her fingers tremble at her chin, and he feels the hurt coming back to her. Lee doesn't want her tears to start again.

I'll pick you some pretty flowers and catch you some perch bait!

Just blue bells, Lee, and watch out for those bad old goat-head stickers. She takes his hand and lets him lead her down the trail to the coolness of the willow-shaded stream. She is laughing now and is prettier than anybody else's mother in the whole world. We need some big old grasshoppers, Lee, if we want to have some big old catfish for supper.

He goes along a secret path to a meadow and kicks at the high grass until a big, gray hopper clacks away, then he runs and pounces. He wraps the hopper in a wad of grass and stuffs it in his pocket. A small grasshopper joins its cousin. As he heads for the tree-shaded side of the meadow, another gets away, but that's all right. Lee is king of the meadow, owner of all the hoppers. Bait for catfish and bream, supper tonight for Momma and Daddy and Lefty, too.

If Will T comes back. And brings Lee's dog. Maybe Will T has gone on someplace else, a place where he could just ride broncs in the rodeo and would only need to find enough money to buy his own supper, and not have Lee and Linna to worry about. And Lefty to worry about, either. A bad dog that runs off every chance the old son of a bitch gets, chasing after smells, jumping out of the car and running across the highway when they stop the car because Lee has to pee and cars almost run over Lefty and nearly run into their car, like the time outside Haskell when Momma screamed, and Will T yelled and cursed and almost got run over himself and kicked Lefty.

Will T wouldn't go off and leave Lee and Linna. Will T will be along, and he'll have Lefty with him. Then, Momma will say the world is just fine again, and it will be.

With the rising sun in front and his shadow trailing behind, the hoppers can't see Lee. He charges into an area of low grass after an especially big hopper until too late to change direction, he is in the midst of grass burs that reach between his sandal straps and grab at his toes and ankles. There are good hoppers all around him, but he has to retreat from the grass burr region and remove the stickers. The burrs try to stick into his fingers, but Will T showed him the secret of removing them. A blade of grass around, pull quickly. And, big boys don't cry.

Away from the grass burr region, Lee catches grasshoppers until the sun is well up and the insects are too energetic for a swift boy. He has a pocketful of hoppers, little green and gray ones, and great big camouflaged hoppers that tickle his palm and even pinch a bit, enough of a hurt that a little kid would drop them. He takes them back to his mother. Linna wraps them in her scarf, except for one of the big ones. That one gets put on a hook, and Lee laughs at the funny face she uses while impaling the hopper.

Through with bait-gathering duties, Lee wades across the shallows and up a high bank to his flower place. There are lots of yellow flowers with little black centers, like eyes looking at him, and on the gravel slopes, tall Indian Paint brushes and beautiful little blood-red blossoms. Apache Tears, his mother calls them. But she likes blue flowers, especially the tiny ones that grow low and scattered, and smell so nice when you get a fistful. Lee picks flowers, some big ones and some small ones, but all of the blue kind, a double armful and starts back across the stream, ankle deep at the most where you walk on gravel jewels just beneath the water. As he squats in the middle of the stream to look more closely at the little pebbles, his bottom gets wet, and he laughs out loud. He gets an echo of his own laughter from the curve of the river, a high bank down the way, the sound just a brief peal like maybe someone mocking him.

The clear water swirls around his sandals and tumbles little jewels, distorts them into flashing greens and reds and blues. A larger blue jewel is moved by the current. It settles on top of his foot, then rolls off and away but he grabs at it and loses some of the flowers so that they float away downstream, bright against the water, but he has the blue gem. The color of his mother's eyes. It is almost round, and has flecks of green and red. As he watches, it dries and becomes a duller blue, then a brownish-gray. He licks the stone, and for a moment, it is blue, but fades. Lee puts it back in the stream and watches as it rolls away in the current, a blue jewel again.

Lee and Linna sit on the edge of a high grassy bank in the shade of willows that arch over the stream. They watch a little stick bobber, hoping for a really big spotted catfish or a bass, waiting for Will T's magic trick to work.

Going to change this ol' bug into a fish, Lee, his mother says in a deep voice like his daddy. They both giggle, and since Will T is not there to see and be jealous, hug one another. After a little while, because Lee and his mother are holding their mouths just right, the magic trick works. The bobber jerks once, twice, then disappears. Linna swings a fish up from the dark water, a shining piece of jewelry that scatters water diamonds all around the pool.

Oh, look, a fine bluegill, she cries. The fish bounces and flips on the sloping bank, free of the hook. It might have escaped, but Lee flops down on top of it. The sharp fins stick his belly and hands as boy and fish slide down the bank into the creek.

Lee! But the water is only waist deep. He has a grip with both hands on the fish and raises it above his head. His mother laughs until tears are again in her eyes.

They watch the bobber for a long time, and after it goes under twice more with no fish on the hook, they consider moving to the deep place farther up the creek.

No, his mother says. Will T might come back and miss us. They move a short distance downstream to a shallow, sunny place in the creek. Linna knots her skirt above her knees and has Lee sit on the edge of the deeper run. She soaps Lee's hair and starts the song that always makes Lee laugh because of the silly part about a chicken head.

I went down to Old Joe Clark's
Found him sick in bed she sings, imitating Will T's voice.
Ran my hand down old Joe's throat,
And pulled out a chicken head.

Lee shivers while she scrubs his scalp in rhythm to the song, soapsuds floating down the creek like snow. She's into the chorus, rubbing his head to match the words.

All around… Old Joe's house…
All around I say…
All around Old Joe Clark's…
Until the break of day--

Will T yells from the car. Linna, Lee?

They scramble back up the trail, a laughing boy and a laughing, crying young woman, her skirt caught up in her hands. Will T meets them halfway down the trail, a limping giant with his rifle in one hand and a brown paper sack in the other. They hug him until he stumbles and sits down in the trail. He smells bad, but they hug him some more.

The sack is full of good-smelling bread, ham slices and a bottle of warm milk. They go back to the creek and eat everything. Will T makes Lee drink as much of the milk as he can because he says it won't be good tomorrow.

Will T is dirty and all scratched up. Linna makes him take off his shirt and jeans and sit down in the shallows with Lee so she can wash them together.

Just like washing Lefty, Lee says. Will T raises him out of the creek, way up high, laughing.

His mother says, Your leg.

Aw, hell, Linna. It'll be okay.

Will, it's worse. We've got to forget that dog and get away from here.

Will T sits on the edge of the bank in a way that shows he's hurting, then eases himself down into the water. That old dog is just off courting, he says, and I know where, now. There's a pack of coyotes running a couple of miles on the other side of the rodeo grounds.

Coyotes, Daddy?

Sure, coyotes, Lee. He'll have to kick hell out of a bunch of boy coyotes to get the girl, and keep 'em fought off while he, uh, gives her some little red puppies.

Linna's voice is angry. We've been car camped for four days now, nearly broke, and that damn dog is off running with coyotes. She puts her hands over Lee's ears and hugs him to make up for her bad word. We've got to get Lee into school this fall.

They are quiet for a little while, listening to the water and the birds up on the hill, and the locusts buzzing in the willow trees. Cicadas, really, not locusts. They come out of the ground and swarm every 17 years. You can dig the white grubs out of soft ground for perch bait, and catfish especially like the grubs.

Will, there are hospitals in Houston that can fix your leg.

Will T looks at his hands under the creek water, then brings water to his face. We don't take charity from anyone. This food…saw an old rancher stringing barbed wire around a calf enclosure. He squinches his eyes, and makes Linna and Lee see the man, kind of hunched and mean and stingy. I walked up and just pitched in.

Cain't pay for no help.

Didn't ask for money. Wouldn't turn down a square meal.

You're the man out lookin' for a dog, the rancher said. Come on.

Goddamn whoever invented bob wire, anyway. We strung that rusty stuff with our bare hands and one pair of pliers. An old geezer and a cripple, sweating and swapping hard luck stories.

You're not a cripple, Daddy.

Gettin' there fast, boy. Anyway, we beat the sun down with the end of the job, and the old man wished me luck, and stuffed a sack full of food, and gave me a quart of milk, too. Said, 'I'd drive you up the road, but that ol' truck ain't got no runnin' lights.

Told him, No problem. I'll fire my rifle and that red dog will come running. He groans, and it's not part of the story.

Wish the old fart had offered some whiskey. He rubs his leg. I hid the food at the rodeo grounds and uncovered my rifle, then hunted coyotes and a dog until the moon went down. Will T gets up and makes them see him hunting, acting out the search as he tells the story. Early on, the pack came up a draw, and there was a big one running at the front of the group. Yelled, you—Lefty dog! Scared hell out of the pack, and they did flips getting back into that draw. One came back to look, though. I found him in the sights and pulled the trigger.

Linna puts her hands to her cheeks. Oh, Will.

Was it Lefty? Lee yells.

Yep. But I didn't cock the hammer, Lee. Will T rubs his bad leg. Tried to run after those coyotes and fell into the draw. Thought I broke the bad leg all over again. Took a while to find the gun and get back out. Didn't fire the rifle until first light, then just to potshoot a couple of rabbits. No bullets to waste, hoping a damn dog—

Oh, Will... Lee repeats everything you say.

Linna sends Lee back to the car for the comforter and some sheets and makes Will T lie down under the trees and rest. While he sleeps, they fish. Before sundown, they fill a pillowcase with nine bream, some punkinseed perch and one big catfish, the kind with spots.

At suppertime, Lee can see that his father's leg is worse. Will T limps around making a campfire by the car, then goes down the slope to take care of the rabbits so Lee can't watch. He is gone a long time, and finally calls up to Linna and Lee to help him back to the car.

It is dark in the valley of the creek, and they have to grope their way along the stream to the shallow area where Will T has cleaned the rabbits. He is sitting with his legs in the water. Just need some balance, Will T says. One leg won't get it. Linna gets under his arm on the bad side, and Lee carries the rabbits and pushes from behind, being very careful not to push on the bad leg. As they move up the trail, Will T sings something Lee had not heard before. Show me the way to go home, I'm tired and I want to go to bed… Linna laughs so hard they all have to stop and rest. Will T continues, laying on his back, an arm over his eyes. I had a little drink about an hour ago, and it went straight to my head. Okay Quinlans, it's up and at 'em. He lurches to his feet and they continue up the trail but have to stop again before they get to the top of the bank.

Linna puts the last of their bacon in the big skillet, and one rabbit and the catfish. The catfish tail hangs outside in the fire and burns and stinks. It is chilly again, but the car is behind them like a big castle, warm from the day, and they are wrapped together in the comforter.

Wonder what the poor folks are doing, Will T says.

Will, we've got to leave that old dog.

Will T nods.

They're going away without Lefty. Can we come back for my dog?

No, says Will T. Lefty's gone, son.

Back Bay Reds   Sam Caldwell

I

We all dream.

He leads a file of men down a winding path. Are they all there? He can't be certain because the path curves up and over a hillside. Form the men up and count them? No. That could get them all killed at one time.

Walking backward, he writes their names down in his mind and checks his rifle. He opens the bolt and ejects a rusty nail. More nails are in his pockets, dribbling rusty ooze through the white sheet of his uniform. At the back of the line of men, John Morgan yells and points. Watch it, Lieutenant—

He turns to face the threat, and sees a man aiming a pistol at him. The force of the pistol feels like a spotlight searching various parts of his body. The impact spot moves from his neck to his forehead, down his left side, then back to the middle of his chest. The man screams incomprehensible words. Quinlan is still holding his rifle and has a pistol in his belt.

Go for his guns, or bow to theirs? The man's eye is steady above the black hole of his pistol muzzle and his trigger finger tightens, tightens— Quinlan drops the rifle. But he stands tall and proud, arms crossed on his chest. He will surrender the pistol in the same gallant manner as General Robert E. Lee surrendered his sword to General Grant at Appomattox. Grant then graciously returned the sword. All of Lee's men were allowed to keep their weapons, or was it their horses, since they would need them to get back to their southern homes alive.

Quinlan pulls the pistol from his belt with a flourish. The man screams and thrusts his pistol forward, jars Quinlan back, shoots him in the middle of the chest.

Above Quinlan, a ceiling fan ticks around. He's awake, ears ringing from the pistol shot. He jerks his tee shirt up and cranes his neck to look at the spot where the bastard shot him, expecting to find a bloody hole oozing red froth from his lungs. There is no hole, no blood.

He pulls the covers onto the bed from the floor, puts both pillows over his head, curls into the fetal position and wills himself back into the dream. Half-awake at first, he flings himself away so that the man's pistol shot misses, then he blasts away unmercifully, killing dozens of the men. But soon he is in their power again. Then he is sitting beside the trail, listening as Dutch Brenner talks to him about life and death.

Quinlan wakes slowly to the same old aching shoulder and a brand-new hangover. He swings lazy legs off the bed, considers running his standard mile. The last time he made a mile, was it two weeks? And it was maybe half running, half walking.

The weather. Maybe there is a mist again, like yesterday, and it would cause pneumonia if he sets forth. Quinlan rolls across the bed, wrestling with sheets and a blanket until he can raise the window shade and glance outside. No hint of daylight. No wind, not even a breeze, or else the bushes would be moving.

The time. The clock hasn't worked since he threw it against the wall a month ago. What was it that seemed important to remember?

Squinting his eyes tight, he pushes the covers into the middle of the bed and stands at attention beside his bed. Hit the deck, you pitiful piece of flab. Give me jumping jacks, fifteen good reps. One, two, three, four — the second repetition is so clumsy that he falls backward across the bed. He pulls a pillow over his face and tries to sleep, but his mind is working now. He finds the phone beneath one of the covers and calls John Morgan.

At Morgan's end, the phone is picked up, then slammed down.

Quinlan dials again. The phone rings a long time before Morgan answers.

What?

The trip —

Not a chance, Lee.

The phone hums again. Must be a little early in the morning for Morgan. Get up and run you lazy puppy.

Five minutes later, Quinlan jogs in place on the west sidewalk of Montrose Avenue. No point in doing all those yuppie stretches and warm-ups, just uses up valuable energy. A silver-haired man runs past Quinlan. Scrawny, bandy legs, gray sweatshirt with an image of the Rice Owl on the back, above the large number 14. Quinlan runs behind the man for a dozen steps but needs to pick up his pace. Quinlan passes the scrawny man clumsily, says, Sorry, but brushes Number 14's elbow. The contact is resented, evidenced by a curt Hey!

Hook 'em horns, Quinlan says as he sprints ahead. Quinlan slows his pace as he approaches the Museum of Fine Art, mindful of the acorns that lurk on the sidewalk like ball bearings. He jogs around the museum to Main Street where the bronze man with the world on his back crouches, pondering the pigeon shit on his shoulders? — then gains speed. He flushes mourning dove, pigeons and grackles from beneath the oaks. After an initial pain in the side, hangover diminishes and health kicks in.

2

She pushes against a huge live oak tree, stretching hamstrings and calf muscles, stressing toes, insteps, tendons. No point in starting cold and tight, and having to limp back to the car. It is still dark and hard to see the tree roots and cracked sidewalks that can be a runner's problem, but the sun will soon begin to filter through the branches, making it a pleasant challenge to run along Main Street. She checks her watch and begins her run. If she can make the loop around Rice Institute in twenty minutes, she will have time for breakfast before she gets Mr. Weiss ready for an early meeting at the courthouse.

Quinlan passes Mecom Fountain at the base of Main Street, then to his left, can just make out the statue of General Sam Houston on his horse, pointing the way to San Jacinto and freedom. He feels pretty good. No chest ache, thighs cooperating with ankles, shoulders, belly. He cruises along the boulevard, nearing Rice University. The sun begins a push through tangled oaks in Hermann Park, and the running traffic picks up. Lazy slugabeds, not tough athletes like Quinlan. Swift footsteps sound behind him and the silver-haired man runs past, glares at Quinlan as he passes, mutters something like I'll show a young fart, let's see you keep up with a real athlete. Number 14 sprints ahead.

Oh, yeah? Give the old son of a bitch a little room, push him for a minute, then blast past. Quinlan picks up his pace, nears the heels of the old fart, starts around but silver-haired Number 14 veers left just enough and Quinlan stumbles, but cuts right and around and picks up speed. What comes out of a Chinaman's butt? Quinlan gasps as he moves ahead of the silver-haired man. Rice, rice, rice.

Asshole, he hears, but Quinlan grins and runs on, laughing to himself, a superb young athlete showing his heels to an envious old man.

Thirty yards along, Quinlan feels the knife thrust of a shin splint begin just above his right ankle. Got to run through the pain. But Quinlan slows, limps, hopes the pain will recede. The silver-haired man runs past, an elbow brushing Quinlan's waist, yells, thirteen to zero! weaves past runners ahead, is out of sight, he's probably not looking anyway and Quinlan eases back to a fast walk. Then to a slow walk.

S'cuse me, sir. A woman coming up behind him veers off the sidewalk onto the uneven ground to get around Quinlan, stumbles on a root, lurches, makes a nice recovery, glances back, grins.

S'okay, she yells. Red hair, a ponytail flipping in rhythm with her steps as she runs on. Thin legs. Nice buns.

Quinlan picks up his pace, a jog becomes a run. Is this a second wind? He manages to stay near the redhead, even gains a bit, can admire her running form as they turn the corner of Main Street to University Boulevard.

Ahead, Quinlan sees the silver-haired man, Rice Owls Number 14 walking, one hand on a hip. The redhead slows, goes around the man in a polite move and continues on. Quinlan grits his teeth and speeds up, passes the man in a whirl of leaves. By God, he'll finish the run at this pace or die trying.

He is close on the heels of the redhead when the ribcage pain starts. Famous Author Felled by Heart Attack While Jogging. Or maybe, Unidentified Man In Coma. Quinlan is doubled over, gasping, when the silver-haired man jostles past him.

Asshole, the man says.

Great vocabulary, Quinlan wheezes and then continues on, head raised, arms clasping his lower back, thinking that he has better things to do than shuffle along in pain while contemptuous people run past. Best to just shut the run down, call John Morgan, fix breakfast, change Morgan's mind about the trip. Quinlan starts limping, a quitter who has met his limit. Then, favoring the aching side and knife-like shin splint, limping, groaning, he finishes the run. He does not see the redhead or Number 14 again.

Back at his apartment, Quinlan's side and legs ache while his stomach growls. He limps to the refrigerator and finds only some moldy cheese, a jar of furry grape jelly and a green lump that once was half a head of lettuce. Breakfast time at Morgan's. Won't have to listen to an argument between Brenda and John. No more Brenda. Before he can limp to the shower, the phone rings.

It's Brenda. What are you doing?

Walking around naked.

Can you come by? I mean, in clothes.

Actually, I'm headed that way. Got some breakfast stuff?

No. I'm packing up to leave.

Uh, right. Need some help?

Only with John Morgan.

I see. Be there in ten minutes, bye.

3

Morgan sulks on the den couch, dark-faced, drinking from a tea glass as Brenda shuffles back and forth carrying stuff to her Volvo station wagon.

You look like crap, Lee, Morgan says. Get you a morning beer.

Nah. I'll give Brenda a hand.

She'll take your arm.

Brenda moves past, straining with a large box. Go to hell, John Morgan.

A busty, sexy woman. Snub-nosed, stocky like her father. Elmo, a tough old son of a bitch.

Bit early for the beer, Quinlan says, but I'll take a handful of aspirin. Refill on the iced tea? Morgan doesn't answer. As Quinlan starts for the kitchen, Brenda's father walks in the front door. Elmo has on golf shoes. The cleats make an unpleasant sound on the terrazzo entryway.

Brenda brushes past Elmo with an armload of clothes. You know how to ring a doorbell?

Elmo ignores Brenda and Quinlan, squinting at Morgan from the entry hall. How come you're still in my house?

My house, Brenda yells from the hall bathroom. You gave me this house as a wedding present, and you know it.

Elmo's cleats change tone as he leaves the terrazzo tile and hits the parquet floor of the living room. A big man gone to pudge, he is accustomed to getting his way in every matter, large or small. He goes out of his way to elbow past Quinlan. Elmo's cleats change tone as he leaves the terrazzo tile and hits the parquet floor of the living room. Morgan is up and across the room, jolts Elmo backward, then seizes his shirtfront and shakes him. He turns Elmo and hustles the dazed man outside.

Brenda follows, holding two ornate lamps from Italy, presents from a honeymoon trip paid for by Elmo.

She's enjoying this, Quinlan thinks. Like father, like daughter.

The older man is regaining his composure as Morgan gets him to the front porch. He steps on Morgan's foot. Morgan throws him against the brick wall. Elmo might have sagged to the concrete porch, but Morgan grabs him by the collar and seat of the pants and marches him to his Cadillac, slams him against the side of the car and opens the front door.

He keeps a pistol under the dash, Brenda yells from the front porch.

Morgan looks into Elmo's eyes from six inches away. Elmo. Listen to me. You listening?

Elmo tries to pull away from Morgan's grip, but Morgan pulls his face closer.

If you pull a gun on me, it will really piss me off. Morgan releases Elmo to the front seat of the car and slams the door.

Elmo burns tire rubber driving away but doesn't pull a gun on Morgan.

Quinlan helps Brenda carry boxes to the station wagon. When the wagon is filled, she gives him a hug, then kisses him flush on the mouth, with a little tongue involved.

I hope the son of a bitch is watching, she says.

I hope he's not.

Brenda burns tire rubber as she leaves the driveway. As Quinlan starts back to the house, he waves, but doesn't see Morgan looking through any of the windows. Morgan is on the den couch, wrapping a towel around his Elmo-cleated foot. The towel is bloody, but Morgan is smiling.

Been wanting to straighten out that old fart for three years.

Maybe I will take that beer, Quinlan says. Want a refill on the Canadian Club?

CC's all gone. Black Jack will do.

Quinlan returns with a beer for himself, a tea glass filled with ice and a bottle of Black Label Jack Daniels. Pour your own. We've got to get the trip organized.

Can't go. Morgan removes the towel. He and Quinlan look at the foot. Four blue indentations ooze blood. Hell, I've had worse on my eyeball, and never left the game. Morgan gets up and starts for the patio door. Make yourself at home while I check on the stock.

After a sip of beer, Quinlan frowns. His stomach wants biscuits and eggs. He goes to the kitchen and locates pots and breakfast material. He dumps two cups of flour in a bowl, but finds no buttermilk or shortening, so he throws in a cup of mayonnaise and a little of the beer. He wads some foil in the bottom of a stainless pot and starts it heating on Morgan's range while he kneads the dough. He plops the ball on top of the foil, then covers it with a layer of foil. He has to search through cabinets for the top, finds it over the refrigerator. The top goes on. Medium heat for twelve minutes. Good practice for Pan Campos on a beach campfire. Biscuits on track, he chugs the remainder of the beer and joins Morgan in the backyard with Morgan's stock. The stock consists of a gray-nosed retriever and a brindle tomcat.

How's my dog? Quinlan asks.

My dog.

Okay. How's your dog?

Old summidge is about worthless. Needs a cortisone shot just to get his butt off the porch. Had to carry him out of the duck spread last season.

If he's a problem, I'll take him back.

Right.

Take him on a hole hunt.

A hole hunt.

Take an old dog, a shotgun and a shovel. Come back with the shotgun and shovel.

Sure you will.

They throw a Frisbee for Sport until the dog finds the right spot in a neighbor's yard. As the dog hunkers, Quinlan says, Third Pass. The primo place for reds and trout in the surf. Snook and tarpon stacked up, hungry

Bullshit. We couldn't get across El Tigre three years ago.

I have a secret weapon this time. And we're gonna do some bird hunting, as well. We pause in South Texas. Jack Voss's place for mourning dove, then on to Matamoras. Margaritas, señoritas, quien sabe?

What are you going to do for gas?

Fill up here. Stop at Brenner's Uncle's place in Freer. That should get us across the border, where there's plenty of Pemex. Then, to the Mexican surf

They auction this house next Wednesday.

You plan to bid on it?

No. The lawyers get everything but my left testicle.

Get your stuff together by this Thursday, make your will, whatever.

Aw, hell, Lee. I can't afford to take off and look after a bunch of drunks. Morgan is silent for a minute then, Who's going?

You are the anal-retentive leader. The trip lawyer is Bill Weiss. Our bird watcher is genteel Dutch Brenner —

Genteel. The only man in Texas I'm afraid of. Don't tell him I said that.

Hey, Dutch is a poet at heart. Beneath that tough exterior is —

A really mean summidge. Who else is on your trip?

Our trip. There's the trip photographer, Crazy Fred Carmichael —

Photographer... he was a spook in Nam, and he's still a spook, unless the CIA has kicked him out.

Quinlan shrugs. Carmichael speaks fluent Mexican. In fact, he's my secret weapon. He says he can get us across El Tigre, no problem. The trip writer is me, and the trip artist works for Dutch Brenner, a kid whose name escapes me right now. And Luck Travis.

Luck is going?

Quinlan grins. Morgan is going on the trip. Actually, Luck hasn't committed yet. But, he'll go.

The trip horny devil, Morgan says. Travis is like old Sport; if you can't eat it or screw it, piss on it.

Wrong. He's the trip lightning rod. If something bad is going to happen, it will happen to Luck Travis.

Cheerful thought, says Morgan. I've never been anywhere with you that something bad didn't happen.

I've never lost anyone— Quinlan feels a wince from Morgan. Didn't mean it that way, John. No one has ever shot at us here. Yet.

Brenner, Carmichael, Travis. And some kid?

A really great artist. Plus, my attorney, Bill Weiss, you and me. A magnificent seven.

Morgan's cat is now a part of the conversation, squalling and rubbing on Morgan's ankles.

Anyway, Quinlan continues, how long has it been since you've hunted South Texas? Jack Voss said your old man used to do a lot of work-overs on his wells.

Silence from Morgan.

You need to pay a business call on Voss. The cat is now working with affection and cat sounds on Quinlan's ankles. Bob, he's called, due to a stub tail. Bob knows that Quinlan feeds cats. Biscuits and eggs, two minutes. As Quinlan turns for the kitchen, he stumbles over the cat. The yowl and scurry of the cat startles Morgan and the dog, and Quinlan.

Clumsy son of a bitch, Quinlan says. The cat glares at him from the patio, eyes full of resentment. S'cuse me, Bob. I was talking about myself. He tries to cajole the cat into petting range, but it is no use.

Morgan coaxes the angry cat to him. Never mind that clumsy asshole, Bob, he says. I'll bring you a sack of fish guts from Third Pass, Mexico. What the hell, Quinlan. I can slip off for a few days.

Ten days.

Six days, max.

Okay, eight days. Meeting Thursday night, your office at 7 p.m. Leave at 8 a.m. Friday from your shop. I'll get Bill Weiss to call everyone. Quinlan starts for the kitchen.

Morgan calls after him. Hey.

Yeah?

Did you mess around with my wife?

No. Did you date my ex-wife?

Aw, hell, Quinlan. She wouldn't even stay in the same room with me.

Reason I asked. Is that a no?

Yeah. Would you lie to me, Quinlan?

Yeah.

Morgan turns away, shaking his head, but smiling. Get out of here before I kill you.

Not till those biscuits are gone.

4

Quinlan drives back to his apartment. Time to go to work. But first, get ready for the trip.

He sheds smelly clothes, showers, finds a reasonably fresh pair of shorts, but clean undershirts are in short supply. He fishes around in the wicker basket meant to collect and air out aromatic garments before they are consigned to the washateria. Several undershirts fail the sniff test. He dumps the basket on the floor, sorts and places the least offensive contestants on the bed.

He chooses a tee shirt and khakis for the day, then begins sorting all the clothes into piles of four. Socks, shorts, tee shirts, times four. Hell, after four days, everyone will smell equally bad. Or, we can get a total wash job before we leave Matamoras.

From the closet he brings two long-sleeved shirts, and—who knows about Texas weather in early autumn—the camo Goretex rain jacket that cost way too much money, even when he had money. A heavy sweater might be good. He finds his brother's wool skiing turtleneck sweater.

Scooter; he'd better remind his brother he is leaving. Below the sweater he finds a pair of boot-foot waders given to him by Scooter. Large. He throws them into the back of the closet. Large waders might fit Scooter, but they are too small for Quinlan. After two uncomfortable days on the water last winter, the nails of his big toes turned blue. He locates an old pair of desert boots and puts them on, sans socks. Floppy, comfortable fit, happy toes. To the assemblage of gear, he adds his running shoes and four pairs of thick socks.

From the pantry, he locates a battered coffee pot. The nested LL Bean cooking kit brings a fond smile. He puts the pot and cooking kit back. Won't need any small cooking gear. Travis will bring too much of everything.

Quinlan stumbles over piles of clothes into the little closet near the stairs. Rummaging in the darkness behind a golf club bag, he finds the Franchi shotgun, but nothing else. Shotgun shells, shooting vest, snake-proof boots, rods and reels—all are at John Morgan's. Sleeping bag, ground sheet, rollup comfort pad; he'll have to call Morgan and get him to bring all that stuff to the meeting place Friday.

He cradles the shotgun and relaxes on a pile of clothes. Rest break. Footsteps start up the stairway. Heavy, hurried. Someone who knows the combination to the front entryway. The landlord, demanding last month's rent? The gay neighbor down the hall, or the neighbor's drunk biker friend? At Quinlan's door, a familiar cadence of seven taps. Shave and a haircut, six bits.

Quinlan sighs, rises from the smelly, comfortable clothes and opens the door. Hello, Scooter.

His brother reaches in, grabs Quinlan by the neck of his undershirt and pulls him into the hallway. Let's go, stranger.

Ever try, 'pretty please?'
Josie's fixing Gnocchi for everyone. She sent me to get you.

Can't go, bro. Got to get packed for the trip, get a manuscript in the mail—

I said, Josie sent me to get you. You want to go like that, or put on some pants?

Give me a minute. As Quinlan puts on what might be the least aromatic tee shirt and least-wrinkled jeans, Scooter walks around the room, checking Quinlan's gear. He opens the shotgun, glances down the barrels. He says, My Franchi.

You're in the will for the gun. What about it?

There's a dirt-dauber nest in the modified barrel, and a spider colony in the full choke. Plus, it's filthy.

That's a protective coating of rust. There's a cleaning kit here somewhere, if it bothers you that much.

Nah, let's go. Little Lee keeps saying, 'Where's Uncle Lee?'

In the parking area, Quinlan starts for his Chevrolet Blazer, but Scooter stops him. Come on with me. That old wreck might not make it, and I'd be in trouble with Josie.

5

Quinlan walks into the melee that is always Scooter and Josie's home. Kids run back and forth but stop to mob Quinlan. Roy, the youngest of five boys, leaps on Quinlan from the couch and the entire swarm collapses on the floor for a loud, happy minute. Josie grabs boys by ears and legs, freeing Quinlan.

Best I've felt in weeks, he laughs.

Josie yells, Lee Boy? Your worthless uncle is here to see you.

Little Lee, the eldest boy peers from a doorway, seems wary of a stranger until Quinlan lowers his palm. Gimme five, Lee Boy.

The boy slaps the hand and grins as Quinlan grimaces in pain, fingers curled into a dead spider.

Josie is moving around the kitchen, dealing with pots on the stove and pans in the oven. Quinlan grabs her, lifts her off her feet, groans theatrically with the effort.

Hugging bandit. Stand and deliver.

Who are you? Josie says. You seem familiar.

Quinlan steals another hug. One for the road. Another hug. That's one for the ditch. When do we eat?

Josie looks past him, a meaningful glance into the dining room.

Ariella is at the dining room table. She is peeling potatoes, sleeves of someone's oversize plaid shirt rolled up to her elbows. Dowdy, the way she always dressed. Painfully beautiful.

After a time, Quinlan walks into the dining room, pulls a chair away from the table across from Ariella and sits down. He'll say something brilliant, make everything right somehow. Words won't form in his mind. He watches her peel a potato, then another.

He says, Scooter didn't tell me you'd be here. Brilliant line, Quinlan.

She doesn't answer.

He leans forward and takes a few potatoes from the pan and arranges them on the table, large potatoes in front, small potatoes behind. Fumbles for his pocketknife. No knife. He rises, says, Excuse me for a moment.

A shrug?

Quinlan goes into the kitchen, opens drawers until he finds a paring knife. Josie sees his face, hugs him and pushes him away toward the dining room.

He sits across from Ariella, chooses a large potato and begins peeling, finds his voice again. Will you ever talk to me again?

A definite shrug, worse than no response at all.

Men are like that, he says. We don't know how much someone means till we've done something stupid, and someone isn't there anymore.

Ariella looks away from the potato, maybe a glance at the window, but not at Quinlan. She says, Allan's coming.

Allan. Are we supposed to joke, or fistfight? Winner takes Ariella?

She doesn't answer, chooses another potato.

He leans across the table, tries to touch her cheek, but she flinches away.

Don't. She finishes peeling the potato, chooses another.

That's an answer.

Quinlan walks out of the house, going anywhere but where he wants to be. Here, with this woman who couldn't stand to let his attention stray from her, wore his shirts, splashed on his aftershave. Wouldn't let him concentrate on driving, once slapped him on the highway to get his undivided attention, to hell with oncoming traffic. This beautiful woman in someone's shirt has only three words for him. Allan's coming. Don't.

Before they were together, she told him, Allan's not coming, and hit him with a shoe when his attention wandered to another woman.

6

He is a bit drunk when he enters the Green Room, but hell, he'll keep his mouth shut and no one will notice, since it will be a drunken party soon enough. There'll be much champagne and grand hors d'oeuvres, maybe those great chicken livers wrapped in bacon, the English cheeses that smell so bad and taste so good, probably Sushi, and this being Texas, whitewing dove grilled with jalapeños tucked inside the breast cavity.

Men and women move around the room, talking, striking poses. Musicians, singers, stagehands, actors. There, Don Giovanni, beaming with happiness, heart not broken. Next to him, Romeo and Juliet, arguing. Near the champagne bar, a Dowager Empress and paying her court, Mephistopheles. Near Quinlan are a large Brunhilde and a small, very blonde Bavarian, her bosom threatening to burst forth from a laced bodice.

Diva Aida in one corner, Diva Mimi in the opposite corner.

Four large, black and silver bottles nest in a crystal bowl of ice, guarded by a tuxedoed tender. The Basso-profundo sings Champagne, champagne, champagne, but the champagne tender shakes his head. The crowd takes up the effort, joining in a chant for champagne, but no champagne is served. Quinlan's stomach growls, but no hors d'oeuvres are apparent.

Most of the men not in costume are in black tie. There are frilled cummerbunds, a few split-tailed jackets, shining stripes on tailored black pant legs. Quinlan fingers a gold button on his tweed jacket. The button dangles by a thread, could pop off if he uses it to close the jacket. He leaves the jacket open, remembers another problem and tucks the lining back into his right jacket cuff. Noise increases, people mill about waiting for champagne.

A girl.

Dark hair, simple black dress, low-heeled black pumps scuffed at the toes. She watches him from the champagne bar, projects Hello.

He mouths back, Hi. He moves toward her, she threads her way through the crowd and stops at his side.

Champagne, champagne, champagne, the crowd chants.

She tiptoes, speaks close to his ear. Hello.

He leans close to her ear. Nice party.

Shitty party.

He laughs and nods, takes her hand, is surprised by her firm grip. Guitar player?

Violin. You're perceptive.

Have to be. I'm a—

I know who you are, Lee. You look different from the photo in your book.

Thanks, uh...?

She smiles but doesn't offer a name.

You play for the symphony?

Principle Second Violin. I'll have to perform for the crowd. She looks around. If the conductor ever shows up and blesses the champagne.

First violin?

Too important to play for us. Probably working right now to get me fired.

Should I ask, why?

He's mediocre. I'm excellent. Here he is now.

A door opens at the far end of the room and the First Violinist enters, smiling, one finger in the air. A sweeping bow from the First Violinist and the Conductor enters, raises both hands, ready for the downbeat.

Silence from the crowd.

Champagne, the Conductor says. Corks pop and bounce from walls and ceiling, women shriek, men shout huzzas.

The dark-haired girl starts away from Quinlan, then turns and says, Don't leave.

Mephistopheles moves past Quinlan. He has four full glasses carried by the stems, winks at Quinlan. No champagne?

No beer?

Mephistopheles rolls his eyes, moves on. The dark-haired girl is back near the champagne bar on a small dais violin in hand. She turns, presents an image that is familiar. Hair up, elegant profile, black dress. Of course—John Singer Sargent's Madame Gautreau. The strap off a white shoulder, ala the first version of the painting. His view of the girl is interrupted by the Dowager Empress, a tall, henna-haired lady, sable-furred to her golden-slippered toes.

The Empress advances on Quinlan. Young man, she says in a commanding voice that doesn't need to be close to an ear, You need a wife. She touches Quinlan's dangling gold jacket button.

Lost one. Can't afford another.

I've met you.

Alan Gould invited you to a reading of my book, ma'am.

Call me Nina. Was I there?

Oh, yes.

I see. I must have been drunk and obnoxious.

You weren't obnoxious, Nina.

The Empress squints at Quinlan and laughs. As she drains her champagne glass, Quinlan sees the dark-haired girl watching from across the room. The girl sticks out her tongue. For a moment, Quinlan forgets the doyen, but she pulls him back into her universe with a tug on his jacket lapel. A wave of her empty champagne glass encompasses the room. I pay the salary of half the people here. I provided all this Perrier something-or-other Fleur '53, at $350 a magnum. The Conductor over there lives in one of my penthouses, and that awful man at the champagne bar refused to serve me until the Conductor made his appearance. What do you think about that?

Quinlan thinks about being disrespected by underlings, and glimpses the dark-haired girl, now with her violin at the ready, still watching him. He plucks the gold button from his jacket, takes the Dowager Empress' hand, places the button in her palm and folds her jeweled, bony old fingers over the button. He looks around the room and says, In honor of one who really matters, we now confer this token of our affection.

The empress looks at the button in her hand, peers into Quinlan's eyes for a moment. How very nice. What do you want?

He shrugs. Nada, Nina.

It's all right. Everybody wants something from me.

Okay, First Violin is mediocre. Get him fired and get everyone else a raise.

The Dowager Empress moves away toward the bar, where the conductor is surrounded by admirers. He sees her coming and raises a champagne glass preparatory to a toast, but the Empress seizes a tuxedo lapel and pulls him aside.

Quinlan hears violin music begin, Bach's Gigue from suite 1 in G major, and remembers the dark-haired girl, but a blonde, very buxom Bavarian girl is now in front of him. She says something to him that is lost in the crowd noise. He cups an ear, and the girl tiptoes.

I saw. Zat vas nice thing for Miss Nina.

Thanks. I was bound to lose that button anyway. He has to lean down to speak in her ear. The cleft between her laced bodice cords is more impressive up close. He says, What did you think of the combo of Handel and Prokofiev?

Bah. Russians haff no rhythm, no timing.

No oompah pah, pah, oompah pah pah.

Yes, she agrees enthusiastically. As she sips her champagne, elbow up, he notices a hint of blonde armpit down. Very interesting, the likely visual relationship of other areas of body hair. A painful whack in his side, and a shoe falls at his feet. A low-heeled black pump with a scuffed toe. He picks up the shoe.

Nice shot, lady, someone yells. The crowd is silent for a moment. The dark-haired girl is frowning at Quinlan from the podium. She is in her stocking feet, violin in one hand and a shoe in the other.

I have one left for Heidi, she yells.

As laughter begins, Quinlan pushes through the crowd to the dark-haired girl and hands her the shoe.

Do you like kosher food? She asks.

I could eat a horse and chase the rider. But I'm waiting for a friend.

Allan's not coming.

Oh, you're, uh...

Ariella.

I met you with Allan at the Sargent exhibition. Your hair was down then, and you were in jeans.

I'm going to give the crowd five more minutes of Bach. If you take me home, I'll feed you.

Two days later, she moves into his apartment.

Now, brakes, a loud horn, curses. Quinlan is in the middle of a Westheimer intersection, a pickup truck hood ornament inches from his waist. The driver, shouting and red-faced rolls down his window and leans out, yells something about almost running over a stupid son of a bitch.

Better luck next time, Quinlan says.

Are you drunk?

Not yet.

Get outta the way.

Quinlan glances at the traffic light and completes the crossing, then gestures at the driver to go ahead. The driver accelerates, truck tires squealing his rage, looking and yelling at Quinlan, and is hit by an oncoming car.

Quinlan walks three miles home.

At the apartment, he finds the downstairs entry door unlocked. He walks upstairs and notes that his door is unlocked. Good. Maybe the landlord or a burglar has taken all his stuff, solving what to gather for the trip. There is a note on the table by his shotgun.

Here are your keys, dumbass. Look in my Franchi before you try to shoot it. Sorry about Ariella, we didn't know. Call me when you get back. Scooter.

Quinlan opens the shotgun. There is a roll of twenties in the breech of the full choke barrel.

He sits at his makeshift desk, the kitchen table, and rolls a sheet of paper into the typewriter. Tough guys work through the pain.

Thirty minutes later, the sheet is still blank. He gets up and checks the fridge, forgetting there will be only moldy cheese, bad grape jelly and a green lump that once was a head of lettuce. There is a Tupperware bowlful of Josie's Gnocchi. In the door of the refrigerator, two quarts of beer are still warm to the touch. Budweiser, dammit. Scooter knows he likes Shiner Bock.

He fills a tea glass with ice and unscrews the cap from one bottle. He pours Budweiser into the glass until foam runs over the lip but saves a few precious ounces with a quick slurp. Back to the typewriter. The sheet is still blank.

To hell with working through the pain. he shuffles through a pile of notes until he finds a telephone number. Good-looking lady, soon to be a lawyer, according to Bill Weiss. And looking, Weiss said.

Miss Kennedy, please. With his luck lately, she'll be a hare-lipped fat girl.

This is Mae Kennedy.

Nice voice.

You don't know me, but Bill Weiss says you will be defending me on a date-rape charge. He said I should take you to dinner.

Nice laugh. Lee Quinlan. The film about your book was, uh, interesting, I liked the other stories that Mr. Weiss brought to the office. He said that you are a very nice person.

I am not a nice person. I am in the mood to meet a new friend. If you don't have a bunch of guys hanging around, maybe you would meet me at Jim Goode's seafood joint, 6 p.m.?

No one is hanging around. I know the place, love their gumbo. But I'm waiting to hear from one of Bill Weiss's clients in the next few minutes.

If you can make it, you'll be watching for a tall guy, prematurely gray like Paul Newman. Quinlan gives her a moment for the image to sink in. I'll be that baldheaded little fat guy.

Feeling gawky and nervous, Quinlan stammers a goodbye and hangs up.

But what does Mae look like, and where do they meet? Maybe he should wear a white carnation. When he dials back a minute later, her phone is busy. Ten minutes later, Mae's phone rings unanswered.

7

The Goode Company bar has Mexican beer, the expensive Dos Equis as well as the cheaper Corona. Quinlan checks the contents of his billfold under the bar. A $20 bill, three singles and a MasterCard that is overdue for a payment. If Mae is hungry, he can settle for a salad.

Corona, Arnold, and give my regards to Jim Goode.

He should be driving for Port O'Connor, and a few days with Dutch Brenner and Fred Carmichael, but what the hell. Who knows what the night will bring? He can go down tomorrow.

At 6:30, no hare-lipped fat girl has shown up looking for a Quinlan. Ever optimistic, he finishes the Corona and watches the yuppies, and looks at the old rods and reels and photos of the coast. Owner Jim Goode walks in the south entry under the painting Quinlan gave him for his wedding. The blackest beard in Texas, fierce eyes under a big, flop-brimmed hat that he must have found after a stampede of millionaires at the Fat Stock Show. Probably too important these days to notice an old friend.

Hey, Quinlan.

Hey, Goode.

Where's your beautiful better half?

She got the house. And the car, and the money, and our daughter—

I see. Goode winces, then glances at the bartender. The bartender jumps to attention. Arnold. This old salt drinks free. But only two more. He walks away, with no long-drawn out goodbyes. You always know where you stand with Jim Goode.

Quinlan drains the Corona and taps the bottle on the bar. Dos Equis, Arnold.

Seven o'clock. The gay guy over by the fish tank has nodded twice, and made eye contact in that certain way, but hasn't bothered to hit on Quinlan. There are two tables of high school kids behind Quinlan, being loud and obnoxious. The boys sport bellbottom pants that a circus clown would throw away, and jut chins of wispy whiskers. The girls are beautiful. Is his daughter laughing in a group like this, or maybe, being groped by a pimple-faced kid? Brailed her in my Beemer, they say nowadays.

At 7: 30, no fat girl has asked if there is a Lee Quinlan present. The bartender, in sympathy, places Mae Kennedy's name on his chalkboard.

By 8 p.m., he has imagined Mae into a beautiful, soft-eyed woman with curly hair. Her voice as he remembers it now is sweet and gentle, with a lyrical quality that reminds him of another treasured woman from the distant past.

By 8:30, Mae Kennedy is a demure yet vivacious beauty who gazes longingly into his eyes. A redhead, Bill Weiss said. Quinlan adds a sprinkle of freckles across her nose. A woman who understands.

His self-description has spoiled a fine evening. Or, maybe Weiss gave Mae's number to one of his other single friends.

Luck Travis? No. Weiss wouldn't give a lady's number to Travis.

Dutch Brenner? Nah. Brenner would have mentioned it. Besides, he's at his Port O'Connor bay house. A last fishing weekend before hunting season. Expecting Quinlan and Carmichael to come down.

Crazy Fred Carmichael. Just back from one of his photo jaunts to some other country. Carmichael with his gawky, angular form and walrus mustache, showing beautiful Mae photos of exotic places as they drink wine in his studio. Evil Carmichael, putting his hands all over Mae. Hating his ex-friend, Quinlan visits the men's room, then stops at the pay phone. He drops a dime in the slot and receives a recorded message. We're sorry, all pay phone calls are now twenty-five cents, please add three nickels

Quinlan has Arnold break a bill into quarters. How long has Ma Bell been gouging us for two bits?

Since the Arabs found out Americans would stand in line for gas.

Carmichael's number gives Quinlan an answering machine after three rings. Mae Kennedy's phone is not answered after 20 rings.

Arnold shrugs and looks away when Quinlan orders another beer. Quinlan figures what the tab should be and puts the money on the counter, but Arnold pushes the money back. Quinlan leaves five dollars.

What's five bucks to a man like him? His net worth. Better drive to Port O'Connor first thing in the morning. Get Dutch Brenner lined up. Run the boat, wet a line, catch a fish.

Moving School Al Barnes

II

She wakes to early morning light. It filters through screened windows, along with an insistent breeze. Nearby, there is a raucous chorus of seabirds. In the distance she hears big motors and deep-voiced horns. Sounds of the sea. She wraps herself around the sofa pillow and pulls the blanket over her head to block out the light and the noise, and drifts back into somewhere else.

2

Aromas of frying bacon and fresh coffee. Baritone voices from the kitchen. The bathroom is on the other side of the kitchen. She needs that bathroom. Now. A cup of black coffee runs a close second. She throws the cover aside, jumps up from the couch, shakes her hair back and gets ready to run the gauntlet of Carmichael and Brenner. Crazy Fred. Nice Dutch.

Across the porch she sees the bed she should have been in, and it makes her angry all over again. A pair of large feet jut from the sheet, and now she sees Carmichael's sleeping, whiskered face. Just beyond him, there is a battered Southern Select Beer mirror, cracked and crazed but still busy reflecting the truths of life.

She avoids the mirror, knowing the image she would see. Pillow wrinkles and wild red hair, elbows and wrists of chafed red, matching red-rimmed eyes. Makeup would help her self-esteem. But she really should take her contacts out and put on the thick glasses.

Hairbrush, toothbrush, glasses, everything is in her bag in the bathroom. If she can just get past the kitchen and the men there — Carmichael. On the bed, snoring. She turns the corner and smiles, hoping to dart into the bathroom, but Dutch Brenner stops her with a grin and an arm like an oak limb. He gestures toward the stove. I want you to meet a friend.

A man with a nice smile is holding a skillet and coffee pot. Hello, Mae. I'm Paul Newman.

3

Mae Kennedy and friends are at BOBBIE'S BAIT LAUNCH COLD BEER ICE, waiting for their turn at the launching ramp. It's on The Ditch, according to Brenner. Looks like a river to Mae, with boats of all sorts running back and forth.

A ditch?

The Ditch, Lee Quinlan answers. Intracoastal Canal.

Another boater completes the process of launching his boat and pulls his empty trailer away. Quinlan steps out of Brenner's Bronco, climbs into the trailered boat and stands at the controls. Brenner backs the boat and trailer down a concrete ramp into the water. Carmichael is busy transferring gear from Brenner's truck. A barge moves past, and in the wake, the boat bangs against the pier.

Asshole, Brenner says.

Lady present, Quinlan says.

Yes, she says. Watch your fucking language.

Quinlan gives her a look, and that impish grin from a photograph on Brenner's kitchen wall.

You'll do, Miss Mae.

Miss Mae is now my attorney, Carmichael says.

A lawyer? Quinlan shakes his head. You seem too nice. Uh, don't take that wrong, Miss Mae.

I won't be anyone's attorney till I get a passing grade on my bar exam.

She'll ace it, Carmichael says. She's been making Bill Weiss look good for years.

As the men get the boat ready, a nice lady at the bait shop visits with Mae.

Bobbie, meet Mae, Carmichael says. Mae's a pollywog. First time fishing saltwater. Bobbie fetches a bucket of water, milling with half-visible little creatures. She reaches into the container and brings out a fistful of the squirming animals for Mae to see. Live shrimp. Mostly whiskers and eyeballs right now, but they'll catch a trout. Bobbie drops a shrimp into the water. One for seed, Quinlan. Do your magic trick and bring me some trout for supper.

Yes, ma'am. Quinlan is now at the controls, but the battery is barely able to turn over the outboard motor. You should take better care of your boat, Quinlan says to Brenner.

Your boat. You never cashed the check, Lee.

Didn't want your money.

The motor starts, and the air is filled with smoke and the smell of gasoline. Mae coughs and moves back.

Hit that girl on the back, Quinlan yells at Carmichael. All aboard.

Brenner points at the bucket of shrimp at Mae's feet. She strains with both hands to get it from the dock down to Brenner in the boat. Brenner one-hands the bucket. Plugs are in, Cap'n, Brenner says, winking up at Mae.

Some response is necessary. Plugs? Mae asks.

Cap'n Quinlan requires his crew to be sure the drain plugs are in, says Brenner.

There was an accident, some time back, says Carmichael.

Minor incident, Quinlan smiles up at Mae from the wheel. Boat sank.

Carmichael tries to take Mae's elbow as she steps down from the dock onto the boat, but she pulls away from him and almost falls. Brenner catches her, then eases her to the back of the boat. She moves away from Carmichael. Brenner nods at Quinlan, and Quinlan raises his eyebrows at her. Perceptive Quinlan.

Contact, says Quinlan looking around. He revs the engine.

Clear, says Brenner. Clear, says Carmichael.

There is a pause.

She learns fast. Clear.

Quinlan pushes a lever down and moves them backward along the pier into the waterway and away from the dock, corrects and accelerates forward. He dodges around a tugboat and they bounce over the wake, smelling fumes. She wrinkles her nose.

Diesel exhaust, Carmichael explains in her ear, hauling coal to make electricity to make cool air for Houston. Mae, I'm sorry about last night. He touches her hand and waits for a response. Quinlan glances around at the pair, and perhaps gets the wrong idea.

Mae moves her hand away. Okay, Fred.

Quinlan maneuvers through a series of small channels bounded by mud banks. Tall grass whips past a few feet away. They are into a huge space of water and sky. The Gulf of Mexico, Mae wonders. Must be a bay, because she can see a pencil line of land on the far side. Quinlan turns the boat and runs near the shore. He glances at his passengers and yells over the motor noise, Vamanos muchachos. And muchacha, then jams the accelerator lever down. The boat leaps forward. Yeeha, yell Carmichael and Quinlan. Brenner grins, winks at Mae and turns his bill-capped hat backward.

Mae is surprised by the jolt of speed and blast of wind, but stumbles forward and holds on next to Quinlan. She brushes hair from her eyes and squints, leaning into the new force, no longer a breeze but a damp hurricane grabbing at her cheeks and eyelids. A group of large birds keeps pace with the boat for a short time, flapping to gain altitude, then soaring in single file. Huge beaks, dark, clumsy bodies. The lead bird folds its wings and arrows into the water.

Oh, she says. The other birds follow the leader and come up, shaking their heads, beaks sack-like, distended with water. Do they turn white later?

Those are brown pelicans, Brenner yells from behind her. Almost gone from here, till the last few years slow down, Lee. He points to a flight of birds on the horizon. Maybe you can tell me what those birds are, Miss Mae. The group of birds moves closer, intersecting the path of the boat. At a distance they seem pink, but as they wing past, their chests and necks are a vibrant crimson.

Flamingos? Mae asks.

Look it, don't they. They're roseate spoonbills.

Dutch never met a bird he didn't like, Quinlan says, slowing as he turns the boat into a small inlet.

Especially in my gumbo, Brenner replies.

How does owl taste? Carmichael asks, tapping Mae on the shoulder and grinning. Mae looks away from him.

Better'n whooping crane, Brenner replies. Just joking, Miss Mae. There, making a line with its beak in the shallow water? That's a black skimmer. Over there are some oyster catchers, and on the bank—the long-beaked, skinny bird? That's a curlew. If we're lucky when we go to Lighthouse Cove, we'll see an osprey, the sea hawk.

Contact, Quinlan yells. Got to get up on plane and over this shallow stretch.

Clear, Mae yells first.

Quinlan runs the boat for a short time in the open bay. Brenner and Carmichael fumble with rods and reels, while Mae holds on next to Quinlan. He shuts off the engine. She falls forward until he grabs her shoulder and pulls her back beside him.

Takeover, Mae. Quinlan gestures at the wheel, then turns away, grabbing a rod and reel, ignoring her as the men rig for fishing. Mae realizes that he expects her to run the boat.

She moves to the controls. The only person paying attention to the idea of a pollywog woman running the boat is Fred Carmichael. He looks at her and then at Quinlan.

Thataway, Quinlan points. And watch out for birds with dry knees.

Birds with what?

Watch for shallow areas, Brenner says.

How will she know a shallow area from a deep area? Contact, she says.

Clear, the men yell. She pushes down the lever. Nothing happens until she forces the lever, then the boat jumps ahead. After a moment the motor accelerates, the bow rises before her and the boat slows, wallowing in its wake.

Drop back a bit, Quinlan says. You're cavitating. Mae slows the engine, the bow drops, the boat accelerates.

Now, drop the motor, Quinlan says. Press your down button — the bottom button on the throttle handle…you got it.

Mae feels a surge of speed as she lowers the engine. At first, she is frightened by the power of the boat, and worried that she will run aground, or have an accident. Boats pass going the other way and their boat slams across their wakes, then wobbles. It is exciting to have a powerful motor at her command. She pushes the throttle all the way down, lets the boat weave left, then right.

Quinlan looks up from a fishing reel and waves a hand. Aim for that channel, Skipper.

She's now a Skipper. Where?

The telephone poles, at the water line? There'll be some shallows where they end. Here — put on these polarized sun glasses, and you'll see under the water better.

Under the water?

Try 'em and see.

She slides them on with one hand. They are too large, and almost blow away.

Oops. Quinlan takes them from her, makes an adjustment of the keeper cord on his own glasses and puts them on her.

Wow. Makes the surface more transparent. The engine coughs and the boat slows. What? What did I do?

Here we go again, Quinlan, says Carmichael.

Sounds like the same old problem, Lee. Brenner doesn't look up from rigging fishing gear.

Quinlan points out a landing area, then moves to the back of the boat. Ease her over there by that shoal, Skipper. Slower… now, kill the motor. Quinlan jumps into the water hip deep. He grabs the side as the bow slides onto a shallow area and grinds to a stop. Mae— there's a spark plug wrench under the console, by your left hand.

Carmichael jumps from the bow onto shore and walks off, casting as he goes.

Quinlan splashes to the back of the boat. Tilt your motor, Skipper. The top button on the throttle handle— the lift whines, and Quinlan says, That's good. He removes the cover of the motor. Wrench. Mae walks to the back of the boat and hands him the wrench. Scalpel. Suture. Forceps. He works with something on the motor for several minutes. Okay, Mae, try the key again.

She turns the key, but the motor doesn't respond.

Neutral? Set the lever in the middle— The motor grinds but doesn't quite catch.

Choke it, Mae.

How do I choke it?

Just push the key in while you turn it— there you go, Skipper. The motor starts and sounds perfect. Quinlan replaces the top, then pushes the boat off the sand. He splashes around to the side and leaps halfway into the boat, head and shoulders in, legs dragging in the water. Punch it, Mae, he grunts, before the wind puts us back on the sand.

As the boat lurches forward, Brenner grabs Quinlan by the belt and hoists him aboard.

They pick up Carmichael down the shoreline, then go full-throttle for a while, Mae driving, Quinlan giving directions. Mae steers into and out of some narrow channels, the four of them leaning with the tilt of the boat.

She could learn to love this.

Now moving through Bar Room Bay, Quinlan says. Hard to port, that's your left. Now moving through Little Mary's Cut. They are soon back in the large part of the bay. Mae can see a surf line on the horizon. The men shout directions.

Steer to port—nah, your other port.

Slow down, more to starboard.

Ease her back, Mae.

Good bait in the water. Kill the engine.

You want to drift or wade, Lee?

We'll drift this deep area, Dutch. See if we can catch a fish before we get our pee pees wet.

Lady aboard, Quinlan, says Brenner.

S'cuse me, ma'am. Our pee pees and our wee wee wet.

Lures or bait? Brenner says.

How about, we save the shrimp for supper.

I'll use bait, Carmichael says. Who made you our guide? He frowns at Mae, and she can tell that his resentment of Quinlan is deeper than a discussion of fishing techniques.

Mae frowns back, thinking quietly but projecting her feelings. Who said you could climb into my bed last night?

Carmichael winces and makes an over-powerful cast. The reel backlashes and he whacks the water with the rod tip.

As Mae turns away, she sees Quinlan looking at the sky with a suppressed grin.

The boat moves slowly with the breeze, as Brenner and Carmichael fish from the front. In the quiet, Quinlan says, You wonder why I've called this meeting.

Not me, Carmichael says.

I've got two words for you, gents.

No one replies, and Mae wonders what Quinlan means. And, why he has excluded her. She frowns at Quinlan, but he is not looking her way.

Quinlan says, Third Pass.

Third Pass, as in Mexico? asks Brenner. If I remember correctly, you can't get there from here.

The greatest ten miles of fishing on this continent, Quinlan says. And this time, Mr. Brenner, I have a secret weapon.

Two words for you, Quinlan, Carmichael says. El Tigre. You can't get across Second Pass, unless you plan to rent a helicopter. Or drive 80 miles of bad roads around it.

There's a ferry now. You explain to the operator in your flawless Spanish that we want to make a donation to his favorite charity. He takes us across, and three days later, brings us back.

Oh? What does that cost? Asks Brenner.

Captain Camo made the trip two weeks ago. Dropped a $20 bill on the operator, going and coming. Had the greatest two fishing days of his life.

Hey, consider the source, says Carmichael. Camo exaggerates worse than Lee Quinlan.

If Camo can do it, Brenner says, We can.

Don't encourage the goofy bastard, says Carmichael.

Quinlan says, I should mention on the way, dove and deer hunting at Voss's place, then Margaritas in Matamoras, before big specks and reds in the Mexican surf.

Who's going? Carmichael asks.

You, Brenner there, John Morgan, maybe Luck

Travis--

Brenner interrupts. Flaming liberal Travis? Count me out.

Need a liberal to keep the argument going. There's me, and Mae's boss, Bill Weiss.

Mae looks at Quinlan in surprise. Mr. Weiss is going?

Yep. I told him about Third Pass.

If my attorney is going, Carmichael says, all I want to know is, when do we leave?

Friday.

Brenner says, I'll think about it.

Quinlan winks at Mae. You have no choice, Mr. Brenner. You'll be pulling this boat with your Suburban.

Brenner nods. Okay, sure, whatever you say, Mr. Hitler.

Carmichael and Brenner cast from the bow as Quinlan works on the motor. Mae watches and hands him tools. He finishes whatever he is doing, wipes his hands on a greasy rag, then rummages around in the cooler and comes up with two cans of beer. Shading his eyes, he glances skyward. Sun's over the yard arm. Cold beer, Miss Mae?

No, thanks.

He pats his shirt pockets, then looks under the console and finds a package of Camel cigarettes. Cig?

Ugh.

I'm not hooked. He stuffs the cigarettes back under the console without lighting one. Does Bill Weiss smoke that stinky pipe at the office?

No. I think he quit.

I'm quitting cigs, after the trip. Let's try something else. Want to fish?

She nods. He hands her a rod and reel and just turns away, like she's an expert. It's a long rod, equipped with a heavy red reel. A strange-looking lure is tied to the end of the line. Mae hasn't had a rod and reel in her hands since she was a teenager, and that was a push-button rig on Town Lake in Austin. She watches what Quinlan does, then casts the lure as hard as she can. The spoon lands ten feet away, and the line on the reel spins into a tangle.

Good looking bird nest, Quinlan says. He plucks at the tangled line until the reel works again. Put your thumb here, he demonstrates, and hold it like this. He wraps his arms around Mae as he shows her how to hold her hands and swing the rod back, then swiftly forward. Try it slow and easy until you get the idea.

He smells like gasoline and cigarettes and sweat mixed with after-shave lotion and beer. As he shows her how to cast the lure, his hand brushes her breast.

She frowns and stops.

Beg your pardon, ma'am, he says. I told you I wasn't nice. He steps away from her and gestures. Give it a try, Skipper.

After a few easy tries, Mae casts the spoon with all her might, thumbing the spool as the lure zips out thirty yards.

Good looking cast, Quinlan says.

Mae laughs, turning the handle of the reel, puffing at a drop of sweat on her nose and at a curl of hair dangling in her eyes. He is still watching her, smiling. The boat bumps along a shallow area, then stops.

Wade fishing time, Quinlan yells, and vaults out of the boat. Wow! Reminds me of that great Galveston High School.

What school is that? Brenner asks.

Ball High. Coming, Mae?

The water is clear and cool looking, and Quinlan is laughing up at her. Mae has on old jeans and sneakers. She eases out of the boat into the water. The shock makes her gasp.

Want to get back on board? Quinlan asks.

She shakes her head.

He puts a belt around her, fitted with gadgets. He is careful not to touch her anywhere.

Hookouts for releasing fish, he explains. Stringer, for keeping fish. Rod holder, knife, lure box. He puts on a white foam hat that might have a pound of lures on it, lures of all shapes and sizes, but mostly spoons.

Crazy? You and Dutch and the Skipper might want to work this area, moving downwind. I'm gonna try the Coast Guard flats for redfish. I'll come for you at the far point. If the boat runs.

Carmichael starts wading just in front of Mae. He has a camera dangling from a strap and swings it around to his back. And stumbles. The camera almost goes into the water, but Mae grabs it and keeps it from being dunked.

No problem, he says. Waterproof.

You're welcome.

Mae, let Mr. Charm go that way, Brenner says, and come on with me. He starts off slowly and glances back at her. Time for our favorite music— C and W.

Country and Western?

Chunk and wind. We'll do the stingaree shuffle.

She may be a pollywog, but Mae knows about the dangerous stingray. They shuffle along and fish, casting strange lures that float. A Jumping Minnow, a Broken-back, a Rattletrap.

They catch no fish. An hour later, Quinlan pulls up in the boat. He yells, Found a few reds. And they want spoons.

They motor off again, Mae at the wheel, and drop anchor in a shallow region. As they climb out of the boat, Quinlan says, Redfish have three principle food groups, Miss Mae. Fish, crustaceans and gold spoons. Mae Kennedy laughs, and Lee Quinlan smiles, and the world changes for both of them.

Quinlan sets off for the shoreline, casting as he goes.

Mae trails Brenner again, casting and retrieving a gold spoon in spots he points out. Only Brenner catches fish. The first is silver and green, with small spots.

Speckled trout, he says as he unhooks it. Too small. Minutes later, he has another fish on, and works for a long time, rod bent, reel occasionally whining, but finally brings the fish to his hands. This one is large and bronze-colored. Redfish. Maybe an inch too long.

Don't release that fish, Carmichael yells as he splashes to their area. He has Brenner hold the fish in certain ways while he composes and shoots photos.

Enough. You're gonna kill this fish, Brenner says. He works with the hook a moment, then gently releases the fish.

That was a great cover shot, Carmichael says, happier now. Texas Parks & Wildlife quality.

Send it to Tide Magazine, or don't use it, Brenner says.

Carmichael stalks away, casting his lure.

Quinlan is nearby as she reels in a lure. He wades to her and hands her his rod. Hold this for me, Mae, while I put a spoon on your line.

The rod jumps in her hand. Lee—there's something on here!

He is fiddling with a lure on his Styrofoam hat. Probably just hooked on the bottom.

The rod is almost yanked from her hand, the reel makes a screeching sound, and the line zips through the water. Yikes!

Big speck, Brenner shouts. Just went past my leg.

Rod tip up, Miss Mae, Quinlan says. Just lean back, let 'im run, and enjoy it.

Mae leans back and watches as the rod curves, tip nodding toward a swirl in the water. The line is taut and musical, in tune with the reel, then the rod tip snaps up and she almost falls backward. Dammit, Mae yells.

Quinlan watches as she reels in the line, then reaches out and takes it from the water. At the end is a curlicue. Sorry, Miss Mae. I tied a bad knot.

The light breeze suddenly becomes a brisk wind. Mae's curls escape her ponytail and scatter around her head, in her face and eyes. I'm sorry about standing you up — she begins, but he brushes the hair from her forehead, then touches her cheek.

Out together, home together. I'm glad you came down with Carmichael, but when we get back to Houston, I hope you'll see me.

Mae nods.

Tailing Reds Capt. Sally Black

4

It is late in the day. Mae Kennedy and Lee Quinlan are waist-deep in the surf. Huge cumulus clouds in the east catch the afternoon sunlight, turning the rushing water into a turmoil of gold and amber.

Fred Carmichael has stalked off so far into the bay that Mae can't see him, but Dutch Brenner is not far away, fishing near the boat. Quinlan looks back at Brenner and jerks a thumb at him.

Knee deep, wearing a flotation vest, he says. Dutch doesn't like to swim. All that Neanderthal muscle and bone, I guess. They are fishing the edge of the current at Pass Cavallo, Quinlan explains, where the bay meets the Gulf. They are hoping for a concentration of speckled trout. Quinlan wants Mae to catch at least one nice speck before the day is over.

She is not sure she wants to deal with another fish. Her thumb has a blister from working the reel and her arm aches from casting. She is hot and tired, and grateful for the relief provided by a wide-brimmed straw hat that Quinlan found in the storage area of the boat. Thank God, the sun is almost down. She's never been so scorched. Her freckles will all run together. And she's dying of thirst.

Quinlan edges out farther, intent on casting into the deeper water. Has he completely forgotten about her? Mae tries to follow, but it is too rough. She feels the current swirling around her legs, and sand shifts under her feet. Quinlan leans into the current and moves deeper, but it is alarming to Mae, feeling the power of the Gulf pulling at her. She has to go back to the boat for a drink of water or perish. Quinlan turns his back to a breaking wave and is looking at her. Mae points at the boat and mimes drinking. Quinlan nods, grinning, one finger up.

Watch Brenner, he mouths.

She walks across the sand beach, nearly to Brenner and the boat before looking back at Quinlan. He is splashing, his rod bent, catching a big fish. As she gets into the boat, she yells at Brenner and points.

Brenner nods his head. I see him.

Mae shades her eyes and finds Quinlan again, spinning in a circle, fighting the largest fish in the Gulf.

He's got his spoon hooked to his wade boot is all, says Brenner. The old Chandeleur Shake gag.

She can't see Quinlan, then sees his hat. He is past the big waves, out where it's deep. Dutch?

Brenner shades his eyes and looks for a long moment, then starts for the boat. It's the first time Mae has seen him hurry.

Get out of the boat, he yells. He gathers the anchor chain and rope as he splashes toward the bow. If we don't come back for you, you'll have to wade across the bay to Carmichael.

No—I'm a good swimmer.

Brenner throws the anchor into the bow, then pushes the boat away from the protected anchorage and vaults on board.

Get off. He turns the key in the ignition, but there is only a series of clicks. He moves to the motor and removes the top, finds a rope in a little pocket and winds it around something. He glances back at Mae. Neutral?

She jumps to the wheel and checks the lever. Neutral. Key on.

Good girl. Now, choke it He pulls the rope and the motor coughs into life, then almost dies, but Mae pushes the warm-up lever high, and the motor roars.

Let's go get him, Brenner grunts as he steps to the console. May I? She moves away from the wheel. The boat vibrates as Brenner guns the motor and the prop churns the sand bottom. The big boat jolts free of the shallow sand. In deeper water, Brenner opens the throttle and yells over the noise of the motor as they run parallel to the surf.

He jerks a thumb over her shoulder at the west shoreline. A sliver of sun escapes through golden clouds, just above the horizon. We could get into the Gulf through Big Pass. Might be ten minutes before we could get back to him. Lee doesn't have ten minutes. We're going across the bar.

Brenner turns the boat so they are looking across the surf line.

Quinlan's hat shines white on a high swell.

There he is, Mae shouts. They see just the hat, then it is gone, past the rolling surf that marks the bar.

Put on my surf vest. On the left, by the bait well. Then pull that little red tab.

Mae puts on the vest and jerks on the tab. The vest puffs up.

We have to cross the bar on a high wave, Brenner yells. If we catch the bar with the prop…

Mae is beginning to understand the problem. What?

Motor dies, no power to head into the waves, she could broach. Roll over.

Mae grips the windshield and Brenner's arm. He eases the motor to half-throttle for a moment, allowing all the carburetor grumbles to work themselves out of the system.

I ought to throw you out of the boat right here. Contact. Clear.

Brenner slams the throttle down. The bow of the boat crashes into the bar. They are thrown forward, gear flying around them as the boat shudders to a stop. The world disappears in a wall of foam and spray. Then the boat lifts on a full wave and they coast down again, past the surf line.

The boat rides easily on the offshore swells, slowing at the crests, accelerating down into the troughs. At the top of a wave, Mae can see Quinlan. Two sea birds are low to the water, winging for shore, almost at Quinlan's face level. She hears him yell, Git. and the birds veer away. Brenner and Mae are almost there, and she leans over the side, reaching out for him. Quinlan turns his back to them. Kicking hard, he is able to get far enough out of the water to raise his rod and make a feeble cast. Brenner stops the boat beside him as Quinlan reels in the lure.

Quinlan gasps, Catch anything over there, Cap'n?

On the Third Bar   Sam Caldwell

III

It is dark when he arrives back in Houston, hungry as a cemetery rat. He stops at a Whole Foods market. A parking place is available close to the front door. Quinlan parks the Blazer and enters, feeling rumpled and dirty. The feeling is not helped by a security guard who eyes Quinlan and ignores Quinlan's friendly nod.

At sampling stations he pauses for chips and salsa, grapefruit slices, raisin clove four-grain bread, a thumb-sized cup of vitamins, then circles back nonchalantly, waiting in line to get a second serving of chips and salsa. He takes a six-pack of cheap beer to the RAPID CHECKOUT STATION. Allison, reads the checker's name badge.

Paper or plastic, Sir?

Paper, and it's Lee. Lee Quinlan.

Quinlan and Allison smile at one another.

She bags the beer. You were here last week.

So were you.

Allison laughs, nods. I have to be here, or they won't pay me.

Quinlan presents his MasterCard. Let's see if they still love me, he says, winking at the checker. Almost as nice as Mae Kennedy. Nah.

Allison swipes the credit card through the reading device. A moment later, the machine beeps. Quinlan leans over and glances at the screen. DECLINED. A worthless tramp, attempting to defraud the system has been caught in flagrant dereliction. Alarms will sound, the Rent-A-Cop will come dashing in and throw down on Quinlan, radio a 319 in progress, request immediate backup. He'll be cuffed and led to a squad car where Eyewitness News captures video footage. All of Houston will watch as the brave officer of the law rudely bends Quinlan's head down and pushes him into the back seat of the patrol car.

Allison says, Card services must be down right now. Just sign here, Lee.

Thanks, Allison.

Quinlan leaves the store, an affluent, card-carrying member of the aristocracy. He puts the beer in the Blazer, then pauses, driver door open, one foot in the truck, looking back toward the munificence of the market. A lady in a gray Mercedes sedan flashes her bright lights and taps her horn impatiently, demanding his parking spot. Quinlan squints against the headlights, reading her lips. Move dammit, can't you see you're delaying an important person?

Aw, hell, Quinlan says to himself. Better get some stuff for the trip. He slams the truck door, waves at the Mercedes lady and saunters back inside. He chooses a cart and starts shopping in the vegetable section. Two spaghetti squash—don't forget to get garlic and real butter— seven pounds of new potatoes, a red-net package of ten tomatoes with the stems still attached at $1.98 per pound, but worth it, according to his sniff test; mushrooms, a quarter-pound bag of large garlic, three purple onions and a bag of mixed greens.

At the meat counter, he chooses ten pounds of smoked sausage, ten T-bone steaks and three packages of Bum Phillip's hickory smoked bacon. Eggs; three boxes of 18 extra-large ought to be enough.

Break time, says his stomach. He heads for the free samples and loads up on chips and salsa. In the dairy section, he nonchalantly pauses at the Stilton cheese and garlic cracker sample table. The lady from the Mercedes sedan rounds the corner of the vegetable aisle and heads his way. Birkenstocks, scrawny ankles, Culottes, loose silk blouse with no tits to hide anyway, a sour expression as she pauses nearby, waiting for Quinlan to move away from the cheese samples.

He selects the largest chunk of cheese, drops it onto a cracker and waggles his eyebrows at the Mercedes lady. My favorite four-letter words, he says. Free food.

The Mercedes lady grimaces and turns away.

What the hell, he grabs a jar of the overpriced salsa that is on special. A large jar of dill pickles. Next, he finds a package of Pioneer buttermilk biscuit mix, two containers of Tony Chachere's seasoning and three bottles of Extra Virgin olive oil. In the tobacco section, he loads three cartons of Camel cigarettes, but at the middle of the aisle, thinks of a new friend who hates cigarettes. Quinlan backtracks and replaces all three cartons.

In the wine section, he studies the labels instead of the price stickers, and selects seven bottles of white wine. STE. GENEVIEVE, one label reads: TEXAS CHARDONNAY / Flavors of tropical fruits, hints of citrus, peach and pear, and a toasty oak finish combine in this rich, round Chardonnay. Off dry and fruity, this golden-colored wine represents an outstanding value.

He will be the judge of that.

Along the beverage isle, considering the options, Quinlan fills the lower section of the basket with ten six-packs of cheap beer and five six-packs of Shiner Bock. Veggies and meat for a few evening meals on the beach, breakfast for three days. If he doesn't have it, they don't need it. He steers the loaded basket for checkout row.

Allison is not on duty.

Quinlan circles back and hits the free samples until a sharp-eyed assistant manager crosses his arms and glares at Quinlan. So much for this shopping trip. Should he put it all back, or just leave the loaded basket and sneak out? He trundles the loaded basket to the vegetable area in the front of the store. Before he can start replacing the vegetables, he sees that Allison is back at her station. She waves at him.

As he aims the loaded cart for Allison's area, the Mercedes lady turns an aisle corner. She picks up speed, frowning at Quinlan, hurrying toward Allison. Lightly burdened with two six packs of Perrier and a carton of Kiwi fruit in a hand basket, she might have beat him to the goal, but a slow old lady crosses her path. Quinlan skids to a halt with three feet to spare and winks at Allison.

2

He stumbles up his apartment steps, places the trip groceries that need to be in the refrigerator along the wall and checks his mail. Three items are stuffed into the rusty box. Two are circulars addressed to Occupant, and one MasterCard envelope is for E.L. Quinlan, marked URGENT, Return Requested.

Sorry, MC. You'll have to wait till I get a check in or hit the lottery. Hey, maybe he overpaid them again, and it's a refund. Ripping the envelope open, he sneaks a look. MasterCard wants their cards back.

He writes all night and through the next morning.

At noon, he is starving. He goes to the refrigerator and brings back a bottle of Shiner and a tea glass full of ice. Sitting at the typewriter, Quinlan smiles fondly at the six-inch electric cord that dangles from the side. Luck Travis taped the wire beneath the manual typewriter. A note is still attached: Happy Fortieth, Lee. We took up a collection after you passed out. Here's that electric word processor you've been wanting. Love, all of us.

Talk to me, Alice, he begs the typewriter, then begins banging out the final pages all over again, this time with fewer words and new thoughts.

Late that evening, he reads over the last page.

Epilogue

It is my party, but no one speaks to me. There's my favorite cousin David, nodding but turning away as I walk toward him. Now I see that many friends are here, and acquaintances, and a few old enemies.

Nancy and Junior, Philip and Joan, the Walkers, by God all of them and the McLeods and Fitzgeralds too, filling up a large part of the garden. Probably arguing Hardshell versus Footwashing Baptistry and threatening blazing hell to non-believers but not drinking, of course, so there's plenty of punch for the rest of the crowd.

The guests are polite, except for the rodeo types, and even they are quiet. No drunk fistfights. Or, none yet. Even Giles of the sour demeanor is being civil, a chore for Giles. I'll thank him for it, if he'll speak to me. But he backs away, raising his eyebrows, looking at the exit. There, near the pool is Clemente, my friend. And his sister Graciela, my life.

Clemente. Handsome devil, with charm, wit and skill in everything except what would be best for Clemente. Scattered across a Cambodian mountainside because he wanted to fight for his country.

Graciela. She sits demurely, not looking at me as I walk up, but aware, and now she does glance at me, but only for a moment.

Gracie.

Graciela puts a hand on my arm. It's heaven being touched by her, being near her and feeling her presence, sensing no disgust from her.

Could you ever forgive me?

Graciela nods, yes, and might have said something to me, but all the guests have left, and Clemente gestures that it's time to go.

End

Quinlan reads through the page. Self-indulgent bullshit, he mutters, then wads the page double-handed into a ball and lobs it at the corner wastebasket. The basket is filled to overflowing. The ball bounces back toward him, rolls to his left little toe and stops.

Aw, hell. He stoops and retrieves the page and un-wads it, reads over it again. He scratches through several words, adds a few more words then writes a note.

DEER VAN: Hears rest of book. Your editor is a lots bettr speler than I am, know you will improove on this anyway, send that third check immediately to my agent, yr. ob. serv., Edward Lee Quinlan, Esq.

P.S.: A middle-finger salute to your Hollywood buddies. Am doing research on a better ending, even as you get this stuff. Will send it along, soon. Or maybe, late. ELQ

Quinlan wraps the manuscript and addresses it, then finds nine dollars in the bottom of a dresser drawer. He drives to a nearby convenience store, gets change from the clerk and buys stamps from a postal machine. He licks what should be enough of the stamps, adds a few more, then walks to a corner mailbox. As the package disappears, the metal door clangs shut and the box echoes for a moment.

He returns to the convenience store and spends the remaining three dollars on a carton of Camel cigarettes. The clerk gives him nineteen cents back in change. He drops all the coins in a box for Jerry's Kids.

Back at the apartment, putting off a telephone call, he rummages around gathering fishing gear, clothes, pans, pots and a large skillet, then stops and makes a list. At the top of the list he writes MAKE LIST

Groceries, skillets, coffeepot, big pot

rods, reels, lures, fishing vest, knife, game shears

quilts, sheets aw hell.

He phones a young artist friend and reminds him of the trip, but that isn't the call he has to make. Since he has the phone in hand, he calls his ex-wife. Jean answers and is coldly polite. Anna Lee is out with a friend. Yes, Lee, a boyfriend. Jean will tell her he called and that he will call back from Mexico. Yes, she will tell Anna that he loves her and misses her.

I miss you too, Jean.

Lee. I'm married now.

You were married in January. To me.

You didn't seem to know that for two years, Lee. And you broke Lloyd's nose—

He was in my driveway. With my wife.

Jean can't talk any longer, she has to go now.

Goodbye, Jean. He eases the phone onto the receiver. Images of the happy times with Jean and little Anna flood his mind.

Quinlan does the manly thing and goes back to work. Finish a short feature for Texas Monthly. The editor needs to fill some space in his magazine, and Quinlan needs to fill some space in the landlord's billfold. The phone rings, and he flinches toward it for a moment. Jean? No, probably Ebert saying, Where is it? Or more likely, Forget it, Quinlan. He leans too far, misses the phone and knocks the receiver off the table.

Hello? It is a woman's voice, tinny with distance from the receiver, yet somehow familiar.

Hello, Mae.

Lee. I just want to apologize again for not joining you at the restaurant Friday evening —

It was all my fault, I say dumb things sometimes, been kicking myself, really enjoyed meeting you.

Anyway, I'm so glad I met you, and thank God you didn't drown—

Not even a close call.

There's a silence.

Well, actually...I may have been shark bait if you and Dutch Brenner hadn't come across the bar. They both laugh, then Mae says she'll be leaving at six tomorrow morning for her mother's home in Austin, will be gone a week for her brother's wedding, hopes she can see him when she gets back—He probably smells grungy, and looks worse from a long work spell, but maybe she wouldn't mind if he drops by for a few minutes, just to say hello again, and she says yes.

Quinlan grabs his billfold and leaves, running down the stairs three at a time. At the Blazer, he realizes he has left his keys. He goes back up the stairs two at a time. At the landing, he pauses for a few breaths and looks at the apartment door. Did he lock the door on his way out? That would be a stunt worthy of Luck Travis. He grabs the knob and twists. The door opens.

3

Luck Travis looks around through one eye, decides he's in a hotel room bed with a woman, and that he's had too much to drink. He goes back to sleep.

4

The woman shakes him awake. Henry.
    Ma'am?
    Turn over. You're snoring.
    It's my turn.
    Did I snore?
    You, or a cave bear. Turn on a light.
    I can't get to sleep with a light on.
    Well, snuggle here, and shake me if you have to.

5

Travis is awake again and hung over. He has an aching head and worse yet, a painfully full bladder. The woman snores in the dark beside him, an arm draped heavily across his belly. He eases the arm gently away, getting a measure of relief for his bladder. He runs his hand slowly up the arm to a cleanshaven armpit. The owner of the arm continues to snore.

Continue exploration. Ah, a firm breast, a plump nipple. Whose nipples had he recently compared to Bing cherries? Oh, right. This is Alice from Dallas snoring beside him. He's in her hotel room. They completed the sale of some of his old equipment too late for her to make a flight, and after getting to know one another a bit better—what the hell? celebrated with dinner and some wine. And some more wine. And damn, he needs to take a leak.

Travis wants to roll out of bed and find the bathroom, and fast, but during earlier activities, he wound up on the left side of the bed. Travis hasn't got out of a bed on the left side since a cot in a bunker near Saigon. Terrible things happened for a week. He'll get out of this bed on the right, and excuse me, ma'am, if I touch you there.

Travis strains and arches carefully, reaching over the woman, planning to support his weight with a hand, then get a leg over and get out of bed on the right side without waking her. But his hand slips off the far side of the bed and his nose makes contact with a breast. Alice mutters something, clutches at his arm.

He eases off the wrong side of the bed, sees the dim outline of a door. He tiptoes across the room and, damn, it's dark. He opens the door and, damn, it's bright. Alice says something. As he steps through the door and closes it behind him, the lock clicks. He's in a hotel hallway, naked as a spring jaybird.

Travis turns the knob gently, pulls and jerks the knob and curses under his breath, but it's no good. He rattles the door and hisses, Alice then listens, ear to the door. There's a soft snore. God DAMN it, Alice. He bangs on the door. Alice, Alice, ALICE. A door opens down the hall, and a man looks out.

Hey, Travis says. I just got locked out of my room. The man starts closing his door. I need to use your phone but the door slams and a lock clicks. Down the hallway to the right is an ELEVATOR sign. To the left, at the end of the hall is an ICEDRINKS sign. Travis still has the problem that brought him into the hall, but there will be no sign in a hotel hallway reading MEN'S ROOM.

He hurries down the hall into the ICEDRINKS room. In the room are two candy and cigarette machines, a pay phone and a stainless-steel ice receptacle. Travis opens the top of the ice container, feeling his bladder scream for relief, right by God now — no, only a worthless jerk would do that. He grits his teeth, does a little jig and sucks his belly up. A stainless-steel ice scoop juts from the mound of ice. He seizes the scoop and is no longer naked. Damn, the scoop is cold, and immediately, he has visions of a trip that Lee Quinlan is promoting. Third Pass, Mexico. Travis fervently wishes that he was on that sun-bright Mexican beach, warm surf rolling up his chest.

He shudders convulsively and decides that he will go on the trip. If he doesn't wind up in front of a judge. A judge, a lawyer. His lawyer, Bill Weiss. The pay phone—he has no coins. The operator can connect him. No. Weiss's number is unlisted.

God, why me? He nods with enlightenment. Got out on the wrong side of the bed. And they call me Luck. He thrusts out his chin and squares his shoulders. By God, he'll make it, somehow. He peeks out the door. The hallway is empty. He heads back for Alice's room, fortified by his new equipment.

But, which is Alice's room?

This one? He puts an ear against the door, can hear a soft snore.

Alice... He taps the door with the ice scoop. ALICE, OPEN THE GODDAMN DOOR. The knob turns, and the door opens an inch. He sees blue-tinted hair in curlers and an elderly pair of eyes looking at him.

Charlie? says the woman sleepily. A stocky, hairy-chested man with a U.S. Airborne tattoo on one bicep is standing at her hotel door with an ice scoop over his genitals. She slams the door.

Travis squares his shoulders, strides to the next door and raps loudly. ALICE?

A man's voice answers, irritably: Who the hell is it?

Never mind, wrong door. There are now faces peering out of several doors down the hall. He walks to the next door, ignoring the faces, and listens at the door a moment. A soft, familiar, female snore. He bangs on the door with his ice scoop.

ALICE.

Someone answers inside, a querulous female voice. Who is it?

Travis hears the whine of an elevator down the hall. He yells, OPEN THIS DOOR, ALICE. The door opens a crack, and Alice peers through, wide-eyed. Travis darts in the door and squints through the little wide-angle peephole. Two blue-jacketed Houston policemen step out of the elevator, cautiously. A gray-haired policeman un-holsters his pistol as a younger cop walks behind him, gun already out. They start down the hall, but there are no naked perverts in the hallway looking to rape old ladies.

6

Quinlan forces himself to drive below the speed limit as he heads for Mae Kennedy's apartment. It's late, and there are drunks out. Damn, he swerves as he turns on Bissonet. Next, a right on Kirby and then a left on Steele. Park in front of the first complex. Go upstairs, apartment 13. Quinlan blinks and squints as he waits for a red light at Kirby. Who needs sleep when a beautiful woman wants to see you again?

Before he makes the turn onto Steele Street, flashing lights in the rearview mirror and a short burst from a siren interrupt his concentration. Behind him are two patrolmen in an HPD cruiser. One cop is gesturing with a flashlight. Quinlan pulls over carefully but runs slightly over the curb before the Blazer shudders to a stop. Both policemen start for the truck, one officer hanging back, a hand on his holster. The other officer approaches the door.

Having a little trouble driving, Sir? The first cop says, not unpleasantly. Quinlan sees gray hair and smile wrinkles.

Put your hands on the wheel, says the second cop as he walks up, and keep 'em where we can see 'em.

Bad cop, good cop? Quinlan winces as the officer's powerful light moves across his face, then around the interior of the truck. No problem, officer. Just sleepy, a long work night—

Shut up, says Bad Cop. Damn. Stinks like a brewery in there. He holds the light in Quinlan's eyes from inches away. Get out of the car, slow and easy. Then, impatiently, Come on, buster, move it.

Get that light out of my eyes.

Okay, Don, back off. A pleasant voice, reasonable, reassuring. This guy seems okay. You need to step out of the truck, sir, and let me see your DL. Quinlan manages a fairly graceful exit from the truck, then fishes his wallet from his pocket.

Edward L. Quinlan, reads Good Cop, his light on the billfold. Sir, your license expired three months ago. That inspection sticker is out of date. You have a broken left taillight, and we observed you driving erratically on Kirby.

Aw, hell, bust 'im. Good Cop glances at Bad Cop. Don, you need to check that transmission coming over the radio. Now.

Quinlan is getting some of his vision back. He sees the younger officer walking back to the police car. The older man is not writing details in his open ledger.   You look familiar; do I know you?

Quinlan considers mentioning a well-reviewed book, a Houston Chronicle feature, but the words stick in his throat.

I do a little writing.

Yeah? The officer closes his ledger. You any kin to Detective Dave Quinlan?

Don't know him.

Good Cop opens his ledger, and his attitude is cooler. We're gonna have to take you in, Quinlan, let you blow up a balloon.

Look, I'm headed for a friend's apartment, one block from right here, you can check it out—

The officer unclips cuffs from his belt. Turn around, then I want your hands behind your back. Move.

Damn. He's going to need an attorney. Mae, could you come get me out of the slammer for DWI? Mae's boss, Bill Weiss. Quinlan invited him on the trip. As Quinlan turns, Good Cop and Quinlan hear the crackle of radio static. Bad Cop yells from the squad car, something about a naked sex fiend running around a hotel hallway, trying to rape old ladies, and they have to get their asses over there right now.

Get outta here, Quinlan. Good Cop sprints for the squad car, yelling over his shoulder, And be careful. If you hurt someone, I'll look you up and beat your brains out. The squad car roars around Quinlan, scattering gravel and forcing him to cringe close to the truck.

Two minutes later, Lee Quinlan is greeted by a shy Mae Kennedy. And as the soft-eyed, demure woman ushers an apologetically stammering, smelly writer into a future lawyer's apartment, he smiles with relief. Her place is a rumpled, comfortable mess.

7

Erwin Baker completes the illustration of a new high rise shortly before midnight, and signs it, Erwin E. Baker, carefully and big, so a viewer can read the name. Then, puts in a copyright mark, tiny. Maybe Brenner will notice it and raise hell. He paints over the copyright.

Baker is proud of the quality, but he put in far more work on the project than he can bill for. Money. Baker could type an invoice and leave the bill on Brenner's desk. Wouldn't get him paid a minute quicker, because Brenner probably won't be back for a week, and he told Baker the price he would pay. Not very much, for a big piece, and on short notice, too.

That's it, Baker, take it or leave it, Brenner growled, then left. It is tough to deal with Dutch Brenner.

Baker cleans his brushes, straightens the area and closes the shop. He figures the charges he would have made for the same project if he had gotten the work direct from the architect. Every day, say ten hours a day times five days, that would be 50 hours. He tries to crank his old Plymouth, but the motor grinds to a halt. He is so accustomed to car trouble, he doesn't miss a beat in his calculations. Multiply that 50 hours by $30 an hour, which is what Brenner charges for this work. That's $1,500. With some luck, he could handle a job like that every week. A year or so, and Baker could go back to fine art.

He finds a set of jumper cables in the back seat, then opens the hood and attaches the leads to his battery. He raises the cables to a passing pickup truck but is spurned. Here he is, a major art talent who will be 25 years old in fifteen minutes, holding his hands out like a beggar.

A Datsun pickup truck pulls over, then backs up beside the Plymouth. The driver gets out and opens his hood. As Baker fumbles in the darkness under the hood of the Datsun, trying to determine which of the battery posts is positive, the driver edges close and puts a hand on his back. Then rubs.

Sure you've got the leads on the right terminals, Bunkie?

Yessir, I've got it now.

When you get it started, the man says, maybe you'd like to drop by my place?

Thank you, sir, but I've got to get home to my wife, it's my birthday, and I'm hours late now. Baker clamps a lead onto a battery post. There is an explosion of blinding sparks. The man whacks his head on the hood as he flinches away, cursing. Baker changes the leads, more by feel than by sight, then hurries to get behind the wheel of the Plymouth. He turns the key in the ignition, and the motor turns over slowly, not quite catching.

Hey! the man yells, Let me crank mine first— but Baker's engine starts. Baker revs the motor a few times, retrieves the jumper cables and slams his hood. Appreciate your help, sir, Baker shouts as he pulls away. The man is behind his wheel now, and is yelling something about his car not starting, but Baker does not look back.

Baker pulls a sign from his apartment door. I LOVE YOU. Inside float a pair of big, silver balloons. Pork chops and French fries have congealed on their special honeymoon plates. He should have called. Baker eats his pork chop and fries, then gulps down Jo Ann's dinner. It is too late for her to eat, anyway. He showers, then goes into their special place, the bedroom, hugs his beautiful, pregnant wife and lies to her.

Jo?

She murmurs sleepily, hugs him and snuggles under his arm, wraps a leg over his waist.

I've got to go on a trip, starting tomorrow morning.

After a moment, Baker feels tenseness in the muscles of her leg and notes a difference in her breathing.

A trip. How will I get to work?

I'm leaving the Plymouth. And, it'll only be a little while. Four, maybe five days. Lee Quinlan, the writer? He's the guy that invited me, he's gonna pick me up at six a.m. Fred Carmichael, the photographer you met? He'll be shooting pictures for Quinlan, and I'll get a chance at an illustration for a big magazine.

Erwin… I was sick again this evening.

Your dad said he would help, if we need it. I need one of his credit cards. Just in case there's an emergency, on the trip.

8

The early morning sun edges across Lee Quinlan's face. He is in a soft, large bed. Mae Kennedy's bed. Mae is gone, must have quietly left for Austin. Her brother's wedding. They talked last night, until he fell asleep in the middle of a thought.

How suave and debonair. Did Mae drag him to bed? Pleasant images come back. She shakes him gently after he nods off in the middle of a sentence. You shouldn't drive anywhere, just get a shower and spend the night. Oh, no, I'm fine, but certainly wouldn't mind a snooze on your couch, just for a few minutes... Mae wakes him a minute later and guides him to the bathroom, where she has a scalding shower waiting. And a few minutes later, joins him in the shower.

To hell with the trip.

Quinlan gets up when his bladder won't let him stay in bed any longer. Damn, it's 7:30, according to Mae's clock. He drives to his apartment, crams all the gear he can think of into a duffel bag, grabs one rod and reel and carries the stuff to his truck. What else? Food, beer. He collects all the groceries and carries them to the truck. Morgan will have room for the meat and perishables, and Travis will have an extra cooler for the beer. They'll have to stop and get ice but can do that on the trip.

Cancel the son of a bitch. Or, send the groceries along, but stay here, work hard, wait for a certain young lady to return from Austin.

Quinlan is almost at the meeting place, MORGAN & SON DRILLING in an industrial park, when he remembers that he promised Erwin Baker he would pick him up on the way. When Lee Quinlan says he'll do something, by God, sometimes he does it. Quinlan goes back for Baker, watching the gas gauge edge toward E.

Quinlan knocks on Erwin Baker's door, and Erwin yells, Be right there, Lee.

Quinlan hears a woman say, Well, just go on and go, then.

Honey, I'll need your dad's Shell card.

Here. Take it and go on. Just go.

9

They are more than an hour late, the last of the group to arrive for the trip. Before Quinlan cuts the ignition, the motor coughs and dies. The Blazer coasts to a halt in the middle of two parking spaces. John Morgan looks up from a clipboard, frowning.

Fred Carmichael says, You're late.

Bill Weiss waves and yells something.

Luck Travis laughs with relief. The grin freezes as he sees Quinlan's glum expression.

Quinlan says, The trip's canceled.

Bullshit. Travis is on him, grabs him around the middle and bearhugs the breath from him.

Come on— Quinlan gasps, I'll take all the small ones first, and the big guys two at a time.

Morgan yells, Bring that late asshole over here. Weiss—get the rope from my truck.

Wait a minute, Attorney Bill Weiss says. This man is my client, and he'll get a fair trial before we hang him.

What are the charges? Quinlan asks.

Travis levels a finger at Quinlan and looks around the jury of outdoorsmen. He's a bad shot, beats his dog and nets fish.

What do you have to say for yourself? asks Weiss, transformed from defense attorney into hanging judge.

I never netted any fish.

That's it, Morgan says. We've got to get going.

Erwin Baker hands Quinlan his wallet and car keys. Did you tell Morgan I'm going on the trip?

Quinlan looks around the group. Mae will be out of town for a week. He will be back in eight days. Maybe sooner. Hey, John, Quinlan yells, fit my artist buddy Erwin Baker in somewhere.

Morgan looks at the young man. Didn't make plans for Baker.

Yeah, that's my fault, not his, Quinlan says. He's sponsored by his boss, Dutch Brenner, and by me. Let's see, I count six guys and three vehicles. Plenty of room.

Travis shrugs. If Quinlan invited him, that's enough for me.

Morgan scratches at his clipboard for a minute, then turns back to Baker and Quinlan. Baker, you're not paid up.

Baker looks at Morgan in surprise. Paid up?

Quinlan has about $300 in groceries. For you, it's $250 cash, like everybody else.

Baker raises his hands. I didn't know—Quinlan didn't say anything about cash. All I brought is sixty bucks, but I have a Shell card.

Won't do. I'm paying cash for food and gas as we go, all from one kitty. Saves time and screwing around.

Quinlan walks toward Morgan, stuffing his shirttail back into his jeans. I never agreed to lump sum financing.

You missed the planning session. And you called the meeting.

Couldn't make it. Now, put me down for Baker's share as well as mine, and cut the shit.

Baker needs to get the money up now, if he's going.

Quinlan nods at the group and turns away. I'll see you assholes when you get back.

Luck Travis looks around the group. Hold up. I want to go on this trip, but I'm not going without Lee Quinlan.

Quinlan starts for the Blazer again. I'm not going without Erwin Baker.

Morgan shakes his head. And I'm not putting up with a Chinese fire drill.

Weiss shoves forward with his billfold open, an attorney seeking compromise. Crazy Fred and I will split Baker's tab.

Like hell, says Carmichael.

Weiss removes his glasses and looks at Carmichael.

Yeah, Carmichael says, we'll split Baker's tab.

Morgan consults his rearranged roster. Hand over the money, Weiss. Mr. Baker, you have the pleasure of our company. Now, gear check. Spread your stuff right here. Baker fumbles with his bag until Morgan squats and scatters the contents. You can leave that cassette player and tapes. I don't want to have to listen to your stuff, or Quinlan's Bach or Travis's rock. Do you smoke?

Not anymore

Good. You can ride or drive with Luck Travis. He shakes Baker's Dopp kit. Is that cologne in the kit?

Uh, yeah.

Morgan pulls the kit open and looks inside. He drops a bottle on top of the cassette player. Put all this stuff in my front office. Quinlan? Get your junk squared away in my truck.

Hey— Travis turns to Morgan. Quinlan is riding with me.

Morgan looks at Travis with raised eyebrows.

His smoking won't bother me, says Travis.

You complained about Weiss's pipe smoking last night.

That was in a restaurant.

To hell with it, Morgan says. I can stay here and solve some of my problems.

Quinlan looks around the group. We don't go without John Morgan leading the way.

Morgan shakes his head. Baker, be useful. Go back inside, get all those CB antennas and radios off my desk and pass 'em out. Then, let's get out of here, before I kill Lee Quinlan.

10

Morgan—what are you guys waiting for? Quinlan yells into Bill Weiss's citizen's band microphone. Oops, bad CB manners. Red Dog One, this is the Quail Shooter on channel 27, have you got a copy, come back? Quinlan is standing at the passenger door of Weiss's station wagon, the only person not seated and ready to leave. After chugging a beer, it was necessary to trot into Morgan's building and take a leak.

Morgan's voice crackles over the CB as he pulls the crew cab truck out of the parking area. Let's dispense with the CB jargon. Now, tell me where we're going to pick up the rest of our troops.

Dutch Brenner is a couple of hours in front of us, unless he broke down on the way, or stopped for a Dr. Pepper and lunch. We'll pick him up at his uncle's motel in metropolitan Freer, copy?

Ten-four, we'll be peeling off at the Beeville exit, next pit stop. Incidentally, if he's not standing right there, we be gone. To hell with Brenner.

11

Break 27 for Kurt Brenner, Dutch Brenner's CB radio hisses at him. Must be a landline put through by the operator. Maybe Lee Quinlan calling. He keys the microphone. It's a request from the operator that he place a call to his shop.

Brenner pulls the truck and boat over before he makes the call. It would be wise to check the axles of the boat trailer after an hour on the road. He walks around the boat and feels the tires and axles. Quinlan was smart to put his Mako on a good trailer with twin axles, but the rig is getting old. The CB hisses again, an operator tells someone to go ahead.

Dutch, you there?

Brenner here.

We've got a problem with the Atkins agency. They say we were supposed to have that new Galleria sign up Thursday.

They were supposed to get a check to me Wednesday.

Allen said you billed him without his extra commission—

Call the chiseling bastard and tell him when all the money is in the shop, his sign goes up. Did Baker finish the painting?

Last night. Looks great. He wanted to get paid early.

No. I'll check back tomorrow on a pay phone that only costs two bits. Clear.

Back on the road. Ahead, Brenner sees a sign bragging about Cold Beer and Hot Food, Turn Off Next Exit. A few minutes later, Brenner turns into the gravel parking lot of MIJALIK'S BARBQ BEER ENTERTAINMENT NIGHTLY. As he locks the truck, the CB hisses at him, the same operator calling for Kurt Brenner. Another money problem? Or maybe, Lee Quinlan. He opens the door, keys the mike and it's Quinlan.

Dutch. Got the boat?

Boat? I'm headed for my deer lease. You're gonna come down and help me fix those tree blinds.

Better have the boat, or I'll stomp your ass.

Better bring a bat and the baseball team, old buddy.

The boat?

Big Mako, about 21 feet long, black Mercury motor?

That's it.

It's right behind me, sitting on a trailer.

Thought so. We'll get you at the motel in Freer. Dinner at Jack Voss's, then on to Matamoras—

Clear.

Brenner walks up a few wooden steps onto the porch of the roadhouse. On the right of the entry hall is a neat, bright cafe. To the left, a stale beer smell oozes out of the darkness. It has been a long time since he had a beer. One wouldn't hurt. Inside the darkness, he can make out small tables from the light of beer signs. Willie Nelson is singing to some pretty girl about her money and his time from a jukebox. A few customers are scattered around, most of them farmhand or cowboy types nursing longneck beer bottles.

In one corner, two women are at a booth table. A middle-aged man in a business suit sits with the women. The businessman is being charming. He lights a cigarette for one of the women with a gold lighter, and glancing Brenner's way, says something that brings a laugh from the women.

A young woman, maybe 18, cute. An older woman, maybe Momma to the girl. Momma looks pretty good, if you don't mind whisky dents on your woman. There's a table in the middle of the room. Brenner turns a chair around, waits for his eyes to adjust to the darkness before he sits down. Now he can see posters on the walls. Rodeos, dances, Country Western singers. A painting of a cowboy being pitched off a bad horse. You can tell the horse is bad because his eyes are wicked and you see his teeth through a snarl.

The bartender is sitting on a stool under a Lone Star beer light. Lazy son of a bitch doesn't get up for Brenner. Brenner scrapes the chair as he sits, making plenty of noise. The girl looks back at him, then concentrates on her drink. The woman glances his way and laughs as she blows smoke at the ceiling. Brenner winks at the woman and lifts his cap to the man behind the bar. A bottle of Lone Star for that pretty lady there, and a case of Lone Stars for me.

The bartender brings one bottle of beer to Brenner's table. The bartender is a round-shouldered man with the scarred eyebrows and puffy ears of a heavyweight boxer, or a wrestler. Must not have won too often, judging from the dirty apron.

The bartender stands next to the table, bald head almost brushing the unlighted chandelier. You want a case of Lone Stars, you'll have to stop down the road. Or drink 'em here one at a time.

Just want a beer and some barbecue, pardner. Brenner flips him a ten-dollar bill, but oops, it goes too far and falls on the floor.

Beer in here, barbecue in the cafe. The bartender lingers a moment next to the table, then stoops, picks up the bill and goes back behind the bar. He doesn't return to his stool. Brenner squints at him, grinning, and chugs the beer.

A woman is setting up for music on the little stage in one corner. Bleached blonde about Brenner's age, somewhere south of 40, carrying an old guitar that Willie might have thrown away. She has spangles on her shirt and wears overly tight jeans. She kicks some wires and moves two loudspeaker boxes around, then taps the mike. No sound.

This stuff gonna work tonight, Barney?

The bartender goes over and is attentive. I don't know, Lacey. Electronics is over my head. Mr. Mijalik will have to look at it. Barney wipes tables, looking businesslike.

When Brenner raises his cap, he gets the big man's eye right away. Another beer, starbender, Brenner says. And save my place. I've gotta git hold of Old Shorty. As Brenner moves toward the men's room, he sees that the businessman has his hand on the girl's thigh and is edging her skirt up. Short skirt, long legs. She glances at Brenner and brushes the man's hand away. The man grips her bare knee, grinning at the woman across the table and laughs about something he has just said.

Brenner frowns. That's no way to treat a lady. The men's room door has a rusty spring that groans at Brenner, then slams the door shut on his heel. Maybe it does something for the electronics, because the sound comes up and Lacey yells, Let's play a lick or two before it quits. She goes into a guitar riff.

Not bad. Maybe he'll postpone the trip for an evening of culture. Hey, might even take one of those little ladies away from that asshole. The older one really likes him, he can tell. Pissing in the old porcelain urinal and listening to the music, Brenner looks over the graffiti. For a good time in Dallas, a phone number. Illiterate scrawls, bad art, insulting references to A&M and University of Texas sexual practices.

Passing the table where the man and the two women are seated, Brenner catches the older woman's eye and gestures at his table. Scraping the chair again, he tilts the longneck and nods at her as he gulps down the last of the foam in the bottle. The businessman leans across the table and whispers something to the woman. Both women are giggling, looking away from Brenner.

A shrug for the bartender. What's a man to do? He wipes beer foam from his beard. Be tidy, Dutch. He grabs the bill of his cap and jams it firmly on his head. In three steps he's across the room standing over the businessman. The man smiles nervously but doesn't look up. Brenner gives him a long moment to consider the situation, but Brenner is not really watching the man. Brenner is more conscious of Barney.

Help you out, pardner? the businessman asks, a catch in his voice.

Yeah. Get up.

Look, fella, we're just havin' a drink, not botherin' you—

You're mistreating some nice ladies, and that bothers me. Brenner jabs the man in the shoulder with a finger. Get up and leave.

The bartender moves around the corner of the bar and across the dance floor and lunges for Brenner's shirt collar but misses. A moment later, the bartender looks up at Brenner, surprised, not used to being the one on the deck. He wipes his nose, looks at blood on his hand and starts to rise.

Be polite, Dutch. Excuse me, but you shouldn't put your hands on my shirt—Someone grabs Brenner's collar and pulls him backward and he is off balance for an instant, then stars explode just before the floor leaps up and hits him in the back of the head. A fat man looks down at him with something in his hand and leans over to hit him again— but Brenner rolls away and there's loud hell, chairs flying, women screaming, glass breaking. Someone kicks Brenner in the head on the way past, the businessman, but now Brenner is on his feet, lurching after the fat man, fending away a blow with his forearm, ignoring the bartender.

Mistake, Dutch. The bartender seizes Brenner from behind in a professional neck hold with a knee between his legs, lifts Brenner up and onto his toes. Brenner is unable to breathe. After a struggle, Brenner relaxes and gasps, Okay, Barney. The bartender lowers Brenner just enough for his toes to contact the floor.

It is quiet in the bar, except for the hiss of the loudspeakers on the stage and the bartender snorting blood down the back of Brenner's shirt.

Well, tough guy, the fat man says. You want some more of me?
I was just leaving.

Bet your ass you're leaving. Fuckin' assholes want trouble
around here, I give it to 'em. Barney, this asshole owe me any bar
money?

Nossir, Mr. Mijalik. He just gimme a ten.

Well, he probably caused a hundred in damages. Mijalik jerks a
thumb at a side door. I'm gonna take it out of his hide. The
bartender drags Brenner out the door and down the steps, then
turns him around. Mijalik looks down from the porch, opens his
jacket to show Brenner a pistol in his belt, then carefully rotates a
large ring to be sure the signet is on the outside of his middle finger.
He places a hand on Brenner's shoulder as Barney lifts Brenner off
his feet again, draws back his fist and smashes Brenner in the face.

The bartender releases him, and Brenner slumps to his knees.

Now, you go ahead and leave, and stay gone, the bartender
says, and you won't have to see our Justice of the Peace.

Brenner wipes snot and blood from his nose with a sleeve.

Mijalik smiles down from the porch. I'm the Justice of the
Peace.

12

Quinlan?

Say what, Bill.

Bladder relief time.

I'll pull over and you can baptize a roadside bush.

That's illegal, Quinlan. Here comes a town, with civilized
facilities.

The convoy is approaching Historical Goliad, Birthplace of the
Texas Revolution, according to a roadside sign.

We don't want to get separated from the other vehicle, Weiss.
Use the CB and let the group know it's pit stop time.

Weiss fumbles with the microphone. He finds a button on the
side of the mike. Uh, Morgan or Baker, come in. There is a long
silence from the radio.

You have to release the key after you talk into the mike.

Oh. Weiss releases the button, and hears, about 80 miles. Come back?

Uh, we missed that, replies Weiss. What'd you say?

This be's Luck, and you're coming in faint and far; who've we got calling, come back?

Quinlan takes the mike from Weiss. The attorney needs a CB handle. Luck, you be's talkin' to the Judge in just a minute, when we get this gadget turned around right. Quinlan hands the microphone back to Weiss. Talk in this side, Judge, and keep it close to your mouth.

Uh, Luck, this is the Judge, and we're gonna have to stop up here. Come back?

Okay, Judge, we got you wall to wall on that transmission. My navigator says we're coming up on Goliad, but Convoy Leader Morgan said our next scheduled stop is Beeville, got a problem, better get back to the leader.

Uh, come in, Convoy Leader? We're gonna make a pit stop in Goliad for my bladder or we'll definitely have a problem. And, Quinlan says there's a Gulf station that may have gas for a top-off. Come back to the Judge?

Judge, big ten four, this is Morgan, turning right at the next git-off. Incidentally, using that CB just dropped your IQ 30 points. Got a copy on a bladder problem, Crazy? Morgan asks.

In the other vehicle, Carmichael keys his mike. Duh?

The caravan pulls off the highway. They pass the Goliad Dairy Queen. No beer, no ice. The Old Trading Post cafe has curtains on the windows and looks like it would be operated by a pair of little blue-haired ladies. The Gulf station has only three cars and a pickup waiting for gas, and there are no Out Of Gas signs. Morgan, in the lead, stops behind the last car. Weiss and Carmichael pull in behind him.

The men's room has three people in line. Across the street is a dusty parking lot surrounding a frame building. Neon blinks, BBQ BEER. In the harsh sunlight of a Texas afternoon, the neon gives the building a cheap, garish look. Just right for this group, Quinlan thinks. There, he says to Morgan.

Morgan hands Erwin Baker a wad of dollars. Stay with the gas situation, kid. We'll be right back. As the men walk into the darkness of the bar area, Morgan goes to the bartender and gives the man a twenty-dollar bill. You guys tell the man here what you want, he says, and we're gone.

Weiss and Quinlan head immediately for the Men's Room. Weiss glances over the toilet wall graffiti. He points to one. WELCOME TO TEXAS YANKEE. NOW GO HOME.

They return to the bar. The bartender has a puffed eye and a swollen nose.

You men take all the time you want to drink your beer, he says, but don't even think about taking the bottles out with you. He dabs at his nose with a blood-spotted rag. Unless you want to see our Justice of the Peace.

At the edge of town, the caravan slows as a railroad-crossing signal comes down and a freight train rackets past. Quinlan's vehicle eases to a halt beside a black limousine. A hearse is in front of the limousine. Behind the limousine's tinted glass, he can make out an angular woman and a skinny boy. A family in bereavement.

The boy glances at the station wagon, turns to see the boat behind them, then focuses on Quinlan's face. Quinlan gestures with a thumb, and mouths at him, Chin up.

The boy gestures with a middle finger.

Quinlan nods and yells at the boy. It's going to be a tough life kid. Keep that finger ready.

Spooked   Herb Booth

IV

The caravan pulls into Freer.

Watching along the highway that arrows through the little
town, the men see neon lights ahead that advertise TOURIST
CABINS HUNTERS WELCOME. Weiss pulls off the highway and
into the center court, parking the station wagon on the caliche
driveway behind the dusty black Bronco of Dutch Brenner. A
Bronco with a boat attached. Quinlan pats the side of the big boat as
he walks past.

Morgan catches up with Quinlan. Your boat?

This is our fuel tanker, John. Forty-gallon gas tank, two jerry
cans full of gas. Quinlan strides through the haze of dust to the
porch. He bangs on the door. Fall out, fisherman.

Sure you got the right door? asks Morgan from five paces back.

If not, I hope someone can take a joke. Quinlan bangs on the
door again.

Dutch Brenner throws the door open, a nickel-plated revolver at
face level. Above the hand, the slits of a pair of puffed eyes glare at
Quinlan. Could you knock a little louder?

God Almighty—

You can call me Dutch.

God Almighty, Dutch, it's good to see you. But you look awful.

Brenner sits on one of the two beds in the motel room as
Quinlan and Morgan enter.

I don't suppose you want to tell us what happened, says
Morgan.

Brenner eases one eye open. Luck failure.

Enough of the gay badinage, Quinlan says. We've got to make it
to Voss's place for supper.

Morgan nods. Dutch, I want you to go on out and get in the
back seat of my crew cab and stretch out. Travis and I will get your
stuff packed and loaded.

How about, I kick your ass instead?

Be a few days before I'll worry about that. Morgan rounds up
Brenner's belongings and stuffs them in a duffel bag. Morgan looks

at the men peering through the motel door. Baker. You're driving Brenner's Bronco. Get his keys. Morgan glances at the puff-eyed Brenner, still sitting on his bed, pistol now holstered. Brenner grunts, stands and tucks the pistol into his bag, then fishes out a set of keys and holds them out for someone to take.

2

Just before 7 p.m., the caravan pulls up to Jack Voss's ranch gate. The ranch foreman is waiting with the gate wide open. The stocky brown man nods at the group of tired men as they drive slowly past.

Welcome to the Good Luck, he yells. Quinlan—que tal?

Arnoldo—muy bien, some days.

A brisk north wind gusts into the vehicles as they get out in Voss's courtyard. It is almost cold in the wind, the first cool front of the year.

Jack Voss shakes hands with each of them as they walk through the double doors of the main ranch house.

Quinlan. How's your behavior? Voss looks like a third-string hired hand. His hat is frayed, his jacket needs a dry-cleaning, or a garbage can, and his jeans were worn out years ago. His boots are in worse shape.

Voss waves toward the bar, an old brass-railed, polished oak triangle in one corner of the high-ceilinged room. But the fragrance of fresh-baked bread wafts from the kitchen and another aroma promises pinto beans. Quinlan sees Travis drawn to the kitchen door and follows, along with Voss. A rotund, motherly little woman is preparing food.

That's Agatha, the housekeeper, says Voss. Best cook between here and Luckenbach. She's kinda straight-laced. We watch our language around Agatha.

Travis whispers to Quinlan and Voss. Looks like my Catholic grandmother. He moves smilingly into the kitchen, intent on winning over Agatha, and perhaps getting an early sample of the bread and beans.

Quinlan also lusts after the bread and beans, but heads for the bar. Brenner, working hard to keep his puffball eyes open, falls in behind Quinlan. The other men have taken seats near the fireplace.

It is an impressive room, all dark oak and native stone, with heavy-racked game animals placed high along the walls. Scattered along one wall are rodeo photographs. Bull riding is the primary subject. In one picture, a younger, leaner Jack Voss is in mid-air, while the bull moves away with straps and mud flying. A few trophies are hung in one corner. A large gold buckle with silver inlays announces that a champion bronc rider won it.

Voss is behind the bar, looking at Quinlan and Brenner over his half-frame glasses. I know John Morgan, the oilman, and Lee Quinlan, the famous writer.

Quinlan nods at Brenner. This is the famous painter, Dutch Brenner.

Sign painter, mumbles Brenner.

Voss frowns at them as he hangs his Stetson on an antler tine. Must be a tough occupation in Houston. What'll it be, gents?

Quinlan eases his elbow gingerly down on the edge of the bar. Aspirin, barkeep.

Dr. Pepper, rasps Brenner, letting his eyelids ooze shut.

As Voss turns to fill their orders, Quinlan reads a gilt-lettered sign on the cabinet. Listen to this, Dutch: Check all weapons with the bartender, to insure their proper working order.

Brenner forces a smile. Hope this bar is friendlier than a certain place back down the highway.

One Dr. Pepper, four aspirins, says Voss. We guarantee the Good Luck Bar to be friendly, or else.

Or else?

We kill you.

Quinlan sees Weiss stoking his pipe as he heads outside. He fumbles for a cigarette and joins him. What the hell; nine days to kick the habit before he sees a beautiful non-smoker again. Halfway through the cigarette, Quinlan drops it into the fire pit. Cold turkey, starting right now.

Voss sends Arnoldo out with a pitcher of Margaritas and a tray of glasses. The other men soon leave the comfort of the bar and the warmth of the fireplace to join Quinlan and Weiss. Travis sits as far away from both as possible, but still coughs from the tobacco smoke when it comes his way.

The wind moves across the patio in sudden gusts. The night sky is cloudless, and the South Texas stars seem to be hanging just above the branches of a spreading mesquite tree. Mesmerized by the glowing coals, the men sip Jack Voss's Good Luck Margaritas and watch as he turns cabrito on the pit. Occasionally, he moves the goat carcass with a small pitchfork, then opens the fire pit and shuffles coals around with a shovel.

Bill Weiss says be damned if he'll eat something that looks like his neighbor's greyhound.

Erwin Baker's attention is riveted on the cabrito. The wind whips the fire and sends a small explosion of sparks scattering. Baker grabs the pitchfork and turns the meat, then pulls off a strip and samples it.

Delicious, he yells, and just about done. Voss peers over his glasses, frowning. No one makes a move to attack the cabrito.

Goaded by Travis, Quinlan begins a story about a recent trip to the Chandeleurs, a string of islands offshore from Louisiana. Baker and Jack Voss are the only listeners who don't interrupt to correct his account. The group pulled six boats from Houston to Hopedale, Louisiana, then ran offshore to the island-- Five and a half boats, someone corrects, Quinlan's boat ran only half the time. They caught hundreds of big surf specks. And five big blacktip sharks, someone adds.

Laughter.

Travis explains the laughter. Someone butchered those blacktips and put 'em in Quinlan's ice chest. Forgot to put ice on 'em. Couple of nights later, we had our leaving celebration.

I had too much silly water-- Quinlan begins, but Travis interrupts.

We had to drag him to his tent. Next morning, a couple of bird watchers showed up at daybreak, bitchin' because we were camped on a bird sanctuary. Saw those two heel tracks in the sand, leading to Quinlan's tent. Accused us of taking endangered sea turtles.

Quinlan finishes the story. These sons of bitches came over and dragged me out of my sack to prove I wasn't a sea turtle, then expected me to fix breakfast.

Voss asks, Why would you fix breakfast for a group like that?

Quinlan thinks about it, surprised that he hasn't pondered the question before. I decided to poison them all on this trip. He looks around the group. Anyway, there I was, scratching up breakfast stuff, in a very delicate condition, when I opened that ice chest full of three-day old, rotten shark carcasses —

I was next to Quinlan when he opened the chest, says Travis. It went 'Poomph!' and a green cloud wrapped around him.

Everyone laughs except Quinlan, remembering the exquisite agony of his hangover. Baker's concentration on the cabrito seems total, and Quinlan decides that he must have missed breakfast at home as well as lunch on the drive. And Brenner doesn't laugh. Brenner's swollen face looks as though it would burst if he smiled.

Quinlan finds a seat next to Baker.

Uh, Lee, Baker begins, I really enjoyed your book — but Quinlan leans around Baker and grabs Carmichael by the shirt collar. Baker's nose is rudely bumped as Quinlan shakes Carmichael.

Crazy Fred — get Brenner's attention, over there. I want to say something to the two of you. And excuse me, Baker. Didn't mean to interrupt your concentration on the roasting goat. Mind swapping seats for a minute? Quinlan smiles at Carmichael and Brenner. I just want to thank my two best friends for something special.

Brenner says, Here comes Mae Kennedy.

We told Mae what a great guy you are, Carmichael says, but hell, I had to tell her about your herpes.

If you're gonna lie, why not leprosy, or AIDS.

Relax, Lee, says Brenner. The nastier we got about you, the saintlier Mae Kennedy thought you must be.

Tell you something else, Carmichael says. When we get back, I'm gonna give Mae a chance to get to know me, and to hell with you. Carmichael moves to the other side of the group.

Brenner says, I think Crazy Fred flipped over Mae.

Quinlan yells after Carmichael— Over my dead body, pard.

Arnoldo brings out another pitcher of Good Luck Margaritas. The pitcher is emptied immediately, and Arnoldo goes back for another.

Dutch Brenner and Luck Travis argue about politics, loudly. You bleeding-heart liberals, Brenner says. You're tearing up America. Makes me puke, listening to all that horseshit about loving a poor, deprived person who has to rob and steal to make it.

Travis looks belligerently around the crowd. Just because you're a bit closer to good resources doesn't mean you own 'em.

Brenner snorts. You've got that cabin near the bay. There are lots of Asians who would love to move in. You could take on a family, teach 'em to set crab traps, maybe concentrate on those stone crabs you like so much.

Travis leans forward, smiling. I like the idea, Dutch. Reminds me of the days when the Irish came over, starving to death. And when the Germans came to Texas, looking for a new life.

The empty land is gone.

Never was empty, Dutch.

Indians. Torture a buffalo to death, then eat its guts. Besides, the Irish and Germans built Texas. Where were the Vietnamese and all those other sons of bitches when things were tough?

I give up. Where were they?

They weren't here fighting Comanches.

Were you, or your father?

Hey, my old man fought Germans in World War Two. And woulda fought the Japs in the jungle, and Chinks in Korea, and Zips in Viet Nam, if they'd have let him.

Good American.

You're damn right.

Dutch, the misery of every person is yours, or else you are a scum organism. Got that?

Baker looks at the ground, expecting an explosion from Brenner.

Brenner surprises even Quinlan by replying quietly. I love you liberals. You are the truth, the way and the light.

Make your point.

Americans ought to tell everyone else to do good or die but stay out of our country.

Okay, God, I'm here now; pull up the ladder.

God hasn't spent any time with you that he told me about.

We don't chat on a regular basis. But you don't have to have the big guy forcing you to be a good person.

Skip the bullshit. Tell me when you're gonna sponsor a family of refugees.

Travis thinks about the question. Good point. As soon as I get back, I'm gonna demand the government send me a family of Viets. Put 'em to work as sign painters.

Everyone laughs but Baker and Brenner. Baker does not want to laugh with Brenner watching. And Brenner nods to himself, feeling that he has won the debate.

With the coals dying down and a fourth Margarita pitcher empty, Voss declares the cabrito edible. Except for Baker, the fishermen move slowly at first, anxious not to seem like rude, hungry guests.

Weiss samples a strip of the meat, still thinking about large dogs. Delicious.

The men watch their language as Agatha comes out among the vulgar crowd and serves fresh bread and pinto beans. Travis helps Agatha carry food from the kitchen and is obsequious, raving about the magnificence of her cooking. Agatha blushes when Travis makes her sit down and eat with the men. He drags his chair next to hers.

Lord, it's unbelievable, Quinlan says, using a fork to peel off another layer of meat, and it's best with just a hunk of fresh bread wrapped around a chunk of goat.

It's best with two chunks of goat wrapped around another chunk of goat, says Carmichael.

Voss smiles with satisfaction. Quinlan, if you and Carmichael don't get some of Agatha's pinto beans, you'll hurt her feelings. She won't let you have any fresh venison tomorrow night.

Quinlan and Carmichael make a rush for the pinto bean pot.

That reminds me, we need some camp meat. Any of you fishermen have an interest in shooting a doe tomorrow, instead of dove? Luck Travis, is it, and Brenner. Voss grimaces at Brenner. Dutch, you won't need a rifle. You can ugly a doe to death. You two men will have to bunk together, in that far room there, so I don't have to wake everybody up looking for you.

He looks around the crowd. We'll stake the two doe hunters out early—the poor bastards will miss Agatha's breakfast—then us lazy hunters will see if we can knock down a few whitewing canapés, and some mourning dove hors d'oeuvres to go with the venison. The host pitches the remainder of his drink on the embers of the campfire. Buenos noches. Y'all can fight one more pitcher of Good Luck Margaritas, then pick a bunk and practice your snoring.

Ambushers   Sam Caldwell

V

Lee Quinlan, John Morgan and Fred Carmichael are stationed along a tree line, overlooking a grain field and a lake beyond. Mourning dove and bigger white wing dove fly past, often in flocks of a dozen. Across the field, they can see Jack Voss and a large black retriever at the edge of a pond. Voss stands and shoots. The dog retrieves a bird from the water.

The retrievers for Quinlan, Morgan and Weiss on the field are two of Arnoldo's nephews. The boys ignore Morgan and Carmichael but are poised and ready to run as soon as Quinlan raises his shotgun. Quinlan has twelve birds, two of them whitewing dove. Quinlan indulged in a running commentary; That's six birds for seven shots. And later, Nine for eleven. One whitewing and two mourners to go. Quinlan is happy with his efforts for the morning.   Morgan is disgusted. Empty 12-gauge hulls are scattered around his feet. He has only two mourning dove tucked in his game bag.

Carmichael is doing better than Morgan and is elated at the shooting. Where the hell is Luck Travis? Carmichael yells.

Quinlan nods. Travis usually beats everyone at bird shooting, and this would have been a fine day for him. Travis and Brenner are off missing deer, Quinlan says. The group may not have a damn thing to eat tonight but my birds. He stands and fires twice. The boys are off into the field, racing to be the first on a downed bird. My limit, he says, picking up his folding stool and moving away from the shooting line.

Come back here, you righteous son of a bitch, Morgan says.

Kill that bird, Quinlan shouts, then says nothing as Morgan wheels and misses with both shots.

The bird boys point at incoming birds from north and northeast. Quinlan drops the stool and makes a clean double kill, then puts two fresh shells into the gun and grins at Morgan and Carmichael.

Hey, Crazy? yells Morgan.

Say what, John?

I like the son of a bitch better when he's drunk and obnoxious.

Jack Voss stops nearby in his truck. Arnoldo gets out of the passenger side, walks to the group and squats down near Quinlan.

Mr. Voss says, tell Mr. Quinlan to let the birds rest, come on and see the new senderos.

2

Dutch Brenner hunts as he watches birds. Being careful, he can look through his rifle scope and his field glasses without too much pain. Through the glasses he spies on a group of cardinal-like birds that has claimed the open Sendero in front of his blind. Pyrrhuloxia, he decides, and the little ruddy birds moving in are Inca dove.

He looks over his hunting area again, noting a few cattle. Two amble closer. Brahmans, the big, hump-shouldered East Indian breed that does well in the harsh Texas brush country. There is a wood thrush across the Sendero; two of 'em. Cock and a hen? Must be like robins, identical boys and girls. No tits on the girls, but the boys can tell the difference. He puts the glasses down to watch a mob of tiny birds moving past the edge of his blind. Chickadees and their buddies, titmice. Titmouses? He can hear the early morning metallic chink of unseen cardinals behind him in the heavy cover.

Coming up the slope of the Sendero are two deer.

Brenner ceases to be an observer of birds. There are three, then six deer in the open. Two are bucks He puts down the field glasses slowly, eases his rifle up and finds the deer in the scope. They are feeding his way, unhurried.

The deer must have moved past Travis's blind, would have provided an easy shot. Travis must be asleep. Brenner frowns, the movement hurting his broken nose and puffed eyes. A man hunts carefully, when he gets the chance.

Brenner focuses on the whitetails. One of the deer is a damn good buck, but the big deer eases back into the brush, as though he was aware of being seen. Two are big yearlings, their spots almost gone now, but also safe. The yearlings seem to be associated with a certain doe, sparing her.

That leaves two barren does. The biggest doe is wary, turns away from him and starts back down the Sendero toward Travis's blind, leaving Brenner only a rear end view. Now all the deer are nervous, have probably picked up his scent. Maybe he should go for a Texas neck shot on the largest doe, a 3006 slug up the asshole. Nah, too messy. Collect some meat for the evening campfire. He shoots the small barren doe through the neck, just below her jaw. The other whitetails vanish into the brush, running back in the direction of Travis's blind.

In three minutes, Brenner has nearly finished the chore of field dressing the deer. Steam from the doe's intestines warms his face, then rises in a small cloud. As he removes the doe's liver and heart, he sees that one of the Brahman cows has moved within twenty feet and is watching him.

Hidy, ma'am. He rolls the doe over to allow the entrails to spill onto the ground. The cow moves a few steps closer, her big ears and hanging dewlap swaying, her nostrils working as she smells the gore. Brenner crosses the doe's forelegs and hoists her upper body over his shoulder to let the last of the blood drain from the body cavity. The big cow watches as Brenner holds the carcass up, the doe's neck lolling over his arm. The cow's dark eyes seem full of reproach.

Friend of yours? The job finished, he lays the doe gently down and waves his arms at the Brahman. The big cow turns and moves ponderously away.

See you around the market, big girl. He wipes his knife blade and his hands on tufts of grass, picks up his rifle and starts for an opening in the brush. Maybe he'll have a chance at that big buck and look after a sleeping hunter.

Daybreak on Good Luck 3   Sam Caldwell

VI

Want a wild dog pelt, Quinlan?

Jack Voss and Quinlan watch from the pickup as two coyotes circle one another far up a hill. The pair is in the center of the cleared Sendero.

Good looking hide on the big coyote, Arnoldo says from outside the pickup, handing binoculars through the passenger window to Quinlan.

Boy and girl, I think, says Quinlan, squinting through the glasses. Definitely. She just sat down, and he's trying to get a sniff.

Jack Voss jerks a thumb at the rifle racked behind their heads. Good optics on that .270.

Quinlan steps from the truck and eases the rifle from its scabbard. He opens the bolt, sees the gleam of a cartridge, then estimates the distance. Three-hundred twenty yards, give or take a foot. He wraps the sling around his wrist, leans against the truck and finds the two wild dogs in the scope. She's playing hard to get, he says, or maybe, 'Quit that, Willie— your nose is cold.'

Those two coyotes will make some pups, and feed 'em a dozen of my fawns next spring. Put a round up his butt, says Voss.

I'll spot with the glasses, Arnoldo says, case you can get off a second shot. Hey, he's getting ready to make out. She's nippin' at him, but letting him take the position—

I hate to interrupt true love, but the big one has a fine coat… Quinlan squeezes the trigger. The small coyote tumbles away, regains her balance and with tail between legs, runs into the brush. The large coyote disappears in a spray of gravel and caliche dust in the opposite direction of the small coyote.

Missed. Sorry, Quinlan lies.

Esta no problema, Voss says. You just created a gay coyote.

Down the slope of another Sendero, driving slow and watching for more coyotes, they hear a distant shot.

Sounds like someone got a doe, yells Arnoldo, riding in the back of the truck, elbows on top of the cab. Probably from Mr. Brenner's area.

Hold on, Arnoldo. We're gonna check on our meat-gitters. Voss picks up speed, and all three of the coyote hunters have to hold on as the truck buckets along a rough stretch. In spite of the racket, they hear another shot. That would be Travis, Voss says. There'll be a warm teepee tonight. We'll give 'em a lift back to camp.

As the truck slows and jolts around a turn toward Travis's blind, they hear three more shots, closely spaced. Arnoldo says from the top of the truck cab, Big buck down over by the arroyo where we put Mr. Travis. Don't see a hunter.

2

Travis wakes shivering, huddled on his side in a ground-level brush blind. There has just been a gunshot. Must have been Brenner, up the Sendero a thousand yards. A pair of sticks are gouging his neck, and he has a headache. Goddamn those last three Good Luck Margaritas, anyway, he whispers. Then he smiles. Better than being in a hotel hallway with your pecker waving in the breeze.

He cradles an old Browning rifle that belongs to Jack Voss. He checks the rifle, admires the rifle's form, an aesthetically beautiful tool for killing large mammals at a distance. He eases the safety off, ready to fire, and lurches to a sitting position. He peers through an opening of the brush blind. The clearing in front features dark undergrowth, marled earth, patches of shinnery. Higher in the Mesquite and Huisache trees across the clearing, golds and greens from the early morning sun are brilliant.

The fog of his breath rises in the chill morning air, then drifts gently behind him, away from the clearing. To his left, he can see open terrain to the edge of a steep arroyo, maybe 100 yards. To his right is an open lane cut in the dense Texas brush by bulldozers. He can see maybe three hundred yards up the slope of the Sendero in Brenner's direction.

Three deer step warily into the clearing on his right.

Squinting, he sees that one is a smallish buck, and two others are doe. Holding his breath, he eases the Browning up and looks through the scope. The deer are very close, living sculptures in beautiful tones of gray and tan. A small mesquite tree has masked two other bucks. Damn—one of the bucks has matching drop tines and a helluva rack. The buck steps into the clearing, quartered away from Travis. He puts the crosshairs of the scope on the shoulder of the deer and eases the safety off. He exhales half a breath and steadies the sight, remembering early training by his father, a Marine in World War Two.

BASS is the slogan, boy; Breathe, Aim, Slack, Squeeze — the rifle slams Travis back, knocking him off balance. He scrambles to his feet and pushes through the brush of the blind. The other deer have vanished from the clearing, but the buck is on its side, kicking. The deer gets to its feet.

He strides quickly toward the deer, not wanting to shoot it again. Hell, wishing he hadn't shot it the first time. At the edge of the arroyo, near the mesquite tree that had first masked the buck, he raises the rifle. The deer is moving clumsily toward the brush. Through the scope, he can see only the deer's rump. He should have stayed in the blind. Without the extra pump of adrenaline from seeing him, it might have lain there and died. At the edge of the brush, the buck slumps to its front knees, falls and is still. Travis takes a deep breath, feeling a shudder that he understands perfectly well, but could not have explained. He walks to the mesquite tree and sits against the trunk. May as well let Arnoldo get messy. That is, leave his chore to someone else. He fumbles in his pockets, finds a folding Buck knife, a longtime outdoor companion that has gutted many trout and redfish, and has seen duty as a tool for cleaning ducks, geese, dove and quail. He imagines himself walking across the clearing, rolling the buck onto its back. The shiny clean blade is inserted just in front of the anus, then, thumb on the outside, knife blade inside, you cut up the center of the belly just under the skin, careful about rupturing the intestines. Split the breastbone at the midline gristle. He helped his father field dress deer and cattle in the old times, before he went off to kill people and have people try to kill him in a different universe.

To hell with it, he says. Arnoldo is an expert who will want to earn his Good Luck paycheck. Travis, a middle-aged businessman, puts the knife back in his pocket and relaxes. As his head contacts the tree trunk, a rifle slug whangs into the rock three feet from his left boot. An instant later, he hears the flat crack of the shot. A middle-aged businessman might have reflected on the strangeness of the situation, but Travis rolls away from his exposed position of the tree trunk and attempts to get a fix on the origin of the rifle shot. He feels himself slipping over the edge of the arroyo. As he goes down, he puts the remaining three rounds from the Browning into a certain small area of the mesquite tangle.

Gravel rolls down the slope with him, lubricating his descent. He hugs the rifle across his body and skids feet first, with some control. Then he slams into a root tangle, and losing all control, tumbles ass over elbows, finally stopping head down a dozen feet from a drop off.

Upside down, clutching the rifle, Travis listens as gravel cascades on down, then splashes into water at the bottom of the arroyo. He waits a few long seconds, then fishes gingerly in his vest, but there are no cartridges in his pockets.

Goddamn son of a bitch, he mutters. He moves around to an upright position and checks the action of the Browning. The magazine is empty. He grabs at his pocket, but the knife is gone. And now he realizes that he has a very bad pain in his left foot, a pain that has to be looked after, no matter what other situation might threaten. He lodges the empty rifle in the base of the brush that stopped his skid and eases himself down the slope to the drop off. It isn't so bad, now that he can look for handholds. He lands in a knee-deep pool of water.

Lurching to the sandy bank of the little stream, he fumbles loose the laces of his boot and pulls it off. The wool sock, blood red up to the ankle, comes squishing part way off with the boot.

Holy Mary-- He gently tugs the sock from the foot. A pink object falls from the open sock into the muddy water. A pebble?

Mother of God-- He wiggles his toes, counting five in the dim light. Above his left ankle, oozing blood is a small gash. And just ahead, glinting in the clearing water of the pool is his knife, and beyond the knife, a rifle cartridge.

He throws the sock to one side, jams his foot into the boot, and with the knife and cartridge clutched in one hand, begins clawing his way back up the slope toward the rifle.

3

Voss and Arnoldo are checking the back teeth of Travis's buck when Dutch Brenner steps out of the brush behind them.

Nice buck, says Brenner.

One helluva buck, except for being gut-shot. Voss looks over his eyeglasses at Brenner. Did you just shoot this deer?

Hell, no, Brenner says. Mine is up the Sendero, dressed out, getting cold.

We heard several shots as we were driving up, says Arnoldo.

I heard 'em.

Where's your hunting partner? Voss asks.

Brenner looks around, then shrugs. Maybe he couldn't stomach a gut-shot deer.

Best buck I've seen in a long time, says Voss. As Arnoldo and Brenner roll the deer onto its back, ready for the knife, Luck Travis limps across the clearing. His rifle is not aimed directly at Brenner, but is not aimed away, either.

You shot at me.

If I had shot at you, I would've middled you, Brenner says.

Hey, amigo, Arnoldo says, hands outspread, stepping between Brenner and the muzzle of Travis's rifle. Chingaderos come over here all the time through a hole in that deer-proof fence. Bastard prob'ly thought you was shootin' at him, he shot back at you—Arnoldo grips the barrel of the rifle, waits a moment, and Travis allows him to take the weapon.

Jack Voss nods. I don't want to hear any more about this deal. Comprende, Mr. Travis?

Travis looks at Brenner, an intense, accusing gaze.

Brenner returns a non-concerned stare. In the silence, Arnoldo tends the rifle. A single cartridge clatters on the limestone.

Mr. Travis, Voss says, the least you could do is help clean this handsome sumbitch you have just gut-shot.

Turning away from Brenner, Travis finds his knife, opens the short blade, and says all one can say in such a situation.

Shit.

4

Tonight, Quinlan announces, we roast venison tenderloin, mourning dove and our host, Jack Voss. Does anybody have an opening statement regarding venison or dove?

Quinlan ignores comments about venison and dove. Standing beside the fire pit, he looks around the assembled group. A side of venison is golden brown, oozing juice onto coals. The bird boys are busy sopping roasting dove. They listen shyly to the strange men from Houston. Between basting sessions, the boys scuffle for a place near Quinlan.

No one has a worthwhile comment, Quinlan continues, so I ask that our host give us a word of wisdom.

Applause. Voss stands and peers over his glasses at the hushed group. I have only a minor comment, but it bears on an important subject. Drink. I won't drink with you tonight 'cause I've got to fly to Brownsville at daybreak. Then I'm going on to the Buena Suerte in Mexico. You young broncs can stay up and drink all the whiskey you want, and fist fight and break up the furniture, but please, no violence.

He sips from his margarita glass. I lied. One last touch of salt and some tequila to wash it down. Ah, drink... He pours the rest of the glass into the fire. I hope to see you all at the Buena Suerte in Mexico. Voss looks over his glasses at Travis and Brenner, Alive, I hope, if not well.

Applause starts, but Voss quiets the crowd. As you go through Matamoras or anywhere in Mexico, you should remember that you are guests in a fine country and that Mexicans are some of the best people on earth, if you don't rub 'em the wrong way. But, being Texans, you'll probably forget that.

Arnoldo nods his head and blushes under his mahogany tan, knowing that all eyes in the group have turned his way for a moment.

Judge Bill Weiss? Voss finds the startled attorney in the crowd. As a cultured ex-Yankee, and an attorney to boot, I expect you to keep these uncouth bastards out of trouble.

Weiss shrugs. I'll try.

Sergeant Morgan?

Morgan jumps to attention.

There's a side of venison for the crowd, and a tenderloin for you, as a consolation award for being the worst shot of the day. Get 'em out of the freezer before you leave.

Lieutenant Quinlan?

Quinlan nods.

Here's the name of a hotel you might consider in Matamoras. Give this note to the clerk, if you go there. Voss scratches his bald spot. Did I forget anything?

Drink, yell Quinlan and Travis.

Oh, yes, drink. I will now attempt to quote from a famous man, whose name I have forgotten, an infamous remark. Voss contorts his face, working to remember the remark. Oh, I forgot to say that the man was a politician. And this was back in the days of the Women's Christian Temperance Union, when Carrie Nation ran around with an ax, tearing up saloons, which is a good example about women remaining temperate... where was I?

Drink.

Oh, yes; the politician was asked where he stood on drink, and he answered something like this: 'You ask me where I stand on drink. If by 'drink' you mean that evil yellow fluid that blinds the minds of honest men, causing their rapid descent into the gutter, thereby forcing their wives and children to beg in the streets, by God, I stand four-square against that devilish poison. But if by drink you mean that golden amber liquid that soothes a man's aches at eventide and provides the lubrication of good fellowship and smooths the wheels of commerce, then I say to you, I am unalterably in favor and shall not veer from my stance.

You missed part of it, says Erwin Baker, and the speaker was— Baker stops as Brenner knuckles him on the back of the head.

And now, says Voss, before I leave, I just want to say I'm going.

There is a round of applause. Their host holds up his hands for silence.

Vaya con Dios and Buena Suerte, Voss says. I've got a feeling this group is gonna need a little help from Dios, and a lot of Suerte before you get back to Houston.

Brownsville Mask Emporium   Sam Caldwell

VI

The caravan pulls into Brownsville at noon. Morgan chooses a storage complex on the outskirts of town and rents two storage units.

Gents, Quinlan yells as the men mill around choosing gear, leave everything in storage that you don't want to lose in Mexico.

All the hunting equipment is stowed in Brenner's Bronco before the truck is to be backed into one of the units.

Carmichael stows items in the truck, then grabs his duffel bag. As he starts away from the truck, Quinlan sees him stuffing something into the bag. A pistol. Bad idea. Quinlan starts for Carmichael, but Bill Weiss has also seen the weapon and grabs Carmichael's arm.

You're not taking that into Mexico, Fred.

Say what?

We're not smuggling a pistol into Mexico.

Out of the way, lawyer. Carmichael shoves past Weiss.

Weiss looks at Quinlan. That's fine. There'll be a Greyhound bus back to Houston. I'll be on it.

Carmichael, Brenner says.

What?

My pistol stays here. Your pistol stays here.

A minute later, Quinlan stops Weiss as the attorney removes his bags from the station wagon. He shows him Carmichael's weapon, a small, black semi-automatic pistol, complete with shoulder holster and two clips. Quinlan tucks it into someone's stored gear. We'll sort it out later. Coming, Judge?

Weiss glances at Carmichael, now angrily going through his gear, throwing stuff back in his duffel bag. Carmichael looks up, hostile, loser in a confrontation. Weiss says, Voss told me to take care of you assholes, and I said I'd do my best.

Quinlan says, Put your stuff in Morgan's truck. He wants you to drive for him.

Weiss thinks about it. When did I sign on as a driver?

Rather ride with a drunk at the wheel, or take the wheel?

You've got a point.

As Weiss stows his bags and fishing gear in the back of Morgan's truck, a new problem surfaces. Morgan wants the boat to stay at the storage complex.

Should be plenty of gas in Mexico, Brenner growls.

Morgan turns on Brenner. We don't need to drag a two-ton gas tank around.

Brenner shakes his head. Pistols stay, but I'm not leaving my boat.

Our boat, Quinlan says, nodding agreement.

Morgan turns to Quinlan, his face dark. We'll have to haul this big son of a bitch across Mexico. Then, we won't be able to get it across the ferry at El Tigre—

John, it floats. We'll run it across El Tigre.

The big Mako remains latched to the back of Travis's station wagon.

Damn, Quinlan says to Brenner. Life is good when you get everybody together.

At the front of the storage building are a couple of pay phones. Weiss and Quinlan head for them at the same time. Weiss beats Quinlan to the phones by a step, and has a handful of quarters out, ready to call while Quinlan is still fishing change from his jeans.

Quinlan looks at his money; two quarters and a dime. Maybe Mae Kennedy will accept a collect call. There is an unused phone next to Weiss, but he will wait for privacy.

Weiss has reached his wife. She's not happy. He is being consoling. Quinlan listens while searching for the piece of paper with Mae Kennedy's number, her parent's phone in Austin. He finds it, light gray notepaper, with her name printed at the top. Lettering of the Austin number with a backward slant, a nice swirl to the letters. A faint aroma? No. Yes, he can smell her perfume, or is it her remembered scent? He could jump on a Greyhound bus and be in Austin late tonight. Would Greyhound accept a maxed-out MasterCard?

Weiss hangs up and is headed for the truck as Quinlan drops in a quarter and reaches an operator. Make that collect, please ma'am.

I love you, Mae.

Is that what he'll say? The number rings seven times before someone answers. It's a young man's voice, laughing over party noise in the background. Yeah?

Will you accept a collect call from Mr. Lee Quinlan in Brownsville, Texas?

Lee who?

Quinlan interrupts. I'm a Houston friend of Mae Kennedy.

Sorry, dude. She's with my best friend. Goodbye.

Quinlan hears the man laughing.

Mae's voice comes over the line, yelling toward the receiver, That's my dumb kid brother— but too late, he has touched the hook and the line is dead.

Quinlan fumbles again for the piece of paper with her number, looking through every pocket, but finds no paper, and one more quarter. What did he do with the number? Several of the men are yelling insults from the station wagon and the truck. The operator asks if he wants to place any other calls, and there's the note with Mae's number, on top of the phone. Yes ma'am. I forgot to tell her something important. But it would be another collect call, and the sons of bitches behind him would spoil it, anyway.

Travis yells, Dammit, let's go, Quinlan.

I'll call back from a hotel across the border, ma'am. You can keep the quarter.

The men in the truck and station wagon watch as he walks to the vehicles. In his path, there's a card on the pavement. It's a playing card, scuffed and pebble-imprinted from being run over. The bicycle emblem is up.

Travis sees the card. Don't pick it up, he yells, thumping on the outside of the wagon for emphasis. Quinlan has the card in his hand and turns it over. Ace of Spades. The death card. Crumpling the card, he tosses it away and walks to the wagon, grinning at Travis. It was for you.

The wagon pulls away from the parking lot, just behind the crew cab truck. After several blocks, they can see the Rio Grande River bridge coming up.

What was it? Travis asks.

What?

The card.

Oh. Queen of hearts.

Ah, sighs Travis, relaxing into the seat. The Lucky In Love Card. I'll take it.

The four-vehicle caravan is now a two-vehicle, one boat convoy. The fishermen cross the Rio Grande river bridge into Matamoras and pull into the courtyard behind an ancient hotel at 12:30 p.m.

2

Lee Quinlan and John Morgan are in the lobby of the Casa de las Palomas. An officious, rat-faced man is behind the desk. He watches the two Yanquis with disinterest. The desk clerk joins the rat-faced man. He speaks at Quinlan in rapid fire Spanish.

No deal, Quinlan says, turning away. There's a problem of some sort that has to do with room availability, or the water pressure. Or something else. We'll take our business elsewhere.

Did you mention Jack Voss's name? Morgan finds the note from Jack Voss in his billfold and hands it to Quinlan with a flourish.

Quinlan spreads the wrinkled paper on the desk and taps it. Juan Voss, he says. The rat-faced man glances at the note and has an instant change of demeanor. He snaps his fingers at the desk clerk and blurts orders. There are some rooms, he indicates, saved for important people such as the bearer of this note.

Quinlan says, Dos muchachos por el, uh, how you say bags—equipaje? And, dos cervezas, amigo. Pronto, por favor. My Spanglish needs some practice, John. Where the hell is Carmichael when I need him? Got some bellhops?

The clerk pounds on a bell and yells up the stairs, then hurries down the hallway.

Bar must be thataway, Quinlan says. He points to the swinging door where the clerk has disappeared.

You want to help, Morgan says, or go to the bar?

Bar and heaven can wait. Quinlan says to the manager, El telefono, por favor? As he reaches for the phone, the manager rushes over, gesturing. No, Señor. La Senora is calling soon.

When for my use?

Presently, Señor.

Two bellboys are now watching as Morgan and Quinlan work. Morgan sorts out the satchels and suitcases, then Quinlan places them in the lobby by twos.

The desk clerk hustles back with a pair of cervezas, hands them to Quinlan and stands there, in the way.

Give the man a few bucks, Morgan.

Morgan fumbles in his shirt pocket, flips Quinlan a roll of bills and moves more gear.

Sip on this brewski and I'll finish up, Morgan.

You drink it. I'm saving my thirst for some Margaritas in that bar. Besides, we're through. Morgan does a nose count. You and Brenner get a room together. You snore, and I'm pissed off at Brenner. Baker with Travis, they're getting along. Let's see, better not put Weiss with Carmichael. Morgan turns and looks at the desk clerk. I'm turning into a Goddamned social director.

Quien es usted, señor—social director?

Let it go, amigo. Weiss rooms alone, because he's a good guy. Morgan drops the keys on top of each set of bags, and gestures to the bellhops. Up the stairs, hombres. Here's five bucks apiece. As the men reach for the bills, Morgan rips the bills in two. Mañana, he says, handing them the half bills. If it's all there tomorrow, you get the matching halves. Morgan watches the bellboys disappear up the stairs with the bags. To hell with y'all, he says. If you can't help with your own gear, the Mexicans can have it.

Let's go to Maria's, Quinlan says. I need some meñudo for my crudo.

Margaritas for me. Morgan points at the bar. The door swings wide and they hear Mexican music and smell booze. Right there in that bar, then a nap. He watches a Mexican woman go into the bar. Maybe she'll join me.

As Quinlan starts away he stumbles over his own bag, and hears Morgan talking to himself, guilt-tripping him.

Care for a cold drink, John? I'll buy. Thanks. Don't mind if I do. The leader of the expedition walks into the bar.

The organizer goes to find the expedition. And a telephone.

3

Bill Weiss and Luck Travis are seated in Quinlan's favorite
Matamoras Cantina, just off the main square. The little place is
packed with noon-time Patróns, Mexicans with enough diñero for a
prepared lunch and two Norte Americanos, Luck Travis and Bill
Weiss.

Hey, gents.

Sit down, Quinlan, we ordered more food than we can eat.

Luck, you can eat more food than I can order. Weiss, how's it
feel to be in a strange new country?

About like it felt to be in England, Saudi Arabia, Costa Rica.

Oh. That bad, huh?

No, it's really pretty nice, Lee. Just strange, particularly the
smells.

How's the ankle, Luck?

Okay. Young Baker's a pretty good medic. He got your first aid
kit out of the boat and wrapped the cut.

Weiss asks, You don't want to have a doc take a look at it?

In Matamoras? I don't think so.

The waitress is looking Quinlan's way, maybe because he's
waving an American five-dollar bill.

Telefoño, Señorita?

She shakes her head.

No? Okay, uno Dos Equis, Señorita. To Weiss and Travis, Best
beer in the universe. Travis nods agreement.

The waitress leans over a table and lets them admire some
cleavage, then squeezes between tables and delivers another round
of drinks. She gives Quinlan a little hip and plucks the five from his
hand.

Where's the gang? Quinlan asks.

Carmichael disappeared as soon as the station wagon stopped,
Weiss says.

Right. He spent time here last year, Travis says. Probably has a
dozen old flames to rekindle.

Brenner and Baker came in with us, Weiss says, but they left to
get something for Baker's wife, or he can't go home.

I got a beautiful peasant-woman dress for my wife, Weiss says.
Vivien is pregnant again. She chose Lee Anne for a name, not after

you, Quinlan, but after a federal judge lady friend. Lee is like Stacey and Meredith and Courtney, popular right now.

Quinlan interrupts to ask whatever happened to Ann and Martha and Jane, or Mae. Now there's a beautiful name, Mae.

And a beautiful person, as well.

I noticed.

She mentioned a recent event. You should be more careful when you fish in the surf.

Yeah.

Weiss looks out of place and uneasy, seems worried about the vibrations he gets from the natives who radiate resentment of Weiss's wealth.

Being poor, Quinlan feels at ease. He enjoys the smells of lard and tortillas and goat cheese burning on a grill; diesel fumes from the street, stale beer and Mexican cigarettes; honest labor, sweat and cheap perfume applied behind ears and under armpits.

Hey, Judge, this is a friendly place, like the Good Luck Ranch bar. Quinlan knocks a half-empty Corona bottle from their table. The bottle spins across the linoleum floor, spraying foam, and ends beneath the feet of a pair of tough-looking Mexican laborers near the door.

Tu Madre... gringos, one says as he retrieves the bottle, slamming it down on his table.

Hey, Weiss says, I'm ready for a shower and the sack. I'll pay for the beer and the food and check it to you.

Travis shakes his head. Smell that, Weiss? That's your lunch.

Quinlan shouts at the waitress over the din of radio music, Una mas Dos Equis, Maria, and how's our supper coming? They are jammed around a table near the kitchen. The waitress-cook-barmaid hustles in and out of the kitchen, brushing past them bearing trays crowded with steaming plates drooling with red and brown gravies. She juggles two arms laden with food and places another golden bottle of beer in front of Quinlan.

He raises the bottle in a courtly gesture to the plump behind of the proprietor- barmaid. Mil gracias, Señora. Ain't this great?

The waitress-chef accomplishes a miracle by somehow placing all their plates and bowls on the small table. She collects a few

American dollars from Weiss for the food and gives him a wad of pesos and a handful of coins in return.

As Weiss searches in vain for a fork or spoon, Quinlan signals the waitress-barmaid. Una mas Dos Equis, por favor.

4

He is back on the streets of Matamoras alone, not ready to leave the evening of this enchanting town. Walking north, he can see the sun easing down at each side street. With each block, the sun appears a bit redder and lower, silhouetting more people. Crowds make way on the streets for cars, grudgingly, each threatened person not looking back as they feel the presence of a fender just a nudge away, the vendors with bicycle-mounted stores, all suicides daring trucks to kill them. Little kids tending littler kids, all alone but for one another's care.

A tall Gringo walking Quinlan's way sees him fumbling in pockets, recognizes the lack of a smoke. He stops and smiles and offers. Cigarette, amigo?

Gracias. They both light up from Quinlan's Zippo, and the tall man moves away, leaving Quinlan looking into a window on the world, a showcase, Photographicas por el Publica, y Pasaportes por El Estados Unidas, the sign says. Tiny photos of people are jammed one next to another, a cosmos looking back at Quinlan through his own image in the glass. Is that a bit of paunch, Quinlan? Look at that elbow there, a fold of skin protruding as the arm straightens, and when did the bag under that eye begin? How could his ancient carcass attract a beautiful young woman?

He remembers a touch of gray in her copper hair. And, why still single? But those special ankles, her hands, her way of laughing. She rubs her nose when telling a story and when she laughs, she's the most beautiful woman in Harris County. Monday, a week from now, he'll be back, and maybe she'll see him again.

Just across the street is a sign above a shop doorway. Telefono. He stumbles across the street, dodging bicycles and taxis.

Three friends wave at him before he can get to the phone booth.

Hey, Quinlan. Travis, Baker and Brenner approach along the crowded street. Travis is limping now. Baker seems a tad drunk.

Brenner's face is yellowish purple across the bridge of his swollen nose. But hell, who's perfect?

Que paso, amigos? They are now a group of four wealthy Texans, swaggering along an avenida with admiring people forced to make way. Judge Weiss was feeling kinda puny, Quinlan says. Went back to the hotel. No staying power.

Travis is the guide. We're headed for whore town, says Travis.

Crude son of a bitch, says Brenner. Actually, we're going to visit a certain old place Luck knows and romance a few beautiful señoritas.

Lead on, Luck. Quinlan will compare beautiful señoritas, young and nubile, to the idea of a certain lady. There will be no contest.

Quinlan leads them into a drugstore, where he has Travis purchase bandages. Better get some hydrogen peroxide, Baker says. And Bactroban is good stuff for cuts. They move along. A doorway or two, Baker is mesmerized by the myriad colors and exotic scenes of a foreign country. Look at that, the color in there. Piñatas! And the people... look at the faces in this place.

Hell, let's go in and be some of those faces, Travis says. He walks into the cantina and buys a round of Mexican beer. The Gringos go back to the street and dodge beggars, taxi drivers, would-be guides, each of whom claims to know the mysterious places of Matamoras like no other. Brenner stops at a shop and buys Quinlan a pack of smokes, then at the cantina next door, buys everyone a round of Margaritas.

The stench of Mexican tobacco, the whang of tequila, the bite of lime and salt. The stumble of feet on curbs. They amble into shops, attracted by stuffed alligators, switch-blade knives and hand-carved chess sets. They wait while Brenner has his boots polished by a team of shine boys.

Just spit? No polish, huh, Pedro. You, peewee, give this to your Madre.

The boys are quarreling over a five-dollar bill when the four men walk on.

That was about $4.50 too much, Travis says. You'll spoil the work ethic.

Not in Mexico.

Quinlan remembers his theory about Mexican cities, or about city Mexicans, really. He explains that it's the time of just after dark when Mexicans are most alive. Maybe not happy-alive, but energized by love or hate or hunger or a need to meet a friend. They all must go somewhere and be there right now, immediately, no time for a story or directions to a stranger, the only time when haste matters. An urge not apparent at any other time of the day, so the streets are jammed with people and produce moving on horse carts, donkey carts and people carts. Ancient cars, cars that never die of planned obsolescence.

Now, there's a car, he says.

An ancient Ford buckets slowly past, a particular car, dents and rust and a crease here and there that mean something. Windows down, a family inside looking back at Quinlan.

See somebody you know, Quinlan?

Just an old beat-up car, Luck. Is this Boy's Town?

Luck Travis had been to Boy's Town years before, a young, swaggering U.S. Army PFC, straight from parachute training near El Paso. Hell, I don't know. Everything's the same, he says, looking down the crowded street, hearing the tinny music, smelling the afternoon stinks and aromas, but everything has changed.

Travis shares less pleasant memories with the group; holding onto a steel plumbing fixture in the latrine, groaning in agony, trying to piss. Later, a corpsman laughing at his pain while the corpsman forces a catheter down his penis. Now, he stops and grins at Quinlan.

Quinlan grins back. What say, Luck?

I'd a helluva lot rather adjourn to the healthy pleasures of our hotel bar. Let's wait for Baker and Brenner to catch up.

Brenner, drinking beer and Tequila; Quinlan worries about Brenner when he drinks anything besides Dr. Pepper. A cluster headache could seize him, or worse for people around him, his sweet disposition could turn sour.

Where the hell are we? Grumbles Brenner. He steps in front of a passing man. A tall man, blonde crew cut, the friendly man who offered Quinlan a smoke earlier. Brenner says, Hey, pardner, you speak any English?

The man looks into the puffed eyes of Brenner.   Shit, no. He starts around Brenner but bumps into Baker.

Beg your pardon— Baker begins, but Brenner has seized the man by the back of the neck. He pulls the stranger's face within a foot of his own battered face.

You gonna speak some polite English, or tell me 'Shit, no,' again?

No! I mean, yes, I speak English. I'm from Encino—

Turn 'im loose, Dutch, Quinlan says. He's a friend of mine.

Brenner releases the man. Which way to Boy's Town?

God, I wouldn't know— Encino clutches his neck, and moves to get away from the broken-faced man. It's gone now, I hear.

Have a nice day, elsewhere, pronto, Travis says.

Baker starts sheepishly out of a doorway. The man from Encino jostles Baker with an elbow as he hurries past.

Son of a bitch, the man snaps at Baker. You pricks oughta keep that animal on a leash. I'm going to the police.

Baker's face is white as he catches up with the men.

What did mister politeness say, Baker? asks Brenner.

Baker walks ahead, hoping the others will pick up his pace, instead of dawdling along. Aw, he just said he would try to be more polite to strangers, Dutch.

What was that about police?

Said the least he could do is warn us about the police here.

Yeah? To hell with the police here.

Wrong, Travis and Quinlan say, in harmony.

To hell with Boy's Town, Travis says. Hotel, hot bath, cold drinks.

In that order, Quinlan agrees.

Ten minutes later, they are in the bar of the hotel, out of order.

5

The bar of the Casa de las Palomas seems familiar, though Quinlan has never been there before. But, hell, all bars with stools and drinks are familiar. Come to think of it, he's been drinking since noon. It is now 8:30 p.m.

Quinlan is aware of the precise configuration of the barstool on which he is perched. There is a lump just to the left of center and forward. In the middle of his right nether cheek is a roughness, and running to the edge of the stool, an uncomfortable crack in the surface. The crack complains silently of many years of bad treatment, then pinches his right cheek. He makes a mental note to maintain most of his weight on the left cheek.

Maybe he should report the problem of the bar stool to the management; that would be a good move, a gesture that would help the management in maintaining the quality of the establishment. In order to form a proper power face that will portray his attitude, Quinlan looks over his countenance. Mildly surprised at the unaccustomed view of himself, he decides that the appropriate combination of forehead wrinkle and lip scowl has not yet been achieved. He adds a left eye squint. Then he ponders the first sentence that will be needed to correct a bad situation, but in the process of creating a grim physical appearance, he has completely forgotten whatever action a prior decision required. Embarrassed, he decides to maintain the present appearance.

Erwin Baker is red-faced, grinning. He sits with Travis at a table just behind Quinlan. Luck? They said you were in Viet Nam.

Travis holds up a finger, shakes his head and sips beer.

I heard you had some rough duty, Baker says.

Quinlan wants to say, You don't want to go there, Erwin, but the words won't jolt loose. He observes that to the right, ranging along the wall, is a group of hand-carved shelves supporting bottles, containers representing all the brands of beer that might be available at this particular bar, or be available for purchase somewhere in Mexico. Quinlan scans the shelf by closing one eye and zooming his vision as though focusing the lens of his camera. It is an ability he has always had but has never been aware of before this moment. In the cabinet are 19 varicolored bottles, many with long necks. Most of the bottles are dark brown, but two display beautiful hues of amber.

Didn't you serve with Morgan?

Kid, I survived a tour in Nam. Had to stomp a drunk biker in a San Diego jail. I don't discuss either subject.

Quinlan zooms to a painting. It is on black velvet with fluorescent reds, greens, intense browns and purples. The painting depicts a man in tight pants swirling a red cape as a huge black bull careens past. Quinlan studies the brush strokes at close range, then zooms back to see the effect of the brush strokes at a distance. Tired of the painting, he examines the bar to the left. There is another cabinet filled with liquor bottles. As he changes his viewpoint, Quinlan realizes that he can now read Spanish fluently. The bar is a friendlier place.

He uses his new awareness to be at the center of the room, while seated at the bar. A Mariachi band begins assembling their instruments around him. Drums, bamboo and other wood things, shiny brass objects. The leader is about to ask Quinlan to move from his central position, but Quinlan says in lisping Castilian Spanish, Toque algunas piezas para mis amigo y yo, el prethidente. Impressed, the band leader makes room for his trumpet elsewhere.

Some of Quinlan's Yanqui friends have moved tables together just behind his seat at the bar. He doesn't have to zoom his hearing. John Morgan is talking about a recent fishing trip to the Padre Island surf, which will be essentially the same as where they're going in Mexico. Big gold spoons, Morgan advises, or maybe MirroLures, M-52's.

Travis squeezes lime juice on his beer can, then salt. He grins at Morgan. Poor man's cheap Margarita.

Cheap man's poor Margarita, responds Morgan.

We've been around Quinlan too long.

Carmichael comes in. He joins John Morgan and lights a cigarette, adding to a dank cloud. It is now hard for Quinlan to see across the room, even with his zoom vision. Some of Quinlan's friends are Norte Americanos, some are Mexicans, others are from Central America. He holds none as favorites nor disfavorites, except for three Cubans at a table near the entrance.

The Cubans are the only sour faces in the room. They earn Quinlan's disfavor because of their attitude. One of the Cubans points out, loudly, that all Latin Americans are inferior to Cubans, and that English-speaking people are contemptible inferiors.

Another Cuban agrees. Yanquis like the big one there and that bearded drunk at the bar are the most inferior of all.

Pfah, Hemingway, the third Cuban says, puffing cigar smoke at the ceiling where it drifts and tempts Quinlan to borrow a cigar from the man, but causes Baker to cough; My black grandfather cursed the Yanqui writer for writing the word Nigger in a book, and he left the place where they were drinking in disgrace, that is, Hemingway left in disgrace, and later, to get even, he wrote about a Mexican fisherman beating my black grandfather in an arm wrestling contest.

Quinlan knows the Cubans are ashore from a loading tanker. They are sober, due partly to a shortage of funds, but mostly because they want to go with a woman later. Each one projects his macho desirability by ignoring everyone, especially the women.

There are women among the crowd. One is Quinlan's age, an imperious lady with a retinue of three men. They sit in the corner opposite Quinlan. A cigarillo is offered the lady and accepted without acknowledgment, as two lighters flash. She meets Quinlan's eyes in the bar mirror for a moment then looks away with disdain.

What is my fine hotel coming to, she says to one of her retinue, the rat-faced manager, that we must cater to Yanqui borachos and prostitutes?

The manager begins an answer. The Americanos spend a lot of dollars, he says, and they are not so bad as the locals who came here until I raised our prices, and then, the women you see are of a better class, and you shall soon see a very fine dancer who attracts much attention— The lady waves him quiet.

In the mirror, Quinlan sees three women enter. The Cuban leader stands as they enter, his chin tilted and head turned so that the elegance and strength of his neck and shoulders show to their best advantage. His eyes are narrowed, a hand gestures gracefully to his table. His companions nod, fetchingly aloof, yet attentive.

Surely, no woman can ignore the quality of these men. But the women have met the Cubans and know of their lack of cash.

One of the three women goes to the end of the bar. Ornately dressed, only her hands and face and a bit of neck and two lovely ankles are visible. She is a dancer. Her two companions are ladies of the evening. Skimpily dressed, they are matched tall and short. They move Quinlan's way, looking into his face in the mirror, perhaps reading his mind, as he reads theirs. The pair moves hip-rubbing close to Bill Weiss and Crazy Fred Carmichael.

Quinlan looks for Luck Travis, and decides he must be in the men's room, or he'd be lusting after these two women. Or, maybe the cigarette and cigar smoke has run him out of the place.

The short woman is dark, plump, shy. The tall woman is fair, angular, freckled. Freckles leans close to Bill Weiss and whispers something in fractured English. Trying to ignore a feeling of nausea, as well as to be polite and find a bridge between cultures, Weiss says to the tall woman, You're part Irish?

No! She says. Soy toda un Mexicano!

She's all-Mexican, Carmichael says.

Quinlan knows that Weiss will soon be violently sick, courtesy of his Mexican salad at lunch. He would like to warn Weiss, but his words come out tangled. He doesn't want anyone to get the impression that he's drunk. He hears the tall woman say, Pouf, homosexuales, about their chances with these two Gringos. The women see Quinlan smiling at them in the bar mirror and move to him. Fragrance of woman surrounds him; Fire and Ice on Freckles, Night In An Arab Boudoir on the dark woman. He can't tell them about the most beautiful woman in the world. Instead, he gestures at the impoverished Cubans near the entrance, and forgetting the Spanish for Lovelorn, says, Except for me, there are the loneliest men in the universe.

The women shrug and move away, then sit down with the Cubans.

Quinlan's Gringo friends have now moved another table together just behind him, are a single group of loud Americans. Quinlan turns around and participates in the group without speaking.

Brenner belches. Purple regions have spread from the bridge of Brenner's nose and surround both eyes. The edges are turning a sulfurous yellow. What are you grinning at, Luck? asks Brenner, looking sideways at Travis, just back from the men's room.

Ugliest face in Matamoras.

You and Morgan are tied for second.

Weiss is now in pain. Quinlan will tell him to get out of here, go to his room and lie down. In a minute. Speaking will take some practice, and he can't do so right now, because the Mariachi band begins playing, drowning out all other sounds. Quinlan is one of their instruments and aids them by keeping time with one finger in the air.

In the mirror, he watches as the dancer begins. The girl is proud, frightened, hostile, wise. She moves from table to table, slapping groping hands, seducing from across the room, dancing to a new heartthrob at each table, then slipping away from an embrace. Men from Mexico, Cuba, Honduras and Panama grab at her and miss as she spins away.

At the table of the imperious lady, Quinlan sees the rat-faced manager sweating, watching for the lady's reaction. She frowns at the dancer, and the dancer whirls away from that table, a teasing, laughing, desirable woman, but a skilled dancer for all that. She visits the table of the wealthy Yanquis last. Weiss ignores his stomach pains, finds a few American bills and tucks them in her waistband.

At the end of the number, Travis catches her around the waist. Crazy Fred, tell her I want to get into her pants.

Carmichael says a few words to the dancer. The girl shrugs away from Travis, and answers with a contemptuous phrase.

What'd she say, Carmichael?

Room for only one asshole in her pants.

The Mariachi band whistles and gestures, demanding a big hand for the trumpet player who is apparently an important Matamoras musician.

The band ignores the dancer.

Morgan stands and yells, Hurray for the little dancer. Get up, you sonsofbitches, and give her a hand. The Yanquis all stand and applaud.

Bravo por la pequeña bailerina, shouts Carmichael.

Travis whistles shrilly, and even Quinlan joins in by clapping.

Weiss stands and stumbles away from the table, a look of panic on his face. Carmichael is watching and is aware of Weiss's problem.

Up the stairs, Judge. Third floor, you're the second door on the right. Montezuma's Revenge strikes again.

Applause fades away as the woman stops behind Morgan. She bows. Through as a performer, she dons her wrap, rests her head on Morgan's shoulder, then takes Weiss's chair beside Morgan.

Quinlan returns to his study of Mexican liquors ranged along the bar mirror. Mescal, one label reads, The Finest in Mexico. Very Ancient and Honored. His vision rotates the bottle next to the Mescal so that he reads Tequila of the Royal Aztecs. Another bottle, made of clay-colored ceramic, is simply labeled Pulque.

Pulque. Bad stuff, not imported to the states. Explodes from the bottle as it ferments. Said to be psychedelic, as bad as absinthe used to be.

Pulque, Quinlan says to the woman behind the bar. She ignores him. He unfolds his hands and lays them flat on the bar with an air of disgust for the quality of Mexican bar service.

Later, he slaps the bar. The woman does not move. He forgets the poor condition of the bar stool and shifts his weight. The bar stool pinches his cheek.

Dutch Brenner stands and peers over Quinlan's shoulder. He waves at the woman behind the bar. Hey, Brenner yells, give my buddy a drink.

The woman says something in Spanish, then shakes her head. Brenner aims a finger at the woman and glares. Now.

Carmichael grabs Brenner's elbow, but gently. Brenner is over his Plimsol line, or he would not be pushing a woman around. Carmichael is aware of macho Mexican types around the room, some of them paying attention to Brenner's bullying of the little barmaid. She said he's already muy boracho, Brenner.

Brenner jerks his sleeve away. Quinlan wants a drink, he gets a drink.

Quinlan focuses on the Mexican woman behind the bar. She is a lady of considerable age, but her hair is untouched by gray. She could be as young as 50 or as old as 70.

Madam? he says, but it does not come out with the force and clarity he intended. The barmaid leans in his direction and seems to be looking at him. He taps the bar in front of him, the property that he owns in fee simple.

Pulque, por favor, gracias.

The barmaid shrugs, then turns away to do his bidding. She places a small glass with a whitish liquid in front of him. He picks up the glass nonchalantly.

Salud.

A sip. Bitter sweetness with a hint of tequila. Another sip, a swallow. An oily pleasantness at the back of his throat, then the fire of chemical hell raging along his esophagus, distinct involvement of every cell, all diffusing into warmth and oddly, a clarity of vision. Inner vision, because his eyes will not stay still on a subject, yet he is piercingly aware of everything and everyone about him.

6

Enlightenment.

Quinlan brushes through the thoughts of those near him and a few who are far away, at first relishing the power, then hating the guilty sensation of watching from hiding. The little dancer worries about her relationship with the Holy Mother, and with the operator of the bar in particular; the rat-faced man wants to force her to dance in whore clothes, to make her sleep with him. He places hands on her, tries to push into her room after the place is closed, mumbles love poems as he sits, leaning against her door when she refuses to open the door. Perhaps the tall, dark, very handsome Yanqui would take her back to the city of Houston. She could continue her studies at that city's famous Music Hall, become a famous dancer. Or, just wash his clothes and care for his children and wife if he has such, like so many other Matamoras girls are doing, and she could also—

Quinlan makes a decision for Carlotta and Morgan and their heirs, then guiltily moves on.

He finds it mildly interesting, but of no import in the final scheme of things that Federico Lopez-Carmichael is a Lieutenant Colonel, KGB, USSR, as well as a spy in the employ of Israel, on temporary loan to the CIA.

He glances through Erwin Baker's substance and irons out a few lumps in the dough of his character. The country could use an artist as president one day. Erwin will do just fine; first though, courage and honesty. Then, Quinlan wanders down many random pathways in the past with ease, looks with circumspect awe beyond the veil of the galaxy and peers, with straining difficulty, through certain curtains of the future.

After a time, clearheaded, he goes to a place in his memory that he had forgotten.

7

Lee sits at the supper table, next to his younger brother. He is picking at a week-old cut on the ball of his thumb, intent on edging the scab off without hurting the tender flesh below the scab. His brother jostles Quinlan as he reaches for the milk pitcher.

Ow, Scooter!

I'm sorry, Lee, his brother says, afraid Lee will whack him. He's safe, with their mother nearby. Back to the scab. Scooter watches as Lee picks at the edge of the cut, both wondering if Lee can dislodge the scab and reveal new, tender skin below, or if it's too early, and the scab will break from raw flesh, allowing the cut to ooze blood. Linna is bustling around, cooking and placing food on the table.

You boys washed up? Linna asks sweetly, her ritual question.

Yes 'm.

She turns from the old black stove to place a platter of pork chops on the table, and 34 years later Quinlan's mouth fills with saliva and he drools on the Matamoras bar.

Lee, don't pick at that.

Yes ma'am.

Mother-- Quinlan yells to his young self, sitting at the table, focusing on a cut finger — let me see mother's face — but young Lee's vision focuses idly on the thumb, investigates with curiosity his fingerprints, unlike anyone's fingerprints in the whole world, then wanders a bit to the familiar texture of the worn tablecloth, drifts to the platter of pork chops. Quinlan's entire being yearns for his mother's face, but young Lee avariciously focuses on a choice pork chop for the moment immediately after the blessing. Linna places another platter on the table, cornbread, then reaching over his shoulder, sets a bowl of black-eyed peas next to the gravy she has made from the pork chop grease.

She gives Lee a hug and smooths his cowlick. Then, idly watching his mother with no concern, Lee looks directly at her face. Quinlan thinks how beautiful she is, so much like his daughter.

His mother looks out the little kitchen window. He's here, boys. Go bring your father in for supper.

At the Matamoras bar, tears well in Quinlan's eyes and for a while, he is filled with happiness. The man smiles at a face in a mirror, and the boy smiles back. It's okay, Lee, he whispers, knowing so much that it fills him and disappears.

8

Watching in the bar mirror, Quinlan keeps track of his friends, just in case they need help. He hasn't had a cigarette for hours, or a drink, but that's good. Maybe he'll return to normal soon. Get his voice back from the Mexican cigarettes and beer and tequila, or was it the pulque?

As Lee Quinlan gets sober, John Morgan gets drunk.

In an unannounced competition, Morgan drinks beer for beer with Dutch Brenner, until Brenner stumbles away from the table, headed with Baker to get their gear. Morgan wants to turn his attention to the young dancer. Small and vulnerable in this room full of men, she is also self-possessed. Most appealing to Morgan, she seems to have no concern for anyone but him. She listens as he talks to the other men, and when he speaks to her, looks at him with soulful eyes. The word Houston means something to her, but she speaks no other English.

Quinlan knows that he could aid Morgan in visiting with the woman, but his voice is not yet dependable.

Carmichael could run interference for him but wants to argue with Morgan about the next day's itinerary. You can stick around here if you want to Fred, Morgan says. We'll find you on the way back.

Like hell. Let's enjoy the hospitality of Matamoras.

These guys want to enjoy the fishing of Third Pass. Me too. Morgan turns to the dancer and smiles. Don't take that personally, señorita.

The señorita is Carlotta, says Carmichael, and she would love for you to stick around.

Erwin Baker stumbles as he comes back into the bar. The kid has been over-served. Quinlan had better look after him. Quinlan practices standing, and it works, but his voice is still on the blink.

Baker looks around the bar. He says, the Matamoras police force just got Brenner.

Morgan stumbles to his feet, knocking his chair backward. Shit, legs are getting drunk. Someone picks the chair up and moves it away from the back of Morgan's legs. What happened, Baker?

Me and Brenner went outside to get my gear. We were at this meter, by the truck, and a little guy was cutting the back-license plate off the station wagon. There were two or three guys in uniforms, cops I guess, and Brenner said to 'em, 'Get the fuck away from there, and right goddamn now.' Baker looks around the assemblage. Anyway, the cops got hostile, a little guy whipped out his Billy club—

Where'd they take Brenner?

They grabbed me and threw me into a wall, and Brenner went berserk, grabbed the big cop and nearly broke the cop's neck, there were cops all over Brenner, and that's when the little guy busted Brenner up beside the head—

Morgan jabs Baker's chest. Why didn't they take you?

I didn't punch anybody. They had to let me go, after they took us in.

Morgan grabs Baker by the shirt. Where is he?

An old courthouse about three blocks from here.

Leave the kid alone, Morgan. Quinlan's voice is weak, but it's back.

He didn't help Brenner, growls Morgan. He grabs Baker's wrist and belt and slings the young man across the bar toward Quinlan. Baker takes down two Mariachi guitarists and the trumpet player, then stops against the base of Quinlan's stool, his head resting on Quinlan's right foot. Morgan pulls a roll of bills from his back pocket and drops the money at Baker's feet. Adios, Baker. Get back to Houston, if you can.

Quinlan leans down to Baker and finds another piece of his voice. I'm sorry you're going to lose your daughter. The Universe is closed and will eventually collapse back on itself.

Lee Quinlan, John Morgan and Fred Carmichael walk into the
Matamoras Municipal Court of Justice and Jailhouse. Quinlan
considers the possibility of bringing off the rescue of Brenner and
walking out of the Matamoras jail as a proud and righteous man
should, head high, a winner.

Then he sees himself bloody and beaten, lying in the corner of a
dark, filthy cell. Rats move along the walls, roaches suck at gashes
in his forehead— squeezing one eye closed, Quinlan focuses on the
other members of his rescue team. To his right is Crazy Fred
Carmichael. One never knows what Carmichael might say or do.
However, Carmichael has guts and speaks Spanish. The presence of
John Morgan seems a dubious asset, but what the hell—Morgan is
in charge.

Ahead, as they move along a tunnel-like hallway, they see
Matamoras citizens formed in a line before an officious-looking
man. Clearly, this is an important man. A judge?

Mexican citizens stand in line, men with hats in hand, women
wrapped in shawls like dark bandages. The Yanquis stop at the
back of the line.

Ahem, Quinlan coughs, jostling Morgan. Morgan squints back
at Quinlan, puzzled for a moment.

Señor, Carmichael says assertively. The official looks up and
over the queue for a moment, then goes back to his work.

The Doctor must be located immediately, Quinlan mumbles.

Morgan glances at Quinlan. The Doctor?

The Mexican official concentrates on the papers before him but
tucks his chin into his collar and gestures toward the person in front
of the line.

You have a very important man locked up here, says Morgan
forcefully. A famous, uh, Doctor. Morgan and Quinlan look at
Carmichael, waiting for his translation.

Hay que largar imediamente al medico!

The official turns and says something to a functionary. The man
scurries to the side of the room, unlocks a door and disappears. The
judge leans forward and says to Morgan, Para adelante, por favor.

Carmichael ushers Morgan and Quinlan into position before the bench of justice.

Morgan speaks quietly, causing the judge to lean forward. Earlier this evening, our friend was brought here by several rude policemen.

Carmichael says quietly and in a reasonable tone, El conductor del doctor es un estupido y el es culpable de estaciando arriba de una de su thoroughfares, por cualno hay culpa el doctor.

The judge shrugs and looks around. The functionary is now at attention behind him. The judge whispers to the functionary. The man nods. The judge taps his thick book of transgressions, opens the book, thumbs through it, looks at the three Yanquis and raises a hand. El nombre de tu amigo importante?

El famosisimo doctor esta mainando abajo de nom de plume de Kurt K. Brenner, replies Carmichael.

The judge nods and taps his book, reading to himself for a moment. Then he tells the Yanquis that their famous doctor has disrupted the peace and tranquility of his precinct and inflicted damage to deputy Martinez, for which the famous doctor will serve five days and be fined $250.

Carmichael speaks out of the corner of his mouth to Morgan: Five days and $250.

Behind the judge a door jolts open and two uniformed officers push through. The larger of the two men has a bandage wrapped across one eye, and a hand on his pistol.

The Patrón Juan Voss has had a heart attack, Quinlan murmurs.

Carmichael crosses himself. Señor Juan Voss—si su corazon palpita por la noche, el Doctor Brenner tendra que Ayudar el Patrón Juan Voss en su hacienda.

The judge places a warning hand across the chest of the deputy, looking at him in disgust, and tells the Yanquis that the Patrón Juan Voss is well known to the court, in fact is a personal friend. He snaps fingers at the flunky. As the aide produces a long-corded phone, the magistrate frowns. He tells them that for their sake, he hopes they are telling him the truth.

Carmichael looks toward the heavens, and raising his arms to an unseen but just God, says reverently to Morgan, I think the little fucker is buying it—

Morgan whispers back, If the little fucker calls Voss, we're screwed.

The judge turns away from the courtroom and dials the phone.

The Yanquis watch as the man talks on the phone for a moment, waits patiently, tapping his fingers on the book of transgressions, then jerks to attention as someone of import speaks to him.

Carmichael gestures for Quinlan and Morgan to listen. He whispers, I'm going into an epileptic fit in just a minute—

Silencio! screams the deputy, drawing his pistol.

Guttierez! The judge turns back to the courtroom, glaring at the officer. The judge tells the deputy to put away his weapon, that these men are on an important mission, a duty that could spare the life of an important friend of Mexico.

Cancel that epileptic fit, Quinlan says.

Morgan seizes the initiative. Mr. Carmichael, Morgan says, tell the judge that my country wishes to provide immediate compensation for any discomfiture which the law enforcement officers of Mexico have suffered. Morgan nods at the judge. We also wish to pay any fines necessary for the immediate release of our friend.

Carmichael yells, El medico del Patrón Juan Voss tiene que ser librado ahora mismo!

The judge winces and removes his glasses. He finds a cloth in an inner pocket and begins wiping the lenses. My friends, it is not...apto? Apropriado? He glances at Carmichael, eyebrows raised.

Not fitting, Your Honor, Carmicheal answers, quietly.

Gracias, not fitting that you men of another place come to our place and... esperar?

Expect, Sir, answers Carmichael.

Gracias, expect to order us about, as though you were our... chieftains?

Chieftains, agrees Carmichael.

Our chieftains, able to affright me with a bad person, such as you. If not for the health of mi estimado amigo, el Patrón Juan Voss, you would now accompañar your ugly medico friend. He frowns at Carmichael, places the glasses back on the bridge of his nose and looks down on the Yanquis. I have no fear of bad persons. The worst persons in Matamoras are my deputies.

Your Honor, says Morgan, fumbling in his billfold, that sums up our case. I think those fines totaled about $250 dollars, American. If cash will do, we request that you release our friend.

10

The Yanquis await the processing, certification and release of Dutch Brenner at the bar of La Casa del Palomas. Quinlan looks on, somewhere between enlightened and drunk. He studies people in the crowd, reads minds, or is it auras?

Although it is after hours, the rat-faced manager is willing to continue providing alcoholic beverages to the men from las Estados Unidos. In return for wads of dark green dollar bills that seem to be of no consequence to them, they demand green limes, free to rat-face from the trees in the courtyard and cheap, clear tequila, along with inconsequentially-priced white salt. And Coronas, and Dos Equis, but no mas pulque por el Jefe.

Their jefe, a lean man with graying beard and dark eyes, remains at the bar, watching while the other Gringos move about, yelling into one another's ears from close range. Each of the men, except for the very tall man with the ugly mustachio, Crazy he is called, go to the Jefe from time to time and yell in his ear. The Jefe nods and smiles.

Apart from the Yanquis, only a few other men remain in the bar. The other men who are not money-flinging Gringos are the Cubans, sailormen who have nursed only a few drinks all evening. And one woman, the dancer remains. The pequeña bailarina, Carlotta. But she is a silly woman who in the past has preferred her own solitary company to his, has often turned her face from him when he smiled at her. Refused him, even when he showed her the depth of his heart. And now, prefers the company of the large Yanqui.

The manager pours himself a stiff drink of Puerto Rican brandy and scowls at Carlotta. She should find admiration for the strength of his will, the depth of his commitment to her security. And, on a very personal side, the potency of his desire for her body. He projects his knowledge of her weakness, her need for him, the desire she must feel for him. She frowns and returns her attentions to the Yanqui.

The manager should challenge that man, see him leave like a cur. Or see him turn on the manager, pull a knife... She weeps when she sees his body. Falling on his bier, forcing aside the wife, the children, she wails and screams, Aieee! I didn't realize the depth of his love.

The Cubans. Quinlan gets the attention of the rat-faced manager and points at the three Cubans, sullen in their corner without women or drink. Tres Coronas, por mi amigos a Cuba.

The manager scowls at Quinlan, but finds the beer, takes the bottles to the table of the Cubans. Quinlan stands and offers a toast. Un trago, para ellos en honor de la grande amistad entre los Estados Unidos y Cuba — salud. His voice is weak, but dependable.

One Cuban shrugs, hoists a bottle in Quinlan's direction. CIA sucks, he says.

Quinlan tilts his bottle, little finger raised, and nods in agreement. To Che.

Travis? Quinlan asks, now that he can speak more than two syllables. Where's the Judge?

Who?

The Judge, Bill Weiss.

Weiss is in his room, puking his guts out, Travis says. Or maybe, fucking his brains out. He winks, having trouble getting one eye closed while the other is open. He says, The two Mexican ladies of the evening helped him up the stairs, Quinlan. He hasn't been seen since.

Carmichael and Travis sit at one side of the long table, while Morgan and the dancer sit across from them, talking quietly. Carmichael facilitates their conversation. Quinlan thinks, Romeo and Juliet have met, or is it Humbert and Lolita?

He is happy with his friends surrounding him, each one a presence, only Dutch Brenner missing. Then he remembers the feel of Mae's cheek, imagines her hand in his, thinks that he should be gone from here, should be back home where she is.

Dutch Brenner stumbles through the door and into the bar.

Our Lady of Guadalupe   Sam Caldwell

VII

Dutch Brenner wakes with a ringing in the center of his head. Lee Quinlan snores in a bed across the room. Good. Brenner had been worried about his friend.

The ringing fades, then returns. He rises slowly to a sitting position and places his feet on the floor. Neon light flickers through a window shade. Brenner pulls the sheet aside in order to rise, but the sheet is stuck to the hair on his chest, up his neck and the side of his face. The sheet is gummy with a sticky mass. He examines his left ear where the ringing is now centered. He tries to pull the sheet loose, but a sharp pain in his ear stops him. The sheet is free behind the ear. Blood must have oozed from the ear while he slept. A hot shower will soak the sheet loose. He stands, and carrying the sheet like a bloody shroud, shuffles to the bathroom.

2

Someone is knocking on Quinlan's door, a polite tap, tap, tap. There's a sock in his hand. He must be putting on his socks. Where is the other sock? A brilliant slit of sunlight under the door provides enough illumination to see objects and hurt his eyes all the way to the back of his head.

Brenner is on a bed near the window, a pillow over his face. Still dressed from last night? No, he has on pressed khakis and a clean shirt.

Quinlan can make out his jeans on the floor by an ancient dresser, shirt draped across a chair, undershirt on the door of the wardrobe, shorts where? He has the shorts on. Still, no second sock. Wondering about his boots, he looks around and there is the missing sock, already on a foot.

Next door, through the thin wall, Quinlan hears someone snoring. Bill Weiss, who has complained about Quinlan's snoring. Apparently, Montezuma's Revenge didn't kill Weiss, and pulque didn't kill Quinlan. But damn nearly. He feels like pounded dog shit, and has a piss hard that demands relief, while someone knocks on the door. He puts on the second sock, then to save energy, crawls a few feet to his pants.

A more forceful knock on the door.

Quinlan looks at Brenner, but the big man seems unconscious. Come on in, damn it, he says. As Quinlan struggles to his feet and begins pulling on his pants, harsh light streams through the door. He squints into the glare. A woman's form, silhouetted. Thin runner's legs. Long print skirt, all white and yellow with little blue flowers, short-sleeved blouse, curly red hair peeking out from a wide-brimmed straw hat he gave her on the bay. Mae Kennedy walks to him and touches his cheek.

Mae?

Are you all right?

God, I don't know. Everything hurts. His eyes are adjusting to the brightness, and he can look into Mae's green eyes, and sees himself as she must, pants at half-mast, hair tangled, eyes bloodshot. And he stinks. I need a shower, Mae, and I've got to get dressed.

I'll be back, after I talk to Mr. Weiss.

Weiss is next door.

I know. Mae takes Quinlan's hand for a moment, then is gone, and the room is dark again, except for the slice of light under the door. There is a hint of woman, a perfumed presence still there. His cheek is warm where he was touched. His palm remembers her warm fingers.

Beside the wardrobe cabinet is a doorway, his shared bathroom with Weiss. There will be soap, shampoo, shaving gear, deodorant, towels, a shower. As Quinlan pushes through the door, he hears Mae tapping on Weiss's door. And faintly, hears their voices. Shouldn't eavesdrop. He pauses, foot in mid-step so as not to miss anything.

Bill?

Who is it?

Mae Kennedy.

Mae. Good God—is everyone all right?

Everyone's fine, Bill. Are you decent?

Quinlan turns on the shower and gets only a trickle, cold and metallic smelling. He lets the water run, but leans against the door, wanting to hear Mae's voice.

For Pete's sake, Mae, Weiss says. Let me get a pair of pants on. Quinlan hears a wordless scuffle, then the door into the shared bathroom opens and a red-haired Mexican woman stumbles through. Freckles hops on one foot while she tries to get her skirt on, clutching her other garments and purse. Next comes the dark girl. He is surrounded by bosoms. Unhappy bosoms. Freckles is angry at being so discourteously treated. And uncompensated; she points to her purse and rubs fingers together.

Ssss, señorita. Es la esposa, Quinlan whispers, trying to cover his boner with a towel. Hay te dejo viente dollars abajo.

Y para mi amiga?

Shhh, dammit. He wraps the towel around his waist and leans close to her ear. 10 dollares para su amiga.

Freckles pouts and stamps her foot. She hisses that she and her friend are not nurses, yet they have attended his sick friend all through the night.

Okay. $20, tambien para ella.

The dark girl tries to give Quinlan a hug but there's no room, because Freckles is all elbows and knees while she dresses. She laughs soundlessly at Quinlan as he tries to hold the skimpy towel closed. She snaps her bra, grabs her purse, waves adios to Quinlan.

The shower trickle is now warm, but Quinlan still listens.

Bill Weiss must be decent now. Mae? Come on in. What in the world are you doing here, anyway?

You need to sign papers on the offshore Gulf platform case. Archer is waiting at the airport.

Archer.

Captain Archer, with Byron Lee's plane. Sign on the bottom of these first two pages—as the attorney of record and here, and on all four of these settlement pages at the X.

This one doesn't need anything but the judge's clerk's signature, Weiss says, and these two could wait. Rustling of paper. Nice dress.

Vivien gave it to me.

You look ravishing. Lee Quinlan's next door.

I know. Quinlan hears a briefcase snap. I'll be at the big hotel on the square till 3 p.m. Vivien asked that you come back on the plane, Bill.

Silence for a minute then, I'll consider that, Mae.

The shower is now lukewarm. Quinlan steps in and gets relief for a previous problem, but finds only a sliver of yellow soap, and a throwaway razor. He does the best he can. When Quinlan returns to his room, Brenner is gone, and Mae is sitting on Quinlan's bed.

S'cuse me, ma'am. Quinlan drops the towel and steps into his pants, then grabs his shirt, wrinkles his nose and fumbles through Brenner's duffle bag. A clean shirt and socks, thank you kindly, Mr. Brenner.

Quinlan and Mae walk away from the Casa de Palomas in the early morning sunlight, holding hands.

3

John Morgan wakes slowly. His dog is barking, wanting a walk and a chance to mark his territory and get a leg up on other dog's marks. But that isn't Sport's baritone bark, and this isn't Houston. Morgan wants to drift back into unconsciousness, but a hanging sheet moves beside him.

Morgan jolts awake. He is in a small bed, a sheet dangling from wire serving as a curtain between the bed and the world. He fumbles the sheet aside. An ancient revolving fan hums, blowing alternately away, then around to his area. The little dancer watches him from a chair at her dresser.

He winces at the sensation of crushed gravel behind his eyes. Through the open window, Morgan hears street sounds and sees sunshine on a stucco wall. He glances at his wrist, but there is only a white strip of skin where the Rolex should be. Must be in his jeans, or maybe in one of his boots. Or on a peddler's rack.

Damn, he has to get dressed, get going. Locate everyone, get their stuff together, if they have anything left. Look for his watch, first thing. No, first thing is to find about five aspirin and a gallon of ice water. The dancer smiles at him and the room seems to brighten. Aw, hell, first thing is to relax just a minute, gather some strength.

Morgan has a vague recollection of stumbling up narrow stairs with Lee Quinlan and the dancer, looking at things in the room. A tour of her life, as Quinlan translates it. A small Madonna over the door, pictures of her family tucked into the frame of a broken-mirrored dressing table. This is her mother, there an aunt and two uncles, twins, both boys dead at 11. A younger sister, holding the dancer's hand and looking up with adoration. A color print of her older brother in Houston who sends American money by Western Union check, earned by hanging mud, that is, he works as a sheetrock carpenter. He perches nonchalantly at the open door of a shiny Chevrolet Impala. In an ornate frame, a faded color picture of her father and mother. Her father's parents in a yellowed newspaper clipping. Polaroid photos of the dancer as a small girl in ballerina costume, bad publicity shots of the little dancer in various poses. Bright dresses and gaudy dance costumes hanging in good order around the room.

She says something to Morgan softly, a question.

He shrugs. Sorry, señorita. She is a pretty girl. No, a striking young woman, aristocratic, even.

Just above her elbow she is wearing his Rolex.

Ma'am, I'll love you forever if you could find me a glassful of aspirin and a handful of water. Uh, cold water, agua, señorita? he says, mimicking drinking and taking pills.

Carlotta, she frowns, shaking a finger at him. The room darkens.

Uh, Carlotta, maybe eight aspirins and a large jug of water? He sees his jeans folded neatly at the foot of the bed, his shirt hanging separately from a wire hanger on the door knob. He is wearing his jockey shorts and tee shirt. He strains to sit up, grabs his jeans and finds his billfold.

He watches as she crosses the room to her table and the closet. She has on a short dress and adds an embroidered shift. Standing, watching him watching her, she manages to gracefully put on high-heeled pumps, then tilts her head, smiles, laughs.

God almighty, Morgan says. You're the most beautiful woman in the world. He finds a $10 bill, then holds his head and rolls his eyes in pain. She accepts the bill, then starts for the door. As she passes Morgan, he crooks a finger at her, then points at his watch.

Carlotta stops, pulls off the watch slowly, eyes downcast. She holds the watch out, waiting for him to take it. The fan hums as it oscillates a cycle, Carlotta to Morgan, then back to Carlotta. She waits, shoulders slumped. Morgan takes the woman's wrist, glances at the time, then slides the watch back on her arm.

Carlotta turns, smiles, and the world brightens again. She hurries from the room.

The drone of the fan is uninterrupted for a time, a slight reprieve from the pressure of his headache when the fan blows directly on him, then a half-minute of agony when the breeze is aimed elsewhere. He could get up and maybe find the control that keeps the fan aimed at his bed. It probably doesn't work, and the effort might cause more pain than relief.

Staccato footsteps on the stairs. Carlotta sweeps back into the room. She is a radiant flower, a bright presence, an angel of mercy carrying a tray. On the tray is a pitcher of chilled orange juice. A pile of aspirin and Alka Seltzer packages surrounds one glass. A large stack of pesos fills the other glass.

Carlotta perches primly on the end of the bed. As Morgan sits up to take the glass, he notices the girl's averted gaze and pulls the sheet up. The cold orange juice chases four aspirin down, then two more.

Carlotta, he says, this trip may not turn out half bad. He puts on his handsomest smile. I have to get dressed and go now, but we'll be coming back this way. He pantomimes putting on shirt, pants, waving goodbye, sadly. Then, mimicking arrival, he throws his arms wide. Carlotta rushes to him, upsets his balance and they fall back on the small bed. A slat breaks, and the bed slants, head down.

Both laugh. Morgan kisses Carlotta.

She kisses him back, but briefly, then gets up.

Sitting awkwardly on the tilted bed, he puts on pants, shirt and boots, the boots with Carlotta's help. He starts out the door, but in an afterthought, tries to hand Carlotta the rolled wad of pesos.

She turns away and he is left standing in the doorway with money in his hand, looking at the back of a haughty woman. He stuffs the bills in his shirt pocket and takes a step away. The door slams, catching a bit of his heel. It is a resounding slam that causes the walls to vibrate.

Morgan stops on the next landing for a short time, then continues downstairs.

Carlotta moves her chair to the door. Tiptoeing, she is just able to reach the Madonna over the doorway and take it down. She wraps the icon gently in a scarf. In one fold of the cloth she nestles the Rolex and a note, then takes the note back out. She straightens the paper and looks over the words. Carlotta knows what the words say. The man called Quinlan read the words to her as he wrote them.

Dear Juan Morgan, the note begins in a drunken scrawl; We belong together. I will go with you when you return.

The note is signed in her small script, Carlotta Morgan, and below her signature is more of Quinlan's writing: Sea Captain Edward Lee Quinlan, Esq. doth hereby officially seal this bond, according to the expressed wishes of both parties.

Below this is the date and John Morgan's looping signature. Carlotta knows the note was written by men who had overmuch to drink and was signed by a man who had closed one eye to grasp the pen. But next week, she will leave this place and go to the country across the river, and there await the return of Juan Morgan.

Today, she will sit here patiently, hoping that he returns to see her before he leaves on his trip. She does not have to wait long.

4

Someone is snoring. Mae? No, it is his noise, fading away, a sore throat to convince him of the culprit. Mae is asleep, her warm, smooth thigh between his legs. They're in Mae's bed in an expensive Matamoras hotel room. About to ease into sleep again, he remembers waking at Mae's place in Houston and finding her gone, and wonders if his snores had sent her away then.

She woke him early this morning with sleeping noises, and knew it and apologized, and he said that even the Queen of England snores, so he had heard. They talk, whispering as though someone might hear. About the past, and the future, and how they can make things work out, now that they know one another he says, and what they could do together, she says.

Maybe I can get my old job back, Quinlan says.

Teaching?

Oh, God, no.

Writing?

Sacking groceries at Weingarten's, the old place on North Shepherd. Maybe I could get you hired as a cashier. Do you count good?

I've been a cashier. I'll get you right here, ma'am. Paper or plastic? There you go. You need some help with that, sir?

I used to make good money. One lady tipped me a full dollar, every time she came in, and she didn't have that much stuff to carry.

Maybe she liked you. Did she ever… you know?

Aw, just a pinch one time. Anyway, I'll talk to Mr. Geizendanner and see if we can get you on, and if the greengrocer, old man Westin tries to grab at you, you just tell me, and I'll take him back of the storage bin and talk to him, and he'll never bother you again.

You'll always be my hero, she says.

Will you marry me?

Right now.

They make love, yelling together, not concerned for any listener on either side of the hotel room walls, or either side of the border.

5

Street sounds waft through the open window. Hello, Matamoras. After two days here, and evenings from other years, the sensations are like home. There's an argument going on two stories beneath the curtain-draped balcony window. Shrill man and loud woman, or two women? But the terrible argument turns into laughter, and the two go away, leaving Quinlan wondering what the verdict was, or if the noise was no more than friendship.

Mae runs in her sleep.

Little jerks of arm and leg and she talks to someone, head shaking, words just a mumble, but intense, then she startles and is awake, nestling into his chest and belly, wrapping arms and legs all over him. She rubs his right shoulder, and he wonders how she knows of the morning agony. Maybe it was a flinch when she touched him there, or just her sense of his feelings. The agony; could have been a fall from a horse, but it's probably just old Arthur Rightus showing up.

She says, This place on your shoulder is so warm. You're hurting there?

He says, Much better now.

Good. Can I hold you here?

Sauce for the gander, sauce for the goose, ma'am. I'll hold you, uh, right here.

Do you have dreams?

Dreaming now.

I mean, hopes, ideas for the future. Places you want to go and things you want to do.

Go somewhere, do things, be with a beautiful person.

Who?

I need a volunteer. Let's see… Quinlan sits up, looks around for potential companions.

Mae raises a hand.

Quinlan frowns at dozens of beautiful women clamoring for his attention.

Mae waves her hand in front of his nose. Me. Take me.

Surprised, he sees her hand. Would you go?

Right now.

We can't leave until we get a good boat.

You have a boat.

A sailboat. To live on.

Oh. You're a sailor?

We could learn.

She holds him as tight as she can. Where will we sail to?

You like the hills.

You like the sea.

Ireland. We'll sail away to Ireland.

6

Matamoras is in mid-day form, the horns of buses and taxis mingling like an out of synch symphony. Charcoal-cooked everything drifts in through the open window, mingled with diesel fumes. Mae is gone. Damn. Did he snore her away again?

Mae walks back into the room. She has wet hair, her body is shiny damp, and she doesn't see Quinlan seeing her. All of her as she turns, fumbling for something on the dresser. The mirror gives him a brain-numbing image of Mae front and back. He hadn't noticed a small scar just below her navel, right side, maybe an appendix scar he'll need to kiss later. She stops beside the bed and completes her hair wrap. Since the navel is just a few inches away, he'll kiss that little scar right now.

Lee... would you care to split another shower?

He wraps one of her towels around kilt style, to mask ugly male appendages and knobby knees.

She pulls the knot loose and drops both their towels.

Bath time, Sir. Steam spills from the bathroom as they enter hip to hip.

Quinlan steps into the shower first. Just right, too hot.

She steps in, smiles and adjusts the knob with her toes.

Beautiful toes.

I have a birthmark on my shoulder.

I love it.

If I don't wear contacts, I'm legally blind. Or else, I wear thick glasses and look like Mole.

Thank God, you're not perfect, like me. That's too flip for this moment. I'm flawed inside, Mae.

They hold each other's flawed bodies.

After a steaming shower, they cuddle in the full bathtub until the water is cool. They towel one another and rest some more, stomachs growling, causing embarrassed laughter. Time for food. Mae picks up the phone and sees Quinlan glance for his billfold.

This is on the law firm, Lee.

What the hell, Bill Weiss makes more money in an hour than Quinlan made last month. In that case, tell 'em, Beefsteak y huevos por tres, and, his Spanish deserting him again, one of their finest bottles of red wine.

Mae speaks into the phone; Señorita, bistec y huevos por tres, Y uno de su mas claro botellas de vino. Rojas vino, señorita. Y andale, por favor.

Quinlan smiles. Always surprises from this woman.

Mae has a glass of wine with their brunch. There is a little steak left, and part of the bottle of wine. Mae helps finish the bottle of wine. When wine is in, wit is out, the French say. When wine and food is in, sex is out.

After lunch, they lie close together and Quinlan tastes her cheek and shoulders while she talks.

You like classical music, she says.

Oh?

Bill Weiss's wife Vivien told me so. You took her and the girls to Rice University, and they loved the music. The girls, especially.

Shepherd School of Music. It was great, he says. And free.

Winifred, the youngest, says she is going to play cello just like that beautiful Asian girl. And Tracy wants to be a singer now, instead of a nurse.

Bill Weiss needs to work less and enjoy his kids more.

Vivien asked me to bring Mr. Weiss back on the plane.

Bill's a sick puppy. He probably ought to go home.

You said you thought about catching a bus for Austin when you called me.

Wish I had.

But, now you're going on?

A little time passes. Yes, Quinlan says.

7

They walk away from the hotel in the late morning sunlight.

You're lovely in the long white dress, with the hat and the ribbon.

You look so different, without a beard.

Feels different. Just shaved it off this morning, too much trouble getting it right, and the shirt is Dutch Brenner's, feels like a tent.

I was sad when I had to leave you the other morning. I hate it that my brother was rude when you called, the wedding was fine, it was nice to see the family, but I just drove home early.

I wish the trip was over.

I came home to see if you were still in Houston.

Oh. Sunday evening, a week?

Mae stops and turns him to her. Be careful, she says.

I wish it was next Sunday now. But there are the men, and the trip.

A flower woman is covered with color, a walking bouquet. Oh, murmurs Mae, and Quinlan feels the sense of her word. Quinlan chooses a white carnation, and yellow flowers of some kind, and has enough Mexican money to satisfy the old lady, but just barely. Mae kisses Quinlan, and people stop, look, frown.

Quinlan feels the disapproval. You don't treat a woman tenderly on a Mexican street. The men resent it, more so the old ones, especially the ancients, who always had at least that bit of superiority over someone, their women walking behind a pace or two. Or, maybe it's the idea of a kiss in front of God and other strangers.

A block further along, Quinlan stops Mae and touches her cheek and kisses her thoroughly, just for the two of them. Mae knows, and melds to him, to hell with all sour non-lovers.

Mae holds the flowers and they walk around the square. A mob of pigeons makes way too slowly even for slow walkers and flies up in a cloud of wings at the last minute, and Mae's dress swirls.

Runner's legs, Quinlan thinks, watching as Mae primly straightens the dress. They stop by a concrete fountain and kiss again, standing there, then sit on the edge of the fountain with water splashing behind them.

Mae takes a ring from her hand and tries to put it on Quinlan's ring finger, but it will fit only on his little finger. It was my father's, Mae says. I have to go to the airport now. Bill Weiss may come back with me, after he talks to his wife.

Weiss will probably go on with us.

They walk back to the hotel, and she leaves in a cab.

Why didn't he go back to Houston with her?

She didn't ask him.

Lee Quinlan, servant to the wishes of friends?

No. He told these men he'd take them fishing, and when Lee Quinlan says he'll do something… He told Mae he'd be back a week from now.

8

At the decrepit Casa de las Palomas Hotel, Quinlan bangs on Crazy Fred Carmichael's door.

Quiet, responds Bill Weiss. There are sick people in here. Quinlan pushes the door open and stomps in.

Weiss is shaving from a basin, slowly and carefully.

Carmichael is sitting on the bed, head in hands. I'm dying, he says.

The air is rank with exhaled alcohol from Carmichael and sour odors from Weiss.

Is this what his room smelled like when Mae walked in this morning? Get your asses in gear, folks. Mr. Morgan will be anxious to move along.

I may go home on a friend's plane.

Plane left twenty minutes ago.

Damn, Quinlan, now you can call my wife and let her know.

Mae will take care of that.

Well, hell. Let's go see about breakfast, or whatever they serve at 3:30 in Mexico.

Quinlan grins. Weiss is going to live.

They start slowly down three flights of stairs. Carmichael descends in front of Weiss, and Quinlan follows.

Looks like you had some fun last night, Crazy.

You could call it fun, replies Carmichael, if you enjoy hammering yourself wit h tequila. The trio limp into the dining room of the Casa de las Palomas.

Look at this, says Carmichael.

Luck Travis and Dutch Brenner are already there, eating. At the same table.

I thought Quinlan would be brain dead this morning, Travis says. As the three join the breakfast table, John Morgan comes down the stairs. He pulls a chair from another table and joins them.

Travis eyes Brenner's leftovers. You want the rest of those tortillas?

Brenner's puffball eyes narrow. Maybe.

Too late. Travis rakes the tortillas onto his plate.

Brenner nods at Quinlan, winks his good eye. Wonder what they're serving at the hoosegow this morning?

Beans with rats and cucarachas, Carmichael says. I've visited similar jusgados before. He taps the face of his watch. I'll be back here by 5:30. Don't leave without me, Morgan.

Give her my love, Fred, says Travis, but Carmichael is striding for the doorway and doesn't seem to hear.

Quinlan does a nose count. The group is all there, except for Erwin Baker. He says, It isn't like Erwin Baker to miss a meal. Where's the kid?

You were really fouled up last night, Quinlan, says Travis. Baker was kicked off the trip. Just before you idiots went to spring Brenner.

Morgan is busy not looking at Quinlan.

John?

Tired of the kid. He let Brenner down. Silence at the table for a minute.

Bullshit, Morgan. Travis frowns around the last of his breakfast. If Brenner wanted to jump the entire Matamoras police force, Baker couldn't stop him.

Brenner winces with the pain of old and new bruises. Damn near whipped 'em all.

The waitress pours more coffee and brings breakfast platters. Scrambled eggs, piles of toast and bacon, fresh fruit, and the inevitable pureed black beans.

Pass the orange juice, Quinlan, says Weiss. And what is this pile of brown stuff?

Chihuahua shit, answers Travis.

Refried black beans, Quinlan explains. Mexicans enjoy serving black beans to Texans.

Gotcha, Quinlan, says Travis. The Drawing of the Beans, after the Alamo. Draw a white bean, you live. Black bean, you die. Morgan?

What?

Baker is a good person, compared to some of the assholes at this table.

Maybe so. But he's gone, and you can join him, Luck.

May do it—

Weiss interrupts. Baker is just down the street, by Morgan's truck. Saw him from my window.

I've had my breakfast and lunch, Quinlan says. I'll check on the kid.

Quinlan walks along the shaded side of the street, watching people, smiling and getting smiles in return. It's a beautiful afternoon, after a beautiful morning. Yesterday's surly crowd seems buoyant and cheerful. Maybe there is a God who cares about each one of us.

In the courtyard behind the hotel are Morgan's truck and Weiss's station wagon, with the boat and trailer behind the wagon. Both outside wheels of Weiss's wagon are bare of hub caps. Walking around the wagon, Quinlan sees that the tailgate looks off-center, as though someone had failed at ripping it from the hinges. Baker leans against an alley wall near the stern of the boat. He seems in worse shape than the wagon. The young man stands slump-shouldered, hands in jean pockets, watching as Quinlan approaches. Baker's satchel is at his feet. Quinlan feels an aura of strength about Baker.

Been here all night?

Yes.

Looks like someone tried to break into the truck.

Twice.

Well, hell. You stopped 'em?

Baker shrugs.

Quinlan realizes that he has taken on the stance of Baker. He shrugs. Cigarette?

No, thanks.

From the shade, they watch the ancient courtyard. Clothes hang gaily from lines across one corner. A small tribe of multicolored hens scratches industriously at the brick surface beneath the clothes line, watched over by a scruffy cock. A screen door slams. A woman who may have been as young as 50 or as old as 70 empties a wash basin, forcing the cock to abandon his dignity and scurry for safe ground.

Luck Travis and John Morgan walk into the courtyard. The intense light causes both men to squint. Baker moves out of the shade toward them.

Morgan.

Baker. Thought you were on a bus back to Houston.

You're gonna have to fight me, Morgan. Baker aims a hard right, straight from the shoulder directly at the middle of Morgan's face, but at the last instant, changes his aim and hits Morgan a glancing blow in the chest.

Morgan chops him solidly in the jaw. Travis catches Baker from behind as the stunned man crumples to the brick courtyard.

Goddamnit, yells Travis. He crouches beside the young man, looking into his face.

Kid tried to hit me. Did hit me, says Morgan, rubbing his chest.

Baker sits up and, eyes on Morgan, tries to rise. Travis and Quinlan keep the young man on the bricks. I'm all right, Baker says. Let me up.

They help him to his feet, and he turns away a moment, then pulls a wadded handful of bills from his back pocket and throws the money in a cloud of ones and fives. Morgan ducks, forearms before his face. Erwin Baker walks away.

9

Quinlan leans from the passenger window of Morgan's truck. Travis drives. Ahead in the crowd, Quinlan sees a tall young man in a rumpled jean shirt. The truck is back in congested Matamoras traffic, moving hardly faster than the pedestrians.

Hey, Baker? Forcing his head and shoulders out of the passenger window, Quinlan thumps on top of the cab, nearly deafening Travis. He yells at a Mexican vendor near Baker. Hey, para es Gringo alli, amigo. The noise of the street drowns him out. He eases the door open and stumbles out.

Through the traffic, Quinlan can see Baker walking toward the bridge that crosses the Rio Grande. He is jostled by passing Mexicans, intent on their own affairs. The narrow sidewalk is crowded with Chiclet vendors, blanket, necklace, shirt, dress, knife, fruit and ice peddlers, beggars with the eyes of poets, taxi drivers with the eyes of hawks, all intent on making a peso or American dollar. Sullen teenagers lounge on cars and in open doorways. The sound of salsa music blares from doorways.

Quinlan hurries past people of Matamoras, intent on a slow-moving Houstonian. Across the street, Quinlan sees Baker rub his jaw and smile to himself. Baker stops in front of a flavored-ice vendor. A soothing wetness of lime ice is being thrust in Baker's face.

Setenta y cinco, the peddler says. Baker fumbles in all his pockets but finds no money. He smiles wanly at the ice peddler and continues walking toward the bridge.

Baker. Wait up.

Lee?

Let me carry that, Quinlan says, taking Baker's duffel bag. How do you feel? Baker's jaw is swollen, and he looks terrible, except for a smile.

Besides some aches and pains, and starving, I never felt better in my life.

Quinlan nods. Hitting back has a certain satisfaction about it. Got any money on you?

No.

Damn. Me neither, Quinlan lies. He has the money that Baker threw at Morgan. But, what the hell, on the other side of the river, I'll make a collect call to my agent. Get us some bus fare back to Houston.

Baker frowns. Thought you guys would be long gone by now.

Travis pulls the truck up next to the two men. He honks the horn and waves impatiently.

I'm not going anywhere with you bastards, Quinlan yells, unless Erwin Baker is welcome.

10

The group watches as Baker, Travis and Quinlan step from the truck in the courtyard of the Casa de Palomas.

Morgan approaches Baker. My apologies, Baker.

The two men look at one another. Baker nods and to Quinlan, it seems that two strong men have agreed on one another's worth. The other men assemble around them, and in their awkward or graceful ways, make Baker welcome.

Dutch Brenner extends his open hand. Baker does not immediately take the hand, but Brenner understands and waits, and when the shock wears off for Baker, the two men shake hands. Don't have any use for a man that won't stand his ground, Brenner says gruffly. You'll do, Baker.

At 4:45, the convoy is loaded and ready to go, but Carmichael is missing. Morgan says, Who does he think he is—Lee Quinlan?

Travis and Quinlan are in the boat arranging gear. Tents refolded and moved up front, less likely to blow out. Cooking equipment in the middle, iceboxes at the rear, with newly purchased crushed ice, beer, soft drinks, distilled water jugs.

Quinlan jabs Travis in the shoulder and says, Look who's coming. From their vantage point in the boat, they see Carmichael hurrying toward the courtyard, head and worried eyes above the crowd, wondering if the group has left without him.

Travis leans down from the boat. Here comes Carmichael.

Weiss— Morgan yells, crank it up. Let's make ol' Crazy Fred run for it. The convoy pulls away from the courtyard at 4:46 p.m., crew cab truck in the lead, station wagon pulling the boat with Quinlan and Travis aboard but not looking back, and last in line, a lanky photographer shouting English and Spanish curses.

After a long block, Bill Weiss stops, and the group welcomes a winded and angry Carmichael back aboard.

They stop again at the edge of the downtown district to buy two lime ices and a large chunk of barbecued goat for Erwin Baker. John Morgan insists on paying for Baker's meal. Then they head west, aimed for the Buena Suerta.

Chicken Champion tonight, or Rooster Soup Mañana?
Sam Caldwell

VIII

At 5:45, Quinlan has Weiss stop the truck at one side of a small Mexican beer joint. He's out of the vehicle before it rolls to a stop and hurries into the old building.

Buenos dias, One Eye, Quinlan says as he hurries past the bar.

A frown and slowed wiping of a glass serve as response from the man. Quinlan smiles to himself. You always know where you stand with One Eye.

There's a door to the left for Damas, one to the right for Caballeros. Inside is a trough at the back of a dark room. Flies, stink, heat. Relief.

Back in the bar, Quinlan sees that One Eye is serving cerveza to the crew of Yanquis, and with this much business the owner seems cheerful.

One-eye talks to Carmichael. Ese, ahi, One Eye says, as Quinlan steps out of the Caballeros door zipping his fly. Ese que esta hay tomo toda la cerveza en una noche... Y su amigo grande quebro lo que no se abilla consumido.

We're fondly remembered from three years ago, Quinlan says to Weiss. To the bartender: Que tal?

El gobeierno se lleva lo que los insectos dejan, Y A mi metoca lo resto.

He says the government takes what the bugs leave. Last time I was here, he had a fight arranged for El Campion. Wonder what happened to his rooster. To the bartender, Y tu gallo?

One Eye shrugs and says there is always one fight too many.

Quinlan turns to Weiss. It's bad form to lose a fight in Mexico, 'specially if you're edible. El gallo campion en las noches, o caldo pollo mañana.

One Eye nods at the line and replies that El Gallo made very tough chicken soup indeed.

Morgan finishes his Corona and slams the bottle on the bar. Vamanos, muchachos, he says, trying some Spanish. Let's get to Third Pass.

Outside the cantina, Travis and Brenner start for the crew cab truck at the same moment. Neither man is willing to turn away and admit any concern for the other. Morgan sits between Travis, the driver, and Brenner, riding shotgun.

Two hostiles, Quinlan thinks. Shoulder to shoulder thinking death wishes. Either one could break Morgan's cease-fire over an idle comment, and there'd be hell to pay. Brenner is already busted up, and so is Travis. It could ruin the rest of the trip.

Quinlan decides to change the seating arrangement in the truck. Swap time, Morgan.

Morgan nods. Judge? he says over the CB from habit, while looking ten feet away at Weiss. You want to trade me Baker for a while. And maybe he'll bring some ice from the cooler in the wagon and look after Brenner.

My pleasure, says Travis, heading away from the truck and Brenner.

First, Quinlan yells at him, as a ticket to ride in the happy wagon, you have to go back into One-eye's joint and buy a case of beer.

Three minutes later, Travis climbs into the station wagon with a case of beer—Quinlan's Mexican favorite, Dos Equis—and Travis is back in his laughing mood. He yells, Vaya con Dos Equis, amigos.

Down the road, Quinlan is on the airwaves, bringing the group new ideas.

VIII

Information break for Convoy Texas, Quinlan says over the CB. As you're aware, my chosen profession is that of stomping out ignorance.

Rude noises from two men.

I will enlighten those ignoramuses within earshot about certain aspects of Texas history. The lecturer snaps his fingers and shakes his empty beer can. A full can of Dos Equis is produced by Travis.

Quinlan nods his thanks. Cold beer for a sore throat. Or, maybe it's throat cancer. Will a beautiful young woman have any interest in an old guy who has to speak by belching?

First, the Drawing of the Beans took place in Mexico, not Texas, and it happened years after ol' General Sam Houston kicked Santa Anna's ass at San Jacinto. Not far from here is a little Mexican town, name of `Me-airrrr'. That's spelled, for you non-linguistically adept Texans, `M-I-E-R.' An expedition of Texans captured Mier. And wished they hadn't. They demanded some stores and ammunition and waited for it, and instead, the Mexican army showed up. Helluva three-day fight. Finally, out of anything to eat or drink or shoot, those Texans had to surrender.

And they shot every tenth man, says Travis.

Nope. In fact, the commander disobeyed Santa Anna's orders to shoot 'em all. Started those 180 Texans for Mexico City. A Scotsman name of Ewing Cameron led a revolt, and most of them got away. But hell, no one knew the country, and they didn't have horses or food. All but a few were recaptured and brought back together at a place called Salado. In irons, over a bowl of beans. A hundred and fifty-nine white beans and seventeen black beans.

Quinlan pauses to sip his beer and eye the countryside. Ewing Cameron drew white. The next morning, he and the other hundred and fifty-eight lucky Texans were lined up on one side of a wall, while seventeen unlucky Texans were shot on the other.

Sad tale, Quinlan.

Yeah. Then, Ewing Cameron got it.

The CB crackles. I thought you said Ewing Cameron drew a white bean, come back to Morgan?

Cameron was a hell of a man, and a fine leader, sorta like Sargent Morgan up there. Even the Mexican officers hated it when the order came from Santa Anna.

Quinlan thinks about that moment at daybreak. The order: Shoot Cameron—Quinlan feels the moment, doesn't hear the sound of the shots because of the shock of the bullets, nor feel the pain as his face hits the rough roadway— nobody knows what really happened to Cameron. Some say he was released and spent the rest of his days with a beautiful Señora and a bunch of little Camerons.

Viva beautiful Señoras, Travis says.

I figure he got a shallow grave, and sent his vital juices back into the earth, pronto. Not that bad, if you think about the option of laying around in a casket for a thousand years, waiting for the same deal.

Brenner speaks from the truck. I've always admired the old Viking funerals. Cremation on your boat. Get your molecules out there working again, quick.

Enough macho death bullshit, Morgan says. I'm pulling over for a piss stop. Quinlan, join us and check on Brenner's ear. Damn things oozing blood, and it's making me queasy.

2

Checkpoint ahead, says Quinlan. We must be 22 kilometers out of Matamoras.

Quinlan is driving for Morgan. He stops the truck, nods at two dark-uniformed soldiers as they approach him, one on each side. Both have side arms. Keeping his distance in front of the truck is a third soldier with an automatic rifle slung across his chest. Near the small checkpoint building, an older man in a tan uniform stands at parade rest. He has a pencil-thin mustache. A hat with a bit of braid. Standing in the shade, while others sweat. Obviously, an officer.

Quinlan looks back, sees two cars and an old van, but no station wagon. Buenos Dias, Quinlan says to the young soldier. The man nods sullenly in return. Brenner leans over the seat from the back, surprising Quinlan. Brenner seemed asleep since Quinlan had swabbed his ear. Or unconscious. A concussion, courtesy of the Matamoras law department?

You okay? Quinlan asks.

Brenner doesn't answer. He points at the soldier on the left of the truck. Sour little bastard. He looks at the braid-hatted man who seems to be in charge. Pompous son of a bitch over there.

Ease up, Dutch, Morgan says quietly from the side of his mouth, at the same time nodding at the soldier with the automatic weapon.

Quinlan realizes that he and Morgan both had calluses from lugging that model of rifle through jungles and across rice paddies and are familiar with the results that occur when the weapon is fired at humans.

Wonder if he ever gets a chance to shoot that gun, says Brenner. He ducks and easing one eye above the back seat, squints at the soldier.

No, Dutch—says Morgan. Quinlan jolts Brenner's gun hand with an elbow. But Brenner rests his hand on the seatback and, index finger pointed at the officer, sights down the finger. The soldier yells something and whips the automatic rifle into firing position.

Brenner fires his finger pistol. Pttshew!

Garza— yells the officer, running toward the truck. Ramon— a sociegate!

Quinlan looks left. Three feet away, the muzzle of a pistol is trembling slightly, a dark eye peering over the gun sight. The pistol is slowly lowered to aim at Quinlan's throat, but the intense eyes of the soldier remain locked on Quinlan's eyes.

Quinlan releases his breath.

Brenner smiles.

I'm going to kill you Brenner, Quinlan says, trying to maintain a nonchalant smile for the officer.

Afuera despacio, yells the officer. Tu— he points at Brenner— las manos en el capacete de la camioneta.

Brenner shrugs.

Abajo, ahora! screams the officer, his voice changing pitch and breaking as he waves his hands, motions understood by Quinlan and Morgan. They step out of the truck. Brenner starts out but bumps into a pistol jammed into his forehead. The soldier gestures at his hands, then at the top of the cab.

Quinlan says, Hands up, Dutch. Brenner slowly places his hands on the ceiling of the truck cab. Quinlan glances at Morgan. We're gonna need an attorney and an interpreter. And some luck.

Bill Weiss pulls the station wagon to a stop behind two ancient sedans and a battered van.

Erwin Baker sits by the open front window. He is nodding sleepily. As the van in front of them starts forward, Baker sees Morgan and Quinlan standing in the shade of a small building, their hands on their heads. Two soldiers are watching them, one with a pistol held at his side. A soldier is walking toward Weiss's vehicle, yelling something in Spanish. The soldier is carrying a machine gun. The soldier gestures with the gun, apparently telling them to go on, follow those cars, get away from here.

Erwin Baker throws open his door and steps out. Uh, Señor, those men are our friends—

In the back seat, Carmichael is now aware of a problem. What's up?

Weiss grips the steering wheel and starts the wagon forward, looking sideways at the young soldier with the gun. Carmichael opens his door, forcing Baker away from the car and closer to the soldier.

Alto! shouts the soldier, swinging the gun from Baker to Carmichael, then back to Baker.

Stop, Carmichael says to Weiss, then says something quietly to the soldier.

Que esta? yells the soldier.

Esta no problema, Carmichael says again, louder so that the approaching officer can hear. Todos somos de Mexico, incluando esos hombres. He gestures with his chin from Baker to Morgan, Quinlan and Brenner. El doctor alli— Carmichael lowers his right elbow to indicate Dutch Brenner. He tells the officer that the ugly man right there is on an important mission for Mexico, a life-saving mission. It is necessary for the officer's future advancement that he immediately make a call to a certain official in Matamoras.

IX

The convoy drives through low hills. They cross a bridge and look down on a small stream. Cattle move along the slope, belly-deep in grass.

Morgan keys his CB. Dull along here, Mr. Baker. No one has threatened to shoot us for an hour.

Baker says, Peaceful valley.

Quinlan agrees. Reminds me of all those westerns where a homesick kid says something like, 'Real quiet, ain't it Sarge?'

Carmichael responds from the truck. Did we wake you again, Mr. Quinlan?

Quinlan continues. The old sergeant, says, 'Yeh, too quiet.' Of course, the kid says, 'Kinda pretty and peaceful. Think I'll bring Molly Belle, settle down in this here valley, and thunk! An arrow hits the kid in the back.

Right, says Carmichael. The good-looking kid always gets it.

Travis nudges Baker. If someone goes down, it'll be young Erwin here.

It won't be Baker, Quinlan says.

An awkward silence.

Baker says, I didn't really read your book, Lee.

Quinlan smiles. Baker wouldn't speak before Matamoras, now won't shut up. Lots of people didn't, Erwin.

What was it about?

Quinlan keys the CB radio to keep the other vehicle in the conversation. Aw, hell, Baker... just sex and violence in the outdoors. Like this trip. Except, on the high seas, in a submarine.

Morgan responds from the truck. Are his lips moving, Baker?

Quinlan continues. There's this U.S. atomic sub, Baker. And a gay Captain, except he doesn't know he's gay—like Luck, sitting next to you.

Don't worry kid. I'm a lesbian.

There's a scientist with a new and terrible AIDS virus, and he's headed for Russia. After making a Moscow connection, he's gonna swap the AIDS virus for a sex-change job in Sweden. Of course, there's a malfunction and the sub nearly blows up, and the Doc solves the problem, except in close quarters with the Captain, and they fall for one another, you know?

Anyway, they decide they'll go off to Tahiti together, after they detonate the sub in New York harbor, blowing up the statue of Liberty and spreading AIDS all over the eastern seaboard. And they do. Except, this courageous young Lieutenant tries to stop 'em. But that's just the first chapter. You have to have a bang-up opening, kid.

Baker laughs. Brenner said you sold the film rights to Hollywood. How was the movie?

Except for changing the title, the story line and the ending, it was just like the book.

You can't believe a thing he says, Baker. Brenner's voice sounds weak over the CB. Cocksuckers rewrote everything, and Quinlan wouldn't go for it. I was looking forward to being the bronc-riding heavy that beats hell out of everyone and screws all the women. But, what the hell, it was a pretty good film anyway.

Travis grabs the CB. Dutch? What you need to do is to get acquainted with your feminine side.

You're gonna die, Travis.

After you, Brenner.

2

The convoy pulls up to Jack Voss's ranch gate at dusk. A little piece of the sun tries to cheer Quinlan, then winks out behind the caliche dust from the vehicles. The men pile out and mill around, stretching, relieving taut bladders.

Quinlan goes to the gate and shakes it. There's no lock apparent, but the gate will not open. Weiss and Carmichael follow Quinlan to the gate. Across the top, a wrought-iron sign spells out Santa Anita de la Buena Suerte.

Weiss asks, What does it say?

Quinlan's Spanish seems to be holding up, so he answers. Transliterally, Judge, it says Saint Anne of the Good Luck.

They can see a distant building, mostly hidden in a grove of large oaks. Robles, the noble trees line the roadway to the hacienda. It seems to be adobe and heavy timber and looks like Jack Voss's Mexican place should look. Old, big, expensive. A plate in the middle of the gate offers a red button. Quinlan leans on the button, expecting a voice to emanate from somewhere. Hello the house? No voice. He rattles the gate, bangs on the button, curses the button.

There is no sign of life from the house, no welcoming committee.

Jump the fence, Quinlan, says Morgan. Get us a sack for the night.

Insulators and wire lead from the gate to the fence line.

Quinlan says, If I touch that top wire, I'll be in worse shape than Brenner.

You should have called from Matamoras.

I hope to see you all at the Buena Suerte. Jack Voss said that, and we don't need anything else. Right, Dutch? Brenner is still seated, head in his hands.

What Brenner needs is a doctor. Worrying about Brenner reminds Quinlan of their host. I hope Juan Voss is okay. He had some health problems last year.

Brenner levers himself slowly out of the back seat of the station wagon, pisses on a trailer tire, then stumbles to the back of the wagon. He sits on the tailgate, holding an ice-filled towel around his head and looks blankly at the bow of the boat.

Quinlan wants the attention of someone in the house. Dutch, is my safety kit still in the boat?

It was soggy. I threw the son of a bitch away.

What about the flare gun?

Rusted shut.

Rats.

So, I bought new flares and a flare gun.

Baker, Quinlan yells at the most athletic member, jump into the boat. The young man steps up on the wheel well and vaults into the Mako.

Look inside the forward compartment. In front, the little slatted teakwood door. Bring me the red plastic case.

A minute later, Quinlan loads a plastic pistol with what looks like a shotgun shell.

Hey, Judge, showing it off for Weiss, we smuggled a pistol into Mexico after all. Angling the gun directly at the house, then up three fists, he pulls the trigger. The bang and muzzle flash startles everybody as a streak of light leaps into the evening, becomes a red explosion, then floats slowly earthward. They watch expectantly.

Nothing happens.

Brenner shakes his head.

Morgan frowns at Quinlan, then turns and kicks one of the trailer tires. Quinlan shuffles into the middle of the group and squeezes into a place between Brenner and Baker.

Nighttime is settling over the Mexican countryside, but no lights are on in the hacienda. Brenner groans softly. No one has ever heard Dutch Brenner admit pain.

That's it, Morgan says. We're headed out.

Quinlan nods his assent, but the men are already moving toward their accustomed seats in the truck and station wagon. The convoy pulls away, headed back to Matamoras.

Two miles down the road, a pickup truck pulls close behind them, lights flashing, then alongside. The driver gestures, points backward.

Don't stop Weiss, Morgan yells. The truck veers in front of them and slows. They see only one man in the truck, and no weapons are apparent.

By God, it's Arnoldo from the Good Luck Ranch. Quinlan whacks Weiss on the shoulder from the back seat. Pull over, Judge.

It isn't Arnoldo, Quinlan discovers at the side of the road. It's his older brother, Esteban.

Ten minutes later the group is in a big living room. It is dark, except for a few coal-oil lanterns. There is a new fire in the huge fireplace. The beer is cold, many cans and bottles floating among ice slush in a metal tub.

Esteban Armendariz bids the men welcome, smiling at questions, but answers only a few. No electricity, amigos. But there is plenty of cold beer. We keep lots of ice made just for no-electricity times.

Quinlan peers through the door of a small anteroom, hoping for a telephone. Two strangers are examining Dutch Brenner. One is a large blonde woman dressed in white, with her hair tucked into a tidy bun at the back of her neck. The other stranger is a little man dressed in black. Brenner looks past Quinlan, gives no sign of recognition.

In the room is a phone, an ancient piece of gilded equipment that might have been there when Poncho Villa was around. Quinlan slips in and waits for a chance at the equipment. Maybe Mae will be home. In Houston. Where he should be. Touching the ring she placed on his little finger, he eases the phone off the hook, but there is no dial tone.

Jack Voss enters in a silk robe. Quinlan nods at Voss, and Voss nods back, but with gravitas. He must have left the run-over cowboy boots and ragged sheepskin jacket back at the Texas Good Luck. Strictly the ruling class Mexican Patrón now.

You'll have to excuse the darkness, Mr. Quinlan. Lights and power are on and off. Mostly off, the last couple of days. As if on cue, the lights flicker, brighten, then go off again.

I thought I had a heart attack a few days ago, Voss says. Called my doctor in Houston, and he sent me this specialist from Transylvania.

From Czechoslovakia, the black-clad specialist says. Now of Tampico. The specialist is looking in Brenner's ear, checking his vital signs.

That's Doc Hlavinka, says Voss, and Nurse Gerta. You do what that little summidge says, or Gerta breaks your arm.

Brenner sits, looking at a distant point, thinking about Christmas Day, 1954. The other men watch through the door.

The Doc decided I didn't have a heart attack, Jack Voss continues. Claims I've been out of the region so long, I'm susceptible to the Tijuana Two Step. He winks at Weiss. That's a variation of Montezuma's Revenge, Judge. Peering over his glasses, he nods at Quinlan, then Morgan. Heard about you and your friends a couple of times, Mr. Quinlan. How's your trip been, so far?

Piece of cake, Jack. Why do you ask?

The doctor is through with Brenner, and gestures impatiently at Gerta. This man is mild concussion, with infected ear drum. The nose... He traces the crooked path of bone and cartilage with an ungentle finger. Brenner flinches. The nose will point different from the face. Unless someone in the future gives it another knock? Next patient.

Zat may happen zoon, Doc, says Travis, stepping forward. Nothing wrong with me but a little nick on my ankle. Travis grimaces as Gerta removes the bandage from his lower leg, unwinding the bandage swiftly at first, then gently as his swollen ankle is revealed. There is an angry red lump above the anklebone, and a blue and white indentation in the middle of the lump.

Septic, says the doctor. Will have to be opened.

Travis's eyes widen. Say what?

Something is still in wound. The doctor turns to Voss. A pan is needed, and hot water. There will be blood. He looks up at the men crowded close around him as he opens his black bag. You want to watch?

Hell yeah, grunts Brenner. The rest of the men turn away.

Now is Quinlan's chance to call Mae, if the line is alive. It is. The operator speaks English, but the lines are all chaos. Please try your call again later, señor. He goes back to the temporary operating amphitheater but looks away from the action.

Travis's face is white. Quinlan says, Cold beer, Luck?

Yeah, Quinlan. One of those good little Coronitas, if they've got it.

You'll have to settle for a Dos Equis. As Quinlan returns with the beer, Dr. Hlavinka drops something metallic in the pan.

Brenner fishes around in the red water and finds the object. He squints at the metal, then nods at Travis. Looks like a piece of my 30.06 boat-tailed Nosler. He hands Travis a small chunk of lead encrusted with brass.

You shot at me, says Travis.

Shot near you, Brenner says, just to wake your liberal ass up. Sorry about the ankle.

Dutch, if I don't kill you before we get back, I'll drink your ass under the table at Rick's.

I'll buy the drinks, says Brenner. You'll pay for the table dances.

The electric lights waver but stay on.

Doc Hlavinka says, This man with the concussion will need attention for the next 24 hours. He looks around the group, but there are only shrugs and averted eyes. So. Gerta?

Gerta takes Brenner's elbow. She is a large woman, urging her patient up the stairs. The men flow out of the room and watch. Brenner pauses midway up the staircase and looks back at them. Quinlan can see an idea working its way forward. Brightness crosses Brenner's face as he looks down at his worried friends.

Maybe this is the night I get lucky.

But nurse Gerta is back downstairs promptly and prepares a hypodermic needle. Sir? She frowns at Travis. The pants, sir. They must go down.

Travis winks at the men. Last time I flashed anyone, I was locked out of a hotel room. He drops his pants and pulls down his shorts. This butts for you, Quinlan. The nurse slaps a cheek and inserts the needle, all in one motion.

That is massive dose of penicillin, Dr. Hlavinka says, then leers at his patient. You may feel free to visit girls in Matamoras, Hong Kong or even Calcutta. Just do so in next two days.

Gee, thanks, Doc, Travis says, but I'll be fishing at Third Pass.

Gerta? Hlavinka glances up as he begins cleaning his operating room. Look after the sick one.

3

Quinlan must be on the east side of the house, because he can feel the morning sun. Yeah, there's a slant of light peeking through thick curtains. Roosters are waking the sun up. Quinlan hears soft words from women, a baritone laugh, then a bit of soprano song from a girl's throat.

He is in a huge bed, sunk deep and spread-eagled on a feather-filled mattress, enveloped by a feather-filled coverlet. Alive and well. Well enough to go for a morning run? He should get his lazy ass up and find running gear. Just do it. Shirt, shorts, thick socks, running shoes, energy. Quinlan decides he has brought none of those items with him. He falls back into the softness of the bed.

Overhead, a high stucco ceiling, crossed by beams that are not just there for looks. Rough wood walls, a big room. Noises float up from below. Dishes, silverware and table-setting sounds.

The smell of food cooking. In Mexico, cooking food seems always to involve frying something, fruit on the table, coffee ready, all aromas mingling with baked bread smells. Quinlan's stomach speaks to him, emphatically. He gets out of the magnificent bed and looks for his clothes. They're in an ornate cabinet, something his mother would call a chiffonier. On the waist-high portion are flowers. Real, fresh, strangely acrid. They reflect like a still life in a silver pitcher, and there's a washbasin, not quaint and decorative, but chipped enamel and serviceable.

Should he look for a bedpan? A thundermug, honeybucket, night soil container. Sure enough, there's an ancient enameled container under the bed. Maybe he'll give it a try. A memorial plaque for the door: Lee Quinlan and Pancho Villa Shat Here.

His billfold—it's beside the basin. Next to the billfold, crushed flowers from a walk with Mae beside a pile of colorful pesos. Hanging on the door is a towel and a bathrobe that looks big enough to wrap Brenner and Morgan together. Scary thought. There's only the one big door, and that means a bath down the hall. Donde esta el baño?

A loud knock on the door. Rise and shine, Quinlan. Desayuna time. Carmichael is going down the stairs as Quinlan opens the door. Breakfast, then we're headed for la palomas, with Jack Voss's escopetas. Andale.

Dove hunting time. But first, a shower and food. The bathroom, baño, excusado, whatever. It's to the left, past Brenner's room. Quinlan knows it's his door, because he hears Brenner talking to himself. To himself? Quinlan stops and listens at the door for just a moment, wondering, and goddamn it, the door opens and Brenner almost walks over Quinlan, looking healthy. Brenner ignores Quinlan's embarrassment at being caught.

How about a little breakfast, Lee?

Not till I scrub off some of this grunge.

Shower's right there, but you'll have to wait till Gerta is through. Or hell, join her.

Quinlan waits.

Breakfast on a shaded patio under small trees. Limes and flowers of limes, all around. Quinlan picks a lime near his head. Key limes. They sit at one of two tables, covered with fruit dishes and platters. Under the platter lids are strips of bacon, thick-sliced bread toasted in different stages of brownness and bowls of black and white stuff.

Black beans again. Quinlan smiles at Weiss, spooning a pile onto his plate. He says, the white stuff is grits.

Spare me, Quinlan.

You're a Texan now, Judge. Got to learn to love grits.

John Morgan and Erwin Baker join the group. Grackles squawk and whistle from the trees, and little ground dove and sparrows are at their feet, hustling for scraps.

The bacon strips are delicious, the fruit sublime. A young woman stands behind Carmichael, waiting to pour juice from a huge pitcher. A demure, innocent woman, who nevertheless reminds Quinlan of Freckles and friend, and their nudeness in a hotel bathroom. Makes him wonder what Weiss is thinking, but Quinlan doesn't look into Weiss's mind.

They are joined by Jack Voss and Esteban Armendariz.

Don't get up, Voss says. He wears starched, pleated khakis and a leather jacket. Polished boots, and by God, a tie.

Make a note, Weiss, Quinlan whispers. When respected gentlemen appear in Mexico, you rise. Quinlan stands, and the others follow his example. As they sit down, three familiar faces watch from the kitchen doorway. They look like the bird boys from the Good Luck ranch, but one is a Niña.

Hey, that's Vicente and Pepe, Quinlan says. And the older one is a young lady. How about the kids joining us, Jack?

Carmichael answers. Those are Armando's cabritos from the Good Luck, and Carmela, daughter of Esteban. And it would just embarrass them.

Jack Voss waggles a finger for the children to join the group. Better get 'em used to impolite company. As the children find chairs around the table, Voss makes a gesture that indicates the entire world outside the confines of the patio and smiles. They may own this place someday.

After breakfast, Weiss and Quinlan amble around the house. Now that they aren't desperate for electricity, every light is on. Someone has a love for food implements. There are ollas and brass pots and pans and skillets holding fresh flowers everywhere. On the entry wall is a vast painting of an outdoor banquet, perhaps with this house in the background. Done in peasant style but sophisticated, it seems to Quinlan.

Good God, says Erwin Baker as he joins the tour. That's a Sequeiros.

On the facing wall is a small portrait, its importance magnified by the presentation of it as the centerpiece of masses of flowers. Weiss looks closely at the portrait. Powerful chin, he says. Piercing eyes. A very strong young woman.

Jack Voss grins as he joins them, and Quinlan understands the grin, if Weiss doesn't. Portrait of a young lady, Voss says. Means more than the big painting.

Very nice, Weiss says. Who is the lady?

Baker peers closely at the small painting. Freida Kahlo?

No. My wife, answers Voss. Done by Freida Kahlo. Younger, by thirty years.

Will we meet the lovely lady?

Not this time. She's in Matamoras, checking some of her hotel properties. She just called me, which reminds me, gents, the phone is now working.

Weiss beats Quinlan to the phone, as usual, and finally gets through to his wife and girls. Waiting, Quinlan can't help but participate as Weiss's call goes along. The girls are fighting, and Vivien is angry. When are the men headed back? A late season hurricane could blow up, or something could happen at the house. Three days, four at the most and we'll be home, Weiss promises. Just ease up, kiss the girls for me and damn, the phone goes dead on Weiss.

No Mae for Quinlan right now. He wanted to thank her for the ring, laugh about the pigeons in the square, tell her he treasured the flowers. Tell her about her chin and eyes, and freckles. And much more. Next Monday. Five days, if this is Sunday.

Instead of talking to Mae, it's time to kill some birds. Quinlan grabs Weiss.

Mata las palomas, Weiss, Quinlan says. We've got to protect our host's crops. And, get some birds for the beach campfire.

The hunters pile into a truck provided by Voss, and once again, Weiss finds himself driving. Morgan is jovial in the front seat, a tea glass in hand, smelling of Canadian Club and lime juice. His knees make it difficult for Weiss to shift gears. There's a shotgun muzzle almost in Quinlan's nose, more shotguns and shell boxes filling the seat. Carmichael and Baker follow in the station wagon, without the boat.

The birds called white wings move in clouds above the grain fields. Setting up at the edge of a field, each shooter has a table and chair, and a handler for mundane chores like providing shells and drinks.

The bird-retrieving boys and the girl of Esteban Armendariz race after downed birds. They come back gory and feather-covered. The young lady brings one live dove to Quinlan and puts it in his hands. There is a drop of blood on its bill, red against the soft gray of the breast. Stroking its beak tenderly, she takes the bird from Quinlan and, headed for the game box, twists off the head.

At lunch, Jack Voss asks the crowd if anyone has an interest in visiting the outskirts of the ranchero. He aims the question at Weiss. Early mañana, Mr. Weiss, or is it now, The Judge? Lee Quinlan says you're the designated driver.

I'd love to drive someone else for a while, Jack.

Lee Quinlan invites himself along.

4

Before daybreak, Quinlan wakes to a thump on the door. Armendariz enters and places a basket with hot bread and fruit on Quinlan's bed. Esteban goes after Weiss, then comes back and re-awakens Quinlan.

I'd like to be wealthy someday, just to have an Esteban Armendariz, Quinlan mumbles as they walk downstairs.

Weiss drives Voss's Suburban for hours. Much of the time they are in four-wheel drive, and often in Grandmaw gear, as Voss calls it. Dead slow, but certain to get over a problem stretch.

Weiss and Quinlan watch the Patrón in action as Voss visits isolated homes. The people of each jacal receive Voss's full attention as they explain their success or failures. Each gets a handshake and a few words of encouragement from the Patrón before they motor on.

The area to the south of the hacienda is green and lush with crops. Mostly corn and other row crops, and an experiment with soybeans, Voss says. One isolated stretch is in sad shape. The crops seem blasted by heat, the rawboned cattle in danger of starvation.

This side of the monte has had bug problems, Voss says.

Insecticides don't work? Quinlan asks for Weiss's benefit, knowing Voss's answer.

Great for the crops. Bad for the people.

Makes them sick?

No. Success makes too many of them unneeded. Speaking of success, Mr. Quinlan. How is that sequel coming along?

Quinlan thinks about the sequel. He says, Dropped a manuscript in a mail slot four days ago, Jack.

Maybe you'd like to work here on the next one, Voss says.

Maybe you'd better read the book. If it ever sees the light of day, you might send one of your guerreros after me.

Oh? Voss says, and Quinlan feels a chill breeze moving down one of Voss's mountainsides. Then, thank God, the Patrón laughs. You couldn't write about me, Quinlan. It would be too damn dull.

I could make up stuff.

That's fine, as long as you skip the facts and tell the truth.

Quinlan, Weiss and Voss are back at the hacienda before noon, where they find that Esteban and Brenner have organized all their gear.

Brenner seems to be in good health. He gives directions as Baker siphons gas from the boat's tank into jerry cans. The cans are handed down from the boat and gas is funneled into the station wagon and crew cab truck.

Hold it there, Baker, says Quinlan. We'll leave some gas in the boat just in case.

The wagon, truck and boat are packed and ready for departure. A group has assembled to bid the Gringoes farewell.

Gerta takes Brenner's hand. He turns to catch the entire group watching. What's the holdup?

Nets and Pangas at El Tigre   Sam Caldwell

X

They must cross El Tigre.

The Rio Grande River is First Pass, Quinlan says. We got across it alive, if not well. Now comes this violent little channel, El Tigre, or call it Second Pass. Farther down the surf will be Third Pass. I don't know about Fourth or Fifth Pass, but maybe we'll find out.

They can cross by a small Mexican ferry, if things work out.

Things didn't work out three years ago, due to the language barrier. This time they have Fred Carmichael to run interference. The ferry is a World War II-vintage barge that accommodates only one vehicle at a time. And the vehicles it was meant to accommodate, Carmichael is told by the surly operator, are official stake bed trucks that haul supplies back and forth between the city of Matamoras and Fifth Pass. The ferry is not here for the recreational use of American fishermen.

Twenty American dollars are donated to the operator's favorite charity. Their new friend says that American fishermen will be his first concern when, God willing, the ferry returns to this side of El Tigre.

Now that passage has been arranged, the group scatters. Weiss, Baker and Quinlan walk through the village that has grown up around the landing. Buildings are cobbled together with driftwood, tarpaper and baling wire. Hovels lean one against another, backing up to ramshackle shops that face the waterway. The shops offer the passerby fruit juices, broiled goat, barbecued chicken, warm Mexican beer and homemade everything imaginable. Every shop features its own radio, tuned to various stations, turned to maximum loudness.

Down the street, the trio looks through an ornately carved doorway. A chapel offers candle-lit sanctuary to huddled forms. One form seems familiar. Baker looks into the darkness. As they continue on, Baker says, Travis was lighting a candle at the altar.

Praying for good fishing, Quinlan says.

Or, to get back alive? Weiss says.

Away from the waterway are small adobe buildings, a better neighborhood. Scrawny chickens wander, hunting, pecking, adding bugs to the El Tigre township food chain. A girl glimpsed through a doorway is changing a one-room home from a bedroom to something else by removing hammocks from the ceiling. On second glance, she is a young woman. Long skirt, a colorful wrap over her shoulders, a mantilla? Seen in side view now, very pregnant. A Señora, not a señorita. The Gringos stop and watch.

A skillet and pot are steaming on a charcoal fire. Ah, Quinlan thinks, she is making a kitchen. The woman raises the skillet lid. Fragrant steam surrounds three hungry Gringos.

2

Rosalia works on the afternoon meal for her family while preparing her business meal. She keeps an eye on the people moving past in the street. At least that part is easy, watching the people, since the doorway is more like an open wall looking into the now-sunny street. Leaning out one side of the opening, she can look all the way to the water, the place where a truck would come up from the landing.

Her neighbor's radio gives her a dancing feeling, and she sways to the music as she adds a touch more water than usual to three masa balls, flattens them into tortillas and lets them sit and dry while she jerks the hammock cords from the ceiling rings and releases the hammocks into a heap, then makes three more tortillas, a bit dryer, because they will all be cooked together. She flattens the masa balls with her palm, pah, pah, pah! and a tequila bottle rolling pin. Straining, Oof! she turns a table onto its legs away from the wall, then rolls the hammocks and pushes them under the table.

This is the way her mother did these things when she was a little girl. Now she is the mama, patting tortillas for her little boy and girl. Waiting for someone very special.

She whispers, Guillermo. Soon there will be another small one for her, and she hopes, for the pride of Guillermo.

Working in this way also allows her to change her point of view often. She doesn't want to miss a thing in the passing traffic. Rosalia is hoping for a visit from her cousin Lupe and an opportunity to hear about the doings of Reynosa, Ciudad Victoria and the road between. And perhaps, see Guillermo driving off the ferry in his big truck. It would be a good day if all those things happened. The Holy Mother has been asked for those things, especially a Guillermo sighting. Asked for more than a sighting; a votive candle was burned at expense beyond reasonable expectation.

She wipes the sweat from her cheeks and leaning away from the tortilla skillet, looks down the street again. Nearby, three Gringos watch her. Big, bleached people of the north, as her sister says. Ugly, compared to Guillermo and Anselmo. They all look the same, she thinks. They wear drab clothes, and stroll along with a haughty attitude, as though the equal of Mexicans.

Rosalia turns the chopped chicken into a small pot that had once been a Buick hubcap, letting the meat scorch and brown for a moment, then drops a palmful of lard mixed with cilantro on top of the chicken. Then a squeeze of lime all over the mixture. Steam and splashes of hot grease leap from the pot. The Gringos, up close, no longer look exactly alike. One is young, tall, fair. Another is thin, freckled, wears glasses, has a pipe in his mouth. La pipa la paz, the Indian peace pipe. Mexicans scorn tobacco pipes. The third Gringo is tall, grizzled, in charge.

The young one and thin one have the transparent eyes that can allow perceptives to look inside the person. She is a perceptive but does not look inside the two men. She looks inside the tall man. He is dark-eyed, grey-whiskered, an older man with gray hair peeking from under his cap. A sad face, though smiling.

The Gringos say something to one another in their guttural language and laugh, and Rosalia blushes, knowing they spoke about her. She can't help thinking of her crazy friend Maria's imitation of a group of Americanos. Gabbledy-gabble, honk honk honk—like geese. Rosalia laughs, looking into the eyes of the tall one with laughter and sadness.

Buenos dias, he says, touching his cap.

Buenos tardes, Rosalia corrects him. She can smell the men, an odor of armpit, tobacco, gasoline mixed with something. It is perfume, or cologne wafting from the freckled man. She wonders if they can smell her private body odors. Rosalia cuts one of the limes she is saving for the prayed-for evening with Guillermo and squeezes it over her arms, down her neck.

Señora, the tall man says, is there a chance of purchasing some of your magnificent food? We are starving, after days of terrible food in Matamoras.

Tch, poor souls, Rosalia says to herself and to the Gringos, because they look like lost souls. She will get the boy to go to the purveyor of chickens later. But the sale to the Gringos means a special wine for the prayed-for arrival of Guillermo. A strong man, Guillermo. At least twice married, but who could say about a man like Guillermo, boss of several work stations. Driver of a GMC truck.

Yes, the food shall be yours in a little moment, sirs, and please be at rest.

There is a swollen jaw on the younger man, gaunt cheeks on the thin man with golden glasses who smells like flowers. Perhaps that one is a man-woman, like Rodrigo, her step-brother. All these things go through Rosalia's mind while she continues her work, and many other thoughts. She plops the tortillas as a stack into her small skillet, then flips the stack, this one up now, that one up again and the center two rotated just so, and finally, all are of the right crispness.

She shakes the pot with the chicken mixture, adds a palmful of salt and ground chile pequins and anchos and a few leaves of cilantro, then squeezes the dregs of the lime onto the chicken. She dumps the pot onto a pile of corn shucks to drain. She loads all six tortillas, then squeezes her last lime over the burritos and hands three to the Gringos.

Twelve pesos. Go with God.

The woman hands them three tortillas piled with food. Weiss tries to pay with a five-dollar bill, but our lady of good food rolls her eyes at the five-dollar bill, goes to a pasteboard box high on a shelf. Weiss insists. Miss, this is so much food, and there's no change coming—tell her, Quinlan. But the woman shifts pots and pans and fakes a search beneath some baskets, then returns counting a wad of Mexican money. Some of the bills look like they have been in the family from Zapata's time.

Uh, no señorita, Weiss says.

Let her do it, Weiss.

The woman finally is satisfied with her accounting, hands the pile of bills and a few Mexican coins to Weiss, then accepts the five dollars.

Quinlan bows, moving between their hostess and Weiss. Bill, just slip her Mexican money into that rolled hammock while I thank her. Gracias, amiga, y que Dios bendiga todo su hijos.

As they move down the street, Baker and Quinlan concentrate on the food.

Weiss, still anguished by intestinal problems says, Were there some vegetables involved?

Mostly chicken parts. Actually, there are some peppers and some cilantro. Delicioso.

Who wants mine? Weiss asks.

Baker and Quinlan share Weiss's food, then look for another vendor. Watermelon and citrus fruits are offered, complete with flies. Baker and Quinlan wave away the flies and eat the fruit. Who wants to live forever?

Ferry time approaches. Back at the waterfront, there are dozens of people jammed into the small launch area. Fishing boats crowd the riverbank, decorated by piles of monofilament net. Over the standard smells of a Mexican marketplace, the aroma of drying fish reigns supreme.

Quinlan purchases cilantro, mangoes, hot peppers of some unknown variety, a large sack of limes. The limes are small, round, rock-hard. Key limes, like Voss's.

Weiss smokes his pipe and watches the commerce of the little port as he and Quinlan sit beside a rack of drying fish. Quinlan eats a mango, drinks warm beer and smokes two Mexican cigarettes, one lighted from the butt of the other.

Weiss shakes his head and frowns. Jesus, Quinlan, just looking at that fruit causes my stomach to churn. And your cigarette smoke smells terrible.

Almost as bad as your Rum and Maple pipe tobacco. If you don't nourish your bad habits every day, you could lose one.

Won't have to smell the pipe much longer. There's not even a can of Prince Albert in Mexico.

They watch as Carmichael, through with his duties as negotiator for passage, shoots pictures. Wearing only cutoff jeans and huaraches, Carmichael looks like an overly tall Mexican native. He sets up a pile of giggling children and shoots photos.

Time to go. Morgan and Quinlan yell for Carmichael to come on or stay behind. A friendly mob of Mexicans accompanies Carmichael to the ferry.

The ferry is maneuvered across El Tigre, slowly, by an ancient craft equipped with a diesel engine. The operator takes the crew cab truck across, then comes back for the station wagon.

The boat is a separate problem, and Morgan has left that problem for last. There are no ramps along the waterway to allow 21-foot boats to be launched. The station wagon and boat won't fit at one time.

Brenner? Morgan yells. No place to launch this bitch. We'll hire a boat watcher and leave it here.

Brenner's face darkens. Our boat goes with us, or I'm headed back.

Quinlan waves a hand at the problem. Nothing to it. We'll take the station wagon across on this shift. Next trip, we'll get together and load the boat. It'll take about a minute.

Morgan frowns at Weiss, standing by for orders in the driver's seat of the wagon. Unlatch the trailer, Weiss. We'll get the wagon across, then figure out the Goddamned boat.

The boat and trailer have to be manhandled down a steep, plank-lined embankment to the water's edge. Every Mexican in Carmichael's friendly group lends a hand, along with the able-bodied Texans.

Brenner is the first to begin pushing the trailer, and the first to stop. He wavers dizzily before he shrugs and walks away. Travis lends a shoulder for a moment, then curses and limps to a seat on the bank. The ankle is worse than Travis has told them. Quinlan makes a mental note to get out his first aid bag, if it's still in the boat, as soon as they get across the channel.

After two false tries and twenty minutes of cursing and sweating, the boat is stowed on board the barge. The ferry pulls away from the landing. Carmichael jumps unsteadily to the top of the boat's center console, blows kisses, shouts Spanish benedictions and throws handfuls of shiny pesos back toward the bank. Travis and Baker jump to grasp his cutoff jeans and steady Carmichael as he dances on the top of the console. The crowd of Mexicans screams arribas, while niños scramble for pesos in the water. The Gringos wave caps and laugh at Carmichael's antics.

Above the din of the crowd and the ferry's engine. Morgan yells, Carmichael, you're a crazy bastard.

What? says Carmichael, cupping his hand around an ear.

Morgan yells, I said, sometimes I'm glad you came along.

Carmichael, the interpreter, yells if I'm the one that goes down, y'all will never make it back.

On the far side of the small bay, they latch the boat to the four-wheel drive truck instead of the station wagon, in case they encounter soft sand. Then, the convoy jolts slowly along a hard-packed roadway, passing through a range of big dunes.

Every man in the party yells as they are finally able to see the Gulf of Mexico. At a distance, it is cobalt blue to the horizon. A light breeze hits them with the whang of dead fish, salt and iodine.

Ah, Neptune's cologne, Quinlan says. They turn south and continue along the beach road for a mile, wanting to get away from the feeling of civilization. The convoy drives off the roadway onto the beach, stopping at the edge of the surf.

This must be Tuesday, Quinlan thinks. Feels like they've been gone a month. Just five days until he sees Mae again. Feels like a year.

Flying High   Ben Kocian

XI

The Mexican surf is emerald green in the near distance, tequila-clear as it rolls up to the wheels of the crew cab truck and hisses to a stop at the station wagon. And begins again.

Carmichael yells, Absolutely fucking perfectamente, Quinlan.

I told you so.

It's about time, says Brenner.

Quinlan clambers to the highest point of the Mako and holds on, shading his eyes, looking across the expanse of the Gulf of Mexico. There's Florida, 741 miles over the horizon, and closer, Cuba.

What do you see? yells Baker.

Birds. Birds everywhere, working the surf as far as the eye can see.

Terns and gulls, says Brenner, searching through his gear.

Quinlan grabs a handy rod and his lure-covered hat. As he splashes past the first surf line, sucking wind as the cold water hits his belly, he is intent on running line through the eyes of the rod. In the calm water of the first deep gut, shivering, he submerges to his neck to get used to the chill of the water, then fumbles a gold spoon onto the line. After he edges past a deep trough, the second surf line stops him. Reeling in slack line, he casts into the swell of a translucent wave. The lure splashes down short, and the reel over-spins into a tangle. The line straightens in front of him, and in the curl of a wave, a silver form moves away. The rod is almost jerked from Quinlan's hand.

Weiss and Morgan are just behind him.

Do you have my rod? Morgan yells at Quinlan.

Graphite rod, with burnt orange wrapping? Quinlan yells back.

Yeah.

Old red Garcia reel? Quinlan holds the bowed rod high as a wave crashes past. He points Morgan's rod at the next wave, allowing the fish to take line directly from the reel.

Would you like to borrow my rod, Quinlan? Use my gun, date my wife?

Get over it, John. Get one of my rods.

The rest of the group is now in the surf around Quinlan. The sun eases down behind them, reflecting light back through the changing thickness of the waves in brilliant patterns of blue and green. Quinlan works the fish, gaining line, rod bent all the way into the butt, winning the battle. Then, the rod has to be held straight toward the fish, line screeching from the reel, as the fish seems to be winning.

Watching anxiously, the men want the fish to be a Moby Dick of a fish, a fish of the magnificence all fishermen desire but mostly, they do not want it to be the inedible jackfish.

Just a big jackfish, Morgan says. To Quinlan's right, Brenner hooks a small redfish, but watching Quinlan's struggle, loses it after a clumsy grab. The afternoon sun spotlights Quinlan's fish for a long moment as it runs along a transparent wave front like an underwater surfer, spots apparent, quicksilver sides glistening. The fish thrashes, leaping free from the breaking wave.

It is a speckled trout.

Now Morgan shouts encouragement. Don't horse 'im. And, If you lose that trout, I'll kill you. Edging closer as Quinlan wins more line, he yells, What did you hook 'im on?

God made sunlight— Quinlan is interrupted by another run of the fish— so trout can see gold spoons flash and shine in the surf. He leans back and feels the electricity of the fish. The rod arcs toward the horizon, then points right and left as the fish fights to go free.

Showboat, yells Morgan. Bring the damn thing in for supper.

The fish is on its side, exhausted, and Quinlan clasps it to his chest. Working with the hook a moment and fighting the surf, Quinlan strains with the weight of the fish and holds it triumphantly above the water.

Brenner stumbles to a position on Quinlan's right, stringer in hand. Quinlan eases the fish down and admires it in the clear water. The fish reflects lavender and silver in the afternoon sun, a jeweled offering from the sea.

Brenner says, Don't— but Quinlan opens his hands and the fish is gone.

As the sun moves toward the dunes, the offshore wind gets stronger. The surf roughens and turns sandy, but the group catches eight good redfish, four speckled trout and a small snook in the remaining light. Two of the reds weigh more than twenty pounds, the maximum measure on Travis's spring-powered scale.

The sun sets behind the dunes. Supper time, Quinlan yells. Come on, Baker. Let's do some cooking. While the men straggle in from the surf, Quinlan and Baker rig Travis's dining fly. Travis limps in with driftwood from the edge of the dunes, and Quinlan starts their first campfire, using the truck and station wagon as windbreaks. Brenner fillets three reds, two of the bigger trout and the snook.

Evening settles over the beach. Baker helps Quinlan grill the fish without waiting for coals. They cover the fillets with sliced tomatoes, purple onions, mushrooms and cilantro. The first fish, scorched and steaming, is torn apart by hands and eaten with limes, salt and appetite as seasoning. For the first time on the trip, there seem to be no doubts about Quinlan's choice of destination.

They cook and eat more fish around the campfire, sloppily, on overloaded paper plates, too hungry to break out tableware. As they finish the last of the fish, they see a stake bed truck rumbling toward them from the south, Third Pass direction. The back of the truck is loaded with stacks of large plastic bags. Mexican workmen perch on the bags or dangle bare legs from the tailgate of the truck and look sullenly at the Gringos. The truck jolts past on the beach roadway.

The driver will know about conditions farther down the beach.

Fred— Quinlan yells, see if you can parleyvoo with el camionero. The truck is now just a dark silhouette, moving past 50 yards away.

Parleyvoo, my ass, Carmichael says. I'll discutir if the hombres don't destruir me. He grabs a bottle of Quinlan's Shiner, runs across the sand and heads off the truck. The Gringos see Carmichael hold up the bottle. The truck rolls to a stop.

The driver steps from the truck and pulls out a knife. But he is grinning, seems friendly. He accepts the bottle from Carmichael with a nod and uses the knife to pop the cap off the beer. The two men squat in the sand. Carmichael accepts the bottle from the driver and drinks from it, then passes it back. The workmen in the back of the truck sit stoically.

At the campfire, Weiss cleans his glasses, tamps his pipe and fumbles for a match, knowing Quinlan will offer him a light with his Zippo. Quinlan lights the pipe, then one of his remaining Camels, instead of an acrid Mexican cigarette. A nearly full moon is rising over the Gulf.

Incredible. This is like being in a three-dimensional mural, Weiss says. .

Carmichael walks to the campfire with the Mexican truck driver. The driver is a paunchy man in dark jeans and plaid shirt. His cuffs are rolled up to show a gold watch and powerful forearms. He has a neat haircut under a rolled-brim straw hat, a jovial face touched by a wispy mustachio and a hint of beard. He wears high-heeled boots with silver points on the toes.

Carmichael waves his hand around the group, then with a flourish says, Gentlemen, I'd like you to make the acquaintance of a very important man, my good friend, Guillermo.

Guillermo stops at the edge of the fire and looks around, diffident in this group of strangers, but arrogant. His eyes say, You men from the north, soft men unaccustomed to hard work and tough duty, are in my territory. This place is not yours to enjoy, if I do not wish it. Guillermo nods at the tall Yanqui who speaks his language. His nod says, My new friend is a good man, careful about the honor of simple men.

Gents, manners are important right now, Carmichael smiles at them, but he speaks with a serious tone. So, be polite.

He bows at Guillermo, then nods at Weiss and says in Spanish, That's Judge William Weiss over there, formerly of el estado del Nuevo York, now a Texan. You two share the same front name, even if it sounds different.

Weiss walks around the fire and grimaces as he feels the powerful grip of the truck driver.

Eh, Guillermo, si? the truck driver grins, wide-spaced teeth shining, the cables in his wrist taut as he grabs William Weiss's hand and pumps once, twice, then claps Weiss roughly on the shoulder. Su es mi tacayo.

You share his given name, therefore are his God-brother, Carmichael interprets. You are now responsible for one another.

Weiss, shaken by the truck driver's friendly blow, smiles back, glad to have the meeting over with.

Carmichael continues the introductions. That's Los Cabrito, Erwin Baker. The hombre with the bandaged leg is Suerte Travis.

The Mexican truck driver stands his ground as each American fisherman steps forward for a handshake.

The ugly man is Malo Dutch—but Dutch Brenner is walking away from the fire and the Mexican visitor.

My turn. Quinlan steps forward, moving around the fire, looking at the group, then at Guillermo, stretching out the moment, covering for Brenner.

Good move, Quinlan. To Guillermo, Carmichael says, I would like for you to make the acquaintance of a very famous and fine writer of stories. Then to all the group, Esta es un hombre especiale, Edward Lee Quinlan.

Quinlan brushes sand from his hand and steps forward. Shake, amigo. Then steps back, gesturing for the next friend of Mexico.

As Quinlan releases the truck driver's hand, Carmichael says quietly, Your turn Dutch, get back here, or I will cut your fucking throat.

Oh, yeah. Delighted to meet you, amigo, Brenner replies, squinting his evil smile at Carmichael. He walks back into the circle and reaches across the fire. Two strong men shake hands through the smoke, a long, powerful squeeze with a bit of push and pull, eyes locked.

Morgan is up, hearing the edge in Carmichael's voice, maybe thinking about Jack Voss's words regarding Mexican hospitality, or remembering a hostile checkpoint. Reaching into the smoke, he rests his hand on the locked hands of Guillermo and Brenner. Brenner winks at Guillermo and relinquishes the truck driver's hand to Morgan.

Carmichael says with a flourish, Guillermo, this is our Grande Jefe, Sargente Juan Morgan.

Eyes smiling, the truck driver grimaces, Aiee! and shakes his hand with snapping fingers, conveying the feeling that his new amigos are powerful men with grips of steel.

Baker. Una mas cerveza for our friend, Carmichael commands. Baker rummages in the slush at the bottom of Brenner's large cooler, and hands a bottle of Shiner to Carmichael. Fred shows the bottle for a moment, then flips it to Guillermo. Their new friend produces his clasp knife and removes the bottle cap. He is comfortable now, a distinguished guest of honor among important people. He sips the beer, rolls his eyes, smacks his lips and squats beside the fire to enjoy the beer.

Quinlan catches Carmichael's eye and points. Behind the truck driver, still silhouetted in the last crimson glow of the west is the truck and the Mexican workers.

Carmichael nods. It would be unseemly to exclude the workers. Para sus hombres si gustan. Nosotros tenemos bebida Coca Cola.

The truck driver considers the idea. He whistles shrilly and yells, Anselmo! He tells Carmichael that nine bottles would be very good, his men are tired from hauling sand for the cement factory and will get no food or drink until they cross El Tigre and reach the village.

Quinlan understands the request for nueves botellas, and immediately gathers a double handful of drink cans and starts for the truck. Anselmo is there at the edge of the firelight, a lean, dark man clad only in long pants. Anselmo takes the drinks.

Quinlan wants to be sure we don't give away any more of his Shiner beer, Carmichael says.

Guillermo waves his bottle at Morgan, sitting in khaki shorts on his cooler. Que te paso a tu pierna, mi amigo?

Carmichael says, John, our new friend is curious about your leg. All eyes turn to the welts that run up Morgan's left leg. Anselmo and Quinlan pause in the exchange of cans, listening.

Tell 'im those are mementos from a disagreement in Southeast Asia.

Nuestro jefe participo en Viet Nam, explains Carmichael.

Guillermo shrugs, sips his beer.

Guerra America en años pasados, si? Carmichael pantomimes shooting. Lots of shooting and dying, he says in English.

Here is a man for whom the words Viet Nam have no meaning. Guillermo does understand shooting, after thinking a moment.

Shooting, Guillermo says solemnly. He stands and chugs his beer, drops the bottle on the sand, then opens his plaid shirt and peering awkwardly down, happy to share an experience with new friends, locates a small dimple beside his navel. Then straining and turning, finds a larger scar on his side. Pulling up his pants leg, he points to another scar below his knee.

Shooting, he says. Face tense, getting into the story, clutching an imaginary pistol, he stalks an invisible foe in the vicinity of Brenner. Carefully edging around the fire and an imaginary corner, he is hit in the belly and staggers, but heroically takes aim at his enemy, is hit again, his leg goes and he sags slowly to the ground, but he is still aiming at Brenner. The truck driver fires, smiles and shrugs. The victor lives.

Brenner looks into the man's eyes and laughs with him. What was the shooting about?

Carmichael repeats the question in Spanish. The entire group, including Anselmo, holding nine cans of cold drinks, waits for the answer.

Guillermo rolls his eyes sadly and says, El corazon de un bella mujer.

Love, Quinlan says.

The truck driver nods at each of his new friends in turn without a formal handshake and returns to his men. The Gringos hear the starter grind, the motor catch and then see the tail lights waver away into the distance.

Most of the fishermen sit at a distance from the fire, lounging on waterproof gear and life preservers borrowed from the boat. Brenner fetches his ice chest from the crew cab truck and moves in between Travis and Baker. Travis has his ankle propped up on Brenner's ice chest, while Baker changes the saltwater-soaked ankle bandage, using Quinlan's first aid kit from the boat.

Looks pretty good, Baker says. Doc Hlavinka knows how to put in a tight stitch.

Looks like a sick football, Brenner says.

Just a few wraps now, and let it breathe tonight, Baker advises. We'll slop on a lot of Quinlan's salve in the morning and wrap it good. Maybe you ought to stay out of the water tomorrow.

Travis winces as he eases a clean sock over the wrapped ankle. Bullshit. A week ago, I had a wet dream about being in this surf. He gestures conspiratorially to Brenner and Baker. Both men put an arm on Travis's back as he relates what seems to be an embarrassing tale for someone. Quinlan overhears something about a Dallas gal in a hotel room. Travis and Baker are laughing at the end, and Brenner's face is contorted as he nods his head and slaps his leg.

Morgan announces that, as the champion fisherman of the day, Lee Quinlan will be roasted immediately after cleanup duties. To avoid the problem of Quinlan getting conceited, Morgan adds, Lee Quinlan will be the cleanup man. There is a round of applause.

Standing, Quinlan nods graciously, accepting the accolades. I thank you for the recognition of my fishing prowess, he begins, but gentlemen, I must say to you now, I owe it all to big Dutch Brenner, who taught me everything I know. Took him about five minutes. Stand up, Dutch, and take a bow. There are whistles and applause from the group as Quinlan grabs Brenner by the collar and pulls him to his feet.

Brenner wavers, shakes his head like a punch-drunk fighter. But Quinlan jars the big man and yells, In recognition of his skills, and for being a rude prick to our new friend Guillermo, I will now be delighted to turn the cleanup chores over to Mr. Brenner.

Brenner walks away.

Later, Weiss nods sleepily as Baker and Quinlan scrub pans. Weiss falls asleep sitting in the sand by the fire, leaning against one of the boat cushions. His glasses dangle from one ear and his pipe is in the sand.

Morgan grins and jerks a thumb at the slack-jawed attorney.

Quinlan eases the glasses from Weiss's ear and picks up the pipe. We'll see that the Judge doesn't lose these. How about a sip of that Canadian Club, Sergeant Morgan?

How about two or three sips, Lieutenant Quinlan?

An hour later, Quinlan wakes Weiss and returns his glasses and a sand-free pipe. They sit around the embers of the campfire for a few minutes. Coyotes. Singing their songs out by the dunes, a thousand yards away.

Real coyotes? Weiss asks.

Enjoying our scraps. Hear that yipe? That was probably some old boss coyote nipping at a pup. Closer at hand, they hear snores from the tent. The rough south wind has stopped. A soft breeze now whispers up the beach from the southeast, off the Gulf of Mexico. Quinlan and Weiss walk thirty paces toward the Mexican surf. They wade into the reflected stars and take a joint piss.

Good distance, Quinlan.

Not bad for an old fart, eh? Add a little salt to this stretch of Gulf.

Incredible stars, Weiss says. There may be stars over Long Island, but you can't see many. Even upstate, and back in Houston, there aren't stars like this. And, diamonds in the water.

The moon edges up from the Gulf, not quite perfect in roundness. The air is cool enough to see a small cloud of moisture as the two fishermen exhale. They both shiver, standing in the mild waves. To the south, a line of clouds is brilliant for an instant with interior lightning.

Too far away to hear the thunder, Quinlan says.

At least, it's too far away now, Weiss replies.

They trudge back through the soft sand, craning their necks to follow the flow of the Milky Way overhead. On the horizon, a sudden flash catches their eyes. A meteor.

Beautiful. Great, Weiss says. He ducks into the opening of the tent and stumbles over Carmichael's outstretched arm, gets a curse, then eases down on his cot. Quinlan locates Brenner's extra sleeping bag, shakes him to stop his snoring, then beds down in a corner.

Marvelous, but I'd rather be at home with my family, Weiss says. My wife and girls smell nice, and they don't snore like a cave full of bears. He struggles into his sleeping bag. Thank God, we'll be home in a few days. Goodnight, Quinlan. Five minutes later, an irritated Brenner shakes Weiss's cot.

We all snore.

Shark-bit specks   Sam Caldwell

XII

Autumn comes along while the men sleep.

Before first light, Quinlan is up and working on breakfast. John Morgan squats near the fire, waiting for a cup of cowboy coffee. He is red-eyed and wobbly, but stiff-backed, a leader who does not sleep while his troops are in need of direction. The troops consist only of Lee Quinlan and Erwin Baker.

Baker shuffles back into the circle of light and drops firewood on one edge of the blaze. Shivering, he holds his hands close to the coals. The knees of his jeans begin to steam. He stands and rotates so his backside can warm.

Quinlan takes the pot from the coals and swirls the contents. The coffee hisses against the sides of the pot. Sounds ready. Smells ready.

Morgan holds his cup toward the pot.

If you can hold the cup still, Quinlan says, I'll pour you some coffee.

Too much Canadian Club last night.

Quinlan grins. How about fetching that bottle and adding a little of the spirits of life to my cup?

That bottle of CC is history.

One night, Quinlan says, God was happy with man, and gave him whiskey.

Weiss and Travis come out of the tent and huddle near the fire.

Quinlan sips his whiskey-less coffee. Of course, man drank all the whiskey, fast as he could. Next day, God gave man hangover.

Travis nods and picks up the thought. One day, God was happy with man, and gave him woman. He winks at Quinlan. Of course, he fucked his brains out. The next day, God was unhappy with man, so he gave woman voice.

Consider the source, Quinlan replies. Luck Travis, that is, not God.

What—not God? Travis says. Not God in the moonlight, in an English garden?

Jesus, Morgan says. As they warm their hands around tin coffee cups, dawn begins. There is little wind. Only an occasional breaker interrupts the quiet. Baker points offshore. The first red sliver of sun edges up from the Gulf, pushing back the darkness. As though to welcome the sun or accompany the view, the shriek of the seabirds begins.

Carmichael tucks his shirt into his pants as he stumbles toward the fire. What's all that tinfoil stuff in the big pot, Quinlan?

Campos, camp. Pan, bread. Pan campos, Mexican biscuit, Quinlan says, to go with our eggs. It's a curse, being a magnificent outdoor chef, forced to cook for unappreciative eaters. The magnificent outdoor chef cracks 14 eggs into a large skillet, an egg in each hand. Breaking two eggs at a time, he gets most of the yolks into the mass unbroken. Good aesthetics. Then, he breaks them all with a fork, and energetic stirring.

I knew the guy had a talent for something, says Travis.

Used to be a short order cook before I found out people would pay good money for stories. Better yet, the chef doesn't do any cleanup. More firewood, Baker, and only hardwood, thanks.

Quinlan stirs the eggs into a golden mass and gently settles the skillet into the coals, next to the pan campos pot. He arranges piles of foil-wrapped lumps on the ashes at one side of the fire and shovels fresh, glowing coals over the foil-covered skillet, and then over the lumps.

Potatoes for lunch? asks Baker.

Morgan's venison tenderloin from the Good Luck? asks Travis.

Better not be my tenderloin, says Morgan.

Quinlan's Surprise. Stay away from those little jewels. Quinlan yells at the nearby tent, Get up, Brenner.

No one stirs in the tent.

Hey, Brenner, time to go fishing.

Brenner slept in the station wagon, Baker says. Said Weiss's snoring was worse than Quinlan's.

John, I want Brenner for cleanup.

Morgan sips carefully from the rim of his cup, inhaling a long breath of hot coffee steam before he gets into the delight of the actual coffee. You like to give all the orders, Mr. Quinlan. I suggest you tell Mr. Brenner to wash up.

You'll do fine on cleanup, Mr. Morgan.

Morgan grimaces as he rises from the sand. There are several audible snaps. Damn knees are getting old. He turns and starts toward Brenner's sleeping place. Over his shoulder, he says, One of us will be back here in a minute for KP. After a few steps, he adds grimly, Might be more than a few minutes.

Hold up, John. I'll discuss this matter with Mr. Brenner, after breakfast.

Ten minutes later, the pan campos is burnt, but the scrambled eggs are okay. Brenner skips breakfast, as usual, and isn't thrilled with the duty, but does an excellent job on cleanup.

Quinlan pitches in. Let's get out of the suds and into the surf, Brenner.

Wednesday morning, Quinlan thinks. Another day here, a day and night driving back to Houston. At noon Sunday he'll be holding Mae's hands, looking at her face, talking to her.

Just your Imagination at the Third Bar Sam Caldwell

XIII

The water is clear after a night of soft southeast winds. Seabirds screech and wheel above the swells, waiting for panicked baitfish. The men wait as well, then move to the bird-designated spot. Under the noisy squads, every cast seems to bring a strike, if not from a speckled trout or redfish, from a 'ladyfish,' the small tarpon of the Gulf. Or less often, from a treasured snook.

Weiss uses a fly rod. He labors against the onshore breeze, keeping a streamer moving through the turbulent water. The others use casting equipment or spinning gear, and some smirk at Weiss as they easily flip spoons and plugs far into the swells. Between Carmichael and Quinlan, Weiss works: double haul, strip, strip, strip—he is on. A solid fish runs for the horizon, getting into the backing before the long rod and heavy drag force the fish close to Weiss's outstretched hand.

Beautiful, he marvels as he leads the large seatrout gingerly in circles, his hand poised to seize the fish behind the gills. Purple and green, a shower of black spots, a yellow mouth, fangs.

Carmichael shoots pictures. Work 'im in—Quinlan, get out of the picture, and Judge, don't frown like that, you'll ruin a cover shot.

I'm working on it. Talk to that big sonuvagun right there, if you want it in.

Weiss reaches for the fish, slowly, then grabs. The fish explodes from Weiss's hand and the rod straightens. Weiss swats the water with his rod.

Wait till you see the expression on your face, Carmichael says, lowering his Nikonos.

Plenty more where that one came from. Weiss starts the lure in, strip, strip, strip, then yells gleefully as the rod again bucks in his hands. There's a powerful surge, Weiss is pulled off balance, then the line goes slack. He reels in a small trout and holds it up, peering at Carmichael through a crescent-shaped bite dripping blood.

Carmichael nods. Mr. and Mrs. Jaws are around. Don't put that bleeding fish on your stringer.

Sharks?

Probably black tips— Carmichael leans back with a solid strike. Whoa, Nelly. A dozen yards away, a form cartwheels from the water. Blacktip on. Probably your bandit.

I don't like sharks, Fred.

You'll love this little guy tonight— but his line goes limp. Too bad. Blacktip fillets make excellent dinner guests. He ties on another gold spoon. Usually, just little sharks come across the bar. If you stick one, pull 'im onto the beach. Quinlan will be on it like a rooster on a June bug.

Weiss eyes the surf around him.

Carmichael grins. Course, a big ol' bull shark may forget the rules and come inside after your fish. Let me show you the quick release hitch, just in case.

The what?

Carmichael rearranges Weiss's stringer on his belt. Feel a little tug on your stringer, whack at the water with your rod. He points at the loose end. If it's a really big tug, and you start for Cuba, just pull this rip cord and make a donation to the shark gods.

Ten four, I got a copy on that last transmission.

Now, go fish, Weiss.

Fish on!

Baker and Brenner drag several ice chests to the surf line, then rig a table with driftwood and a plank. As the fishermen bring in stringers, they convert thrashing red drum and spotted seatrout to quiet pink fillets on ice.

Baker swims out through two sets of breakers to the chest-deep bar. With a full stringer, he swims back in to care for his catch.

Baker, Weiss yells as Baker splashes past. Don't you worry about sharks out there? Baker pauses to catch his breath, and ostentatiously compare his heavy stringer of fish to the few on Weiss's stringer.

Judge, swimming around with sharks is the safest I've been for a week.

I see your point. Weiss shakes his head as he watches Baker start back out to the third bar.

The kid's a strong swimmer, Quinlan says, but things can happen in the surf. He points at Brenner, wearing a flotation vest.

Wears it in the boat, even in the bay when we fish knee-deep. Maybe in his shower. It's just that he sinks like a rock. No, like a boulder.

Morgan and Quinlan are now fishing near Brenner. They both see the quicksilver glint of a fish moving through an approaching wave, see the flash of Brenner's lure near the fish. The spoon disappears in a swirl of foam a dozen feet in front of them. They hear Brenner's surprised yell above the soft thunder of the wave as it breaks at their waists, then hear the drag on Brenner's reel releasing line.

Silver King Surprise Sam Caldwell

A tarpon, the silver king of the Gulf, smashes out of the turquoise curl of an incoming wave. The fish twists wildly in the early morning sun, throwing the lure high above their heads, then splashes back into the Gulf, free. Brenner looks at the lifeless rod in his hands.

Quinlan takes a break at the edge of the surf. He smiles, watching the fishermen from a folding chair, beer cooler close at hand. Travis drags a full stringer ashore and drops the fish at Quinlan's feet. There are shining speckled trout on the stringer, copper-hued redfish and two line-sided snook. Travis laughs, unfastens one end of the stringer and, grunting with the effort, pulls the stringer free. The fish thrash around Quinlan's bare feet.

Quinlan grins up at Travis, squinting against the sun. Are we having fun yet?

Here's my Texas limit, right out of your Coastal Conservation guidebook, Travis replies. He grabs the can of Mexican beer from Quinlan's hand and drains it, then drops the empty container back in his lap. Now, to hell with you and the CCA. I'm goin' back into this surf and get me a Mexican limit.

Luck?

Say, what, Quinlan?

Are you sure you want me to take charge of your fish?

Travis has almost reached the surf. He stops, fetches his own cooler, returns to the pile of fish and carefully ices them down.

Weiss and Carmichael stake their stringers in the first gut where calm water reigns, walk to the beach and relax beside Quinlan.

Cold beer for your chauffeur, Quinlan?

Y una mas por el fotografico, adds Carmichael, getting two beers from Quinlan's battered Igloo. Damn, I got the last Shiner.

What— Quinlan starts to his feet, sees Carmichael's wink at Weiss, relaxes again. Don't mess with me or my Shiner, Fred. He points at a jellyfish that has washed ashore nearby. I'll give you a facial.

Carmichael pats Quinlan's shirt lying in the sand next to the lawn chair and finds a pack of Mexican cigarettes. Quinlan produces the Zippo and lights Carmichael's cigarette. Weiss is smoking the last shreds of his American pipe tobacco. The pipe gurgles and stinks, but Weiss is downwind and catches a lungful of second-hand Mexican cigarette smoke from Quinlan and Carmichael.

You guys are too tough for me. As Weiss moves to the upwind side of the smoking section, he stops, riveted by a scene. Hey, look at this.

Two men push a bicycle down the beach. They are using the bicycle as the carrier for four plastic jugs of pink liquid.

Headed for Fourth Pass, maybe eight miles thataway, says Carmichael. Gonna sell that lemonade to a work crew.

Weiss watches the men, unable to turn away. The Mexicans have no hats, shoes or seemingly any possessions beyond their ragged pants and the bicycle. Quinlan makes a brief mental inventory of assets the Americans have scattered haphazardly across the Mexican beach. There are electronic contraptions perfected by use in outer space and manufactured in Taiwan. Cogs, wheels, cams, valves and bearings machined to precise tolerances in Detroit, optical instruments produced in Berlin and Tokyo, petroleum products from thousands of feet below Arab sands.

At their feet, the force of a powerful wave that began in the Sea of Japan dies out, leaving another jellyfish stranded at Quinlan's toes. The animal pulsates slowly, a translucent grayish mass. He nudges the animal with a big toe.

Hell, we're all just blobs of protein, like this jellyfish, except our species has a little more calcium for stiffening, and a different arrangement of DNA, and some of us may be a bit smarter. Poor little bastard here can't see a beautiful sunset and isn't aware of anything but this instant.

Quinlan glances at the two natives moving away down the beach, takes a gulp of cold beer and inhales a lungful of cigarette smoke. On the other hand, the lucky bastard isn't aware of bad things in the past, or death ahead. He drains the beer, then gingerly picks up the jellyfish with the tips of his fingers. Holding the blob away from his side, Quinlan wades out to the first gut and releases it. The Good Samaritan starts back ashore, but something is wrong. He splashes shoreward, struggling to get out of his jeans, then thrashes the water with his pants, ducks underwater and rubs his waist and legs with sand.

Let this be a lesson, Quinlan yells at Weiss and Carmichael, laughing on the beach. Never help a dumb animal in distress. They always turn on you.

There's some first aid spray in my bag, Weiss says.

Carmichael grabs him by the shirt collar. Think about his last words, Judge.

Weiss picks up his fly rod and follows Carmichael back into the surf.

Thirty minutes later, Quinlan joins them. Catching fish in a clear, soft surf could convince a doubter that God lives and favors mankind.

Surf Helmet   Sam Caldwell

XIII

The fishermen watch as groups of baitfish move past in the crest of every wave, never knowing what their next cast will bring. After his encounter with a tarpon, Brenner nods at Quinlan, then toward the boat. Tarpon stuff. He whistles at Baker and walks slowly out of the surf. At the boat, Brenner gestures to Baker. Get your young carcass up there and look through the forward compartment. I need my offshore box. The big one under the console.

Baker jumps into the boat and locates the tackle box. He balances it on the gunwale of the boat and leaps lightly to the sand below, then has to clamber back up on the wheel well of the trailer to hoist the box off the gunwale. Baker is straining, off balance, falls backward as the box comes down, but Brenner is there with a steadying hand in Baker's back, grabs the handle and swings the box to the sand.

Thanks, Erwin.

Baker watches as Quinlan and Brenner make fishing rigs.

Like this, to start, Quinlan demonstrates, and Baker clumsily follows suit as he bends wire in certain ways. In a few minutes, they have three large plugs. Shading his eyes, Brenner finds Morgan in the skirmish line of fishermen. They return to the surf.

Morgan. Here's something special for our leader.

Helluva rig, says Morgan, frowning at the contraption. Queen Bingo, two big hooks. Three feet of wire. Nothing will hit this mess but a tarpon.

Courtesy of the boat.

Helluva way to haul fishing tackle around.

I owe you one for the boat. Maybe more than one for springing me from the jailhouse. The two men laugh, glad to be together in the Mexican surf, fishing, free.

Yours was made by Quinlan and young Baker, Brenner says. I'm keeping the best one.

Hell, tarpon, come on.

Waves later, Quinlan has just brought in his lure and is ready to cast again. There, he yells. Shadows loom through the incoming wave, large silver forms move along the force of the wave.

Uumph, Morgan grunts, had a hit, but missed him. Then Morgan's line hisses away in a different direction. Twenty yards upcurrent, a fish explodes from the water and crashes back. Morgan's rod jumps and the tip jerks toward the splash. Shaking its head, the tarpon jumps again, cartwheeling, then heads out to sea. Morgan leans back on the rod and, laughing aloud, listens to the taut line hum in the wind. The big silver fish jumps again, farther away. Other fishermen converge in Morgan's area, watching the struggle with his tarpon, as they watched the day before with Quinlan's trout.

Line should be going out or coming in, Quinlan advises. Put some muscle on that fish, John. Morgan maintains pressure on the rod, and gains some precious line back on the reel, pumping and winding, a few turns at a time. The big fish thrashes on the surface, not far away. Then, in a continuous run, it takes all the line on Morgan's reel.

That's it, Morgan gasps, looking at the shining spool of his reel.

The line will give you some stretch, Quinlan yells. Hold on to the rod. He grabs Morgan by the belt. Gimme a hand, Brenner.

Let him go. Brenner pulls Quinlan's hand from Morgan's belt. You could ruin a record if you aid the angler.

There is a moment when Morgan and the tarpon are at an impasse, and Morgan must choose between releasing the rod or being dragged into the Gulf of Mexico. He gains a turn of the reel, and a dozen more. The fish does not jump again. Morgan can crank and pull and work the tarpon in. The men assemble around Morgan as he gradually eases the fish into the shallows.

Good grief, says Weiss, looking at the fish as it wallows in the wash near the beach. How could someone bring in an animal like that with a little rod and reel?

What's the line you have there, Morgan?

Twelve-pound Stren.

Hotdamn almighty, might be a 40-pound tarpon. Worth a mention in the IGFA records, yells Travis.

The fish looks at them, eyes rolling. Aware?

You gonna kill this fish, or look for a record, John?

Last thing I care about is someone saying I caught the fourth largest anything. Out of the way, Quinlan. Morgan pulls a scale from the gill plate of the tarpon. The men help him move the big fish out to the second bar, supporting it all around. The tarpon ceases to be a captive and moves away, then is gone.

They return to the deeper surf, where birds show the way to gamefish. The fishermen drag Texas limits of reds and speckled trout up the slope of the beach. By midmorning, they have filled four coolers with fillets of trout and reds.

One cooler is reserved for a few snook. In Texas, the snook is a fish of rare distinction. To avoid the anonymity of fillets, each snook-catcher scratches an initial in the side of his prize, then they are gutted and gilled and placed carefully on ice.

What the hell is this? Travis asks, holding up a bag full of pink and red intestines.

Guts for Bob, answers Morgan.

Travis looks at Quinlan.

Quinlan shrugs. Old friend with peculiar tastes.

Before noon, the light southeast wind veers to the east and strengthens. The soft curlers become breaking waves that make standing difficult. The fishing slows as the men are forced back to the shallows inside the rough surf line. Across the Gulf from the east, a high overcast moves across the sky, and with the overcast, the wind changes to an angry near-gale that roils the surf. Sand whistles past ankles and covers exposed gear with grit. At mid-afternoon, the Mexican beach seems cold and wintry.

As the stragglers wade ashore, Quinlan yells, The chef needs a volunteer. Don't everyone rush forward at once... thank you, Mr. Baker.

The fishermen convene in the lee of the boat, where Baker and Quinlan rig two tarpaulins as a windbreak. Wind thrashes the tarpaulin flaps, and the men dodge inside, grinning, jostling, squatting in a circle around the coals of Quinlan's cooking fire. One tarpaulin is flung aside by the wind, and the men curse as they wrestle it back into place.

Reminds me of my father, Quinlan says, trying to ranch but losing his land to weather. Quinlan balls his fist and yells at the sky, Go ahead and blow, you old gray-haired son of a bitch.

Travis moves away from Quinlan. Be my luck for a lightning bolt to miss you and get me.

Quinlan pulls the pot of foil-wrapped lumps from the ashes of the campfire. Gather round for lunch. He juggles two onto Travis's camp table and opens them. Each contains a dove with a small piece of bacon tooth-picked to its breast, roasted in its own juices.

First course, two apiece He is jostled by Brenner's greedy hand and one of the birds falls into the sand. Okay, homosexuals served first. Brenner turns away in disgust, but Travis pushes forward.

I'm a lesbian. Does that count?

You get three. Counting the one in the sand. Quinlan hands out the lumps. The men rip open the foil and begin to devour the birds.

Mine are cold, says Carmichael.

Give 'em to me, Travis says. I'll warm 'em for you.

Aw, hell, they're just right, replies Carmichael, his voice muffled by broiled dove breast.

Hey, says Baker, This one has an olive in the breast cavity, and the other has a cheese-stuffed jalapeño.

This one has cocktail onions, says Morgan.

Now, jump on this course, Quinlan says. He takes the cover from a long pan. Garlic spaghetti squash, with Bum Phillips sausage au cilantro. Mr. Baker will now uncork the Texas wine.

No wine glasses? Carmichael says, as Baker passes out tin cups.

No applause? Quinlan says.

Both bottles of the wine are drained, as the squash and sausage disappear.

Quinlan, you should give up writing and take up cheffing, Travis says.

The chef pulls a jar of dill pickles from a sack and puts the jar in the middle of the eaters. The jar is assaulted and emptied immediately in a vinegar-splashing feeding frenzy. Baker and Brenner vie for the last pickle, but Baker's smaller hand wins the trophy. He breaks the pickle in two and eyeing the pieces, hands the lesser portion to Brenner.

Not bad, eh? Quinlan says. How about a round of applause for the gent who provided all these birds? Several fishermen applaud clumsily, but hands and mouths are too full of Jack Voss's provender for a big demonstration.

Quinlan frowns at Brenner. I'll drink a six-pack to Jack Voss, first chance I get. If I ever see another six pack.

Brenner smiles back. In favor of filling coolers with crushed ice from Voss's icemaker, Brenner left most of the beer and other items he deemed nonessential.

Hell, we still have plenty of ice, Morgan says. And, this weather's bound to let up during the night. He holds up a hand for silence. I have some bad news, and some good news.

Let's have the bad news first.

I have a case of Carta Blanca hidden in the truck.

Whistles, shouts, laughter.

Morgan looks around the group. Now for the good news; we're staying over another day.

Hold up, says Bill Weiss. He looks back toward the ferry, the road home, but avoids looking at Morgan. We've got more fish than we can ice down.

Quinlan gives it a moment's thought. They'll be back on Sunday, if late. Or Monday morning, very early, if he can get everyone to share driving all night. No problem, since he'll not be drinking, and can take two shifts. He wipes his hands on his shirttail and grabs Weiss, wrestles him until he is turned in the other direction, facing Third Pass. We may not see fishing like this again for years. What's one more day, either way?

Travis has a bad gash on his leg. And Brenner is hurting.

How about it, Luck? Quinlan says.

Travis shrugs. Ankle's okay.

The men turn to Dutch Brenner. Would his weakness allow him to go on?

I came here to fish Third Pass.

Piss on the fire, Morgan yells, and call up the dogs. We're going across Third Pass.

Hang On! Sam Caldwell

XIV

The convoy is forced to stop before Third Pass. A concrete mass crosses the beach and thrusts into the surf for fifty yards. The men climb out of the wagon and truck. Baker and Carmichael jump down from the boat, followed gingerly by Travis. They look at the barrier. Gusting wind roils the distant waves and sends breakers crashing onto the crumbling cement. The surf thunders up a steep beach, then rolls past an embankment to the wheels of the vehicles.

Quinlan kicks at the cement. The Mexicans have put in a jetty.

Tried to put in a jetty, says Carmichael. They used big bags of concrete without reinforcing, and it went to hell on 'em. Heard about it from our truck-driving compadre.

Quinlan splashes through a slime-covered tidal pool and scrambles up the embankment. Shading his eyes, he looks across the beach and Gulf to the east and back into the bay to the west. Morgan and the rest of the men follow him to the top. At the crest of the man-made hill, the roar of the surf is thunderous.

Caused a helluva channel, as far as I can see back into the bay, Quinlan yells above the noise of the surf. How do we get past this son of a bitch?

Weiss looks angrily at Morgan. There's no point in trying to go any farther.

Tire tracks. Morgan points and they all turn to look. Baker. You want to take that young, healthy body and see how the Mexicans get around this channel? Baker skids down the slope recklessly, in a run for the back of the pass.

Wrong, yells Weiss. Hold up, Baker. Baker stops, knee-deep in the pool, looking up the hill to Morgan for instructions.

Go, Baker, commands Morgan.

Baker shrugs, goes, splashes green water and kicks up sand.

We can ford this ditch somewhere in the truck— Morgan says.

No, Brenner says. He eyes the horizon, across the channel. We can cross Third Pass in the boat.

The men turn and look at the big Mako, trailered behind the crew cab truck.

The bank down there past the jetty looks as good as any boat ramp, Quinlan says.

Water's way up, says Brenner. All we'd have to do is back the trailer down and float the boat off.

You've got a strong tide now, shouts Weiss. Might not have another good tide until tomorrow night. That means we couldn't leave until the next day.

That would give us another day here, yells Morgan.

Right, Quinlan says. We can fish tomorrow and leave Saturday.

Today is Friday, Travis says.

Brenner smiles. You lost a day somewhere, Lee.

That makes everything different, Quinlan yells. It's time to get out of here and go home. He looks around the group. Carmichael?

Carmichael jostles Morgan with a bony elbow as he drags a toe in the sand, scuffing a line between Morgan on one side and Weiss on the other. Carmichael, then Quinlan steps over the line to stand beside Weiss.

Fuck being wet and cold, Travis says as he joins the deserters. I'm staying on this side of the pass beside a warm campfire. Morgan and Brenner are two against four, on the wrong side of a faint line gouged in the sand.

Morgan steps across the line, grabs Weiss by the shirt and throws him down the hill. Weiss rolls down the slope, then splashes into the pool at the bottom. He sits up, coughing green water. His glasses hang from one ear. Quinlan grabs Morgan by his elbow and belt, and leaning hard downslope, tries to throw Morgan after Weiss, but Morgan drops to a knee and grabs Quinlan's shirt collar. Quinlan sees the world whirl.

Weiss starts back up the slope, yelling. By God, he will kill Morgan—but Quinlan takes Weiss down with him. They splash back into the tidal pool.

Quinlan feels vibrations bouncing around the universe of his mind, sits up, choking on the bilious water, hears a voice screaming with rage—his voice—as he follows Weiss back up and over the crest.

He sees a melee down the hill at the edge of the surf. Brenner is fending off Carmichael and Travis while he stands over Morgan, a foot on his neck. Weiss crashes into the big man, followed a moment later by Quinlan.

2

The wind hampers Quinlan's dinner preparations. The gusting wind whips the smoke stream, scattering sparks for yards and forcing the group to move away, out of the firelight, into distant groups.

Dutch Brenner sits morosely on one side of the fire.

John Morgan leans against his cooler on the other side. He grimaces, hawks and spits red into the fire, then fingers his neck.

Erwin Baker jogs back into the new camp Quinlan has established in the lee of the jetty.

He says, There's a wide, shallow crossing about two miles past the dunes, where the Mexican trucks go back and forth. He waded all the way across, at most knee deep, all on hard bottom. When are they headed for Third Pass?

Forget Third Pass, croaks Morgan.

Quinlan pours cooking oil into the frying pan and begins dredging steaks in another big skillet that contains a flour batter.

Travis limps around the group, parceling out the remainder of the Mexican beer. Each man has two cans of Carta Blanca dropped at his feet.

Where's my lime and salt? asks Brenner, glancing up as Travis moves around.

Plenty of salt right out there, Travis nods toward the surf. Carmichael stands and grabs his cans so they will not explode when opened.

No one speaks at supper. Afterward, Brenner moves to help Baker with cleanup chores, but four other men are already busy scrubbing skillets and pots, burning paper plates and replacing gear in ice chests. Brenner accumulates empty beer cans from the sand in a trash bag, then stomps the bag flat for burial.

With the fire down to coals, the men gather upwind for the evening bullshit session.

Quinlan settles the coffee pot on the coals. I don't ever spend time outdoors without thinking about my father. He squints into the coals. And my mother. And an old red dog. And coyotes yelling somewhere over a hill. A sudden blaze pops up in a small area of the coals, then fades away. The surf seems to be easing back, along with the wind. Quinlan leans forward and retrieves the soot-coated coffee pot from the edge of the coals, shakes it next to his ear.

Couple cups left. Anyone? He pours himself a cup of the coffee. I saw an old Ford in Matamoras that brought back trying to get across West Texas to Houston. My Dad got busted up fixing power lines in a sleet storm. Lost everything but me and Momma, and that old car. And Lefty. I guess no one wanted a big old red-colored retriever.

Quinlan eases the pot back into the coals. Will T—my Daddy— had been following a rodeo, picking up a few dollars. He would cripple around and rig the electricity and lights. We ran out of luck near Haskell, or it might have been Tuxedo. It was before Abilene, I know, 'cause he was worried about getting back to the rodeo before it got there. I think he had the idea his bad leg was going to be good enough to make a few rides for Abilene's big money and pick up a stake. Quinlan looks around the group. Times were kind of tough for the Quinlans. Then, Lefty ran off.

He discards the last dregs of his cup onto the coals. Dad looked for that dog for days, while Momma and I stayed around a little creek, catching perch to help out with supper. Camping out, eating wild game around a campfire… haven't been inside since, if I could avoid it.

Baker adds a few chunks of driftwood to the fire. Travis holds out his cup and shakes it. Quinlan grabs the pot with a rag and pours coffee into Travis's cup.

Gracias, Travis says.

Por nada. Must have been tough on Momma and Daddy. The morning after he gave up on Lefty, Will T couldn't get up. His leg was swollen so bad, he couldn't even get into his jeans. Listen— hear those coyotes? The men had been hearing the wild dogs when the wind made a shift from the west, the direction of the sand dunes.

Wouldn't be surprised if there's not some retriever blood in every coyote on this continent. Anyway, Momma rigged a cover over Will T, and put me in the back seat of that old Ford. She pulled out the choke and pumped the gas pedal and got a rolling start off our little hill. By God, if that old clunker hadn't cranked, I think she would have kick-started it. We made it into town. She sold Will T's rifle and traded the spare for a tank of gas. Bought some food and some Paregoric for Will T, and then we went back and parked on that hill for another two days, waiting for Lefty to show up. He did.

By God, says Travis, It must be sack time. The beer is all gone.

Morgan throws his bedroll on a pad in the back of his truck, away from the other men.

Brenner is snoring when the rest of the men are ready to turn in.

Baker has a few blankets and a sheet in one corner.

Quinlan appropriates Brenner's extra sleeping bag, rolls a shirt for a pillow and turns the Coleman lantern to OFF. The gasoline lantern hisses as it runs out of fumes and radiance. Quinlan says to the group, Better than a room at the Shamrock Hilton.

Better than a hooch on a hillside, says Travis.

Listen to that surf out there, says Baker.

They listen to the surf crashing onto their beachfront for a while, and might have been asleep in another few minutes, but Carmichael says, Where does all that energy come from?

Quinlan knows. Energy is love on its way to death.

Baker speaks up. I like that.

Here comes another one... love is the only thing that really exists.

Carmichael speaks from his corner. Must have come as a surprise to those redfish and trout this afternoon, when you cut their guts out and sliced off their sides for supper.

Laughter.

The lantern has run out of fumes and the light winks out. How about this, Quinlan says: There isn't really any death. There's just an absence of love. And those beautiful reds and trout were eaten with love.

Think they loved it as much as we did? asks Travis.

They did — in a cosmic sense.

A pause, then laughter again.

Wait a minute, says Travis. What did you say about energy and death?

I forget.

Baker remembers. Energy is love on its way to death.

That's a contradiction, Travis says. He pulls the sheet over his bare chest and turns away from the conversation.

Quinlan says, Time and tide wait for no man. The surf of a Mexican beach thunders nearby, then recedes and thunders again.

Got the bumper sticker, says Travis.

Tides are part of time.

True, answers Travis.

Time has tides that ebb and flow. We're part of the tides, and part of time.

Gettin' deep.

We move on the edges of a triangle, energy. Always stepping from past to future, each moment a bit nearer the apex of the triangle, yet each moment closer to the center of the circle, time.

The surf crashes nearby on the beach. In the quiet between breakers, they hear coyotes yelping near the dunes.

Brenner is awake now. He says, Must be time for Quinlan's fortune telling.

Quinlan fumbles for a cigarette but gives up on the idea. My best friend, Dutch Brenner, is going to have a sandy sleeping bag tomorrow, he predicts, lying on the sleeping bag. And, he'll make it into 2020, healthy.

Big deal. You couldn't stretch that another thirty years?

'Fraid not. Next person?

Travis asks, Who's gonna win the super bowl?

Sorry, Luck; you'd bet on the other team and lose your life savings. All seventy-eight dollars.

Travis is silent for a while. Then, Missed it by nine dollars.

Weiss says, Will I ever see my girls and my wife again?

Yes. And you'll have another girl, and rule on international matters, Judge.

A round of laughter.

How about me? Travis asks.

A pause. Quinlan says, Sorry, Luck. Next person?

There is an uncomfortable silence, broken by an embarrassed cough from Travis.

Baker listens to the crash of another breaker, then speaks up. I want you to predict something for me, and I don't care how bad it might be.

You'll be shot by a mental patient out on her Christmas leave, late in your second term of office. Silence for a moment, then uncomfortable laughter.

Carmichael says, Gimme a reading, Quinlan.

Bad news, or good news first?

Always bad news first.

Good news first. You'll be caught and shot.

The men feel the jolt of surprise from Carmichael, hear the creak of his cot as he flinches.

Pay no attention, Fred, says Travis. The swami over there always makes predictions on these trips. Hasn't had one come true yet.

Carmichael eases back on his cot. Quinlan, you'd cause a man to beat a blind baby with a brick. Now, tell me the bad news.

They'll torture you. You'll tell them everything they want to know.

Shit. All I know is, fish a rising tide on a full moon, stay home when the south wind blows.

Morgan peers into the tent. What's all this ruckus?

Some of us are getting readings from the Swami, replies Weiss, happy with his reading.

I predict one of us is going to kill the Swami, replies Carmichael, unhappy with his reading.

If you've got a reading left, Swami, let me have it, says Morgan. His voice is hoarse.

You'll kiss your grandchildren.

Hell, I don't even have any children, Morgan replies.

Next year, Quinlan says, you will. Then, Hate—remember all this, Baker—death is the simple fact of hate, and both death and hate are black holes that devour love and truth.

Travis speaks up again. I'm glad ol' Quinlan knows all that stuff about love. When we get back, he can come over to my shop and meet with me and a couple of bankers, and love 'em into lending me a few dollars to keep the place open.

Luck, you're talking about concrete, says Baker. Quinlan is talking about—

Cosmic bullshit.

He's talking about the truth in life. And I want to hear him out.

That goes for me, too, says Carmichael.

Remind me to stomp both your asses when I wake up mañana, says Travis.

How about right now? says Carmichael.

You missed Quinlan's point about love, says Weiss. Now, I want to hear more from Quinlan.

Swami's closed.

3

Hearing Carmichael's cot creak, Baker says softly, Fred?

Erwin?

Sounds like those coyotes are just outside the tent.

Probably a thousand yards away. Workin' on Quinlan's garbage dump.

Where did you learn to speak Spanish?

Mother's milk.

Uh...

His mother was Spanish, says Travis.

Oh. Why do they call you Crazy Fred? Seems like you're the only sane person in the bunch. At times.

Travis answers. Baker, you missed Carmichael in action the other night at the bar, after you were, uh, asked to leave.

Two men cough uncomfortably. Baker laughs.

Travis continues. Anyway, Crazy Fred gave a dance performance worthy of the Bolshoi Ballet, led the Pledge To Allegiance, then threw three Cubans out of the joint. Besides, says Travis, he's always looking to get himself killed.

Horseshit, says Carmichael.

Brenner snores. Carmichael reaches across the tent and jabs Brenner in the ribs.

See what I mean? says Travis.

I'd rather fight the son of a bitch than listen to him snore, says Carmichael.

Brenner sits up, looking around in the darkness of the tent. What?

Time to go to sleep, says Travis.

Can't sleep with you assholes talking all night.

Dutch?

Erwin?

You're about the toughest human being I've ever met.

Travis and Carmichael laugh.

Brenner wheezes softly. Comes from my old man, says Brenner.
Quinlan's story about his father made me think about my old man.
He was tough. And meaner than Carmichael there. But I loved him,
always tried to be just like him. Brenner rubs his whiskers
reflectively, then lies back down. I guess.

Be damned, says Travis quietly.

Luck?

Say what, Erwin?

How come they call you `Luck'?

Travis snorts. I'm like that ad for a lost dog—three legs, blind in
one eye, neutered, answers to the name of Lucky.

Laughter.

That started in Nam. Tet time. A Cong jumped in our hole and
stuck his rifle in my belly— just my luck, there were eight of us—
and pulled the trigger. Click. Jammed round.

Morgan says, Luck took the rifle away from the Cong, and beat
his brains out with the butt.

Silence for a while.

Jesus, says Carmichael.

Amen, says Brenner. I'll be looking for Luck to protect me at
Rick's when we get back.

If I get back, snorts Travis. Quinlan doesn't like my chances for
the future.

Nor mine, says Carmichael.

That's a good sign, croaks Morgan. I've been through a Quinlan
seance before. On a hillside in Nam. Show you how wrong he can be,
he predicted I would die richer than three feet up a bull's ass. As of
last Monday, I'm poor as a skid row wino.

Laughter.

Brenner is snoring again in his corner.

Morgan stumbles to his feet and brushes sand off his jeans. I
want to tell you men, he begins, but the sand from his jeans drifts
across the inside of the tent and there are a couple of curses. He says,
Wind has changed back to southeast and slacked off. Goodnight.

Don't let the bedbugs bite, mumbles Weiss from his cot, as Morgan ducks through the tent flaps, causing another flurry of sand to drift across the inside of the tent.

Did we wake you, Weiss? asks Travis.

Caught the last part of Morgan's story about a Viet Cong and a machine gun. I'll dream all night about guns and blood... makes me wonder what might have happened on this trip if we hadn't had Fred's linguistic talents.

Carmichael's cot creaks as he turns over.

Weiss asks, You still awake, Fred?

No. But I answer in my sleep.

If I ever have any more adventures in faraway places, I want you to be there, interpreting.

Better pick the right languages.

Which ones?

Aw, I speak Italian, it's a lot like Spanish. And pretty good German. Had a Deutschland nanny, back there. Dad was with the foreign service.

Carmichael is quiet for a while. My folks moved around a lot when I was a kid. I mean, around the world a lot. But I was usually in Texas schools till later on. Dad was from Austin, and wanted me to be a Texan, you know?

Yeh, answers Weiss.

Anyway... Pop did some tough duty in a lot of bad places. But he loved the Texas Hill Country. He could have done something else, and we could have been together. You know, milking cows or pumping gas at a service station.

What did he do, Fred?

Translated for a company.

Oh. Runs in the family?

I guess. If Quinlan's prediction comes true, and you wind up in an international judicial role, you might give me a call.

The future international jurist is snoring.

Quinlan, at the edge of sleep, asks, Speak any Russian?

Отьебись.

Which means…?

Go fuck yourself, Quinlan.

4

Quinlan wakes before daybreak. Damn, he feels good. Could it be because he gave his beer ration to Travis last night? Maybe he'll never drink again.

It's Sunday morning. He has to get moving, start people packing. A beautiful woman in Houston is expecting Quinlan to pay a call tomorrow. Lying on the cold, damp sand alone, he fumbles for a cigarette, then remembers that he's quitting. May as well start right now. Carmichael smokes, when someone else provides the cigarettes. Quinlan flips the package of Camels onto Carmichael's cot.

All this way, and no Third Pass. What the hell, he could go across, at least for a fish or two.

Tiptoeing on the gritty canvas floor, he reaches outside the tent, grabs his still-wet jeans from the tent rope and shivers into them. He pulls on the shirt, equally damp and cold, then his sodden desert boots. Damn, he's freezing. Through the tent flap, he can see Travis and Baker huddled at the campfire, feeding driftwood scraps to a small blaze. He kicks his bedroll under Weiss's cot and shakes him gently.

Wake up call, Weiss. Your day to do something for breakfast.

Outside, it's goose-pimple cold. In the east, a rose tint is growing in brightness, pushing the night sky back. In the west, the full moon is turning gold as it nears the horizon, is about to graze the dunes.

Good morning, fishermen. Quinlan hunkers beside the small campfire.

Morning, Lee, says Baker.

Up your ass, Quinlan, says Travis.

Hostile this morning, Luck, Quinlan replies. Somebody piss in your boots?

Quiet. Good people are still sleeping.

Quinlan huddles close to the small blaze. Haven't met any good people lately. Oops—I take that back, kid.

During the night, the wind has softened but is much colder. The three shiver at the fire, rubbing their hands in the warmth.

We'll be out of here by noon, drive in shifts. Home late Sunday, Quinlan says.

Guess we won't see the other side of the pass, Baker says.

I will. Are you wooses gonna hang over this fire, Quinlan asks, or be macho tough guys and come with me across Third Pass?

This comfortable fire is history, says Baker, jumping to his feet and heading for his fishing gear.

If you're waitin' on me, Travis answers, you're walkin' backwards. Travis starts for the equipment area in the blackness between the tent and truck, then curses as the tent shivers and he gasps, Jesus, Mary.

A tent rope victim. Quinlan jumps to help him, but Dutch Brenner is already there, his flashlight showing Travis's white face, grimaced in silent agony. Travis grips above and below his ankle bandage. As they watch, a pink stain on the white bandage spreads and turns crimson.

Fuck Third Pass, Travis says.

I wasn't invited, Brenner says, but I'll take Luck's place.

Ten minutes later, three macho tough guys wade across Third Pass.

Big Surf, Big Sky   Sam Caldwell

XV

As the three fishermen splash out on the far side of Third Pass, wet to the waist and shivering, the great red ball of the sun begins edging out of the Gulf of Mexico. The sun silhouettes thousands of birds, all of them working past breaking surf. The men amble along the edge of the surf, studying conditions and enjoying the beauty of the sunrise, aware that they are consciously delaying the moment when they will again step into the cold water.

Farther down, the surf line moves away from the shore along a vee-shaped bar. Quinlan studies the breakers.

Great birds out there. Good gut in here.

A lagoon, says Brenner. Oughta be jam full of fish. Maybe I'll take that big speck you released, Lee.

Good luck, Dutch.

Inside the protected area will be easy fishing. Out on the bar it will be rough and tumble, with any action past the breakers, under the birds. Someone should try it, though.

Quinlan says, Where's your floatation vest, Dutch?

In your boat.

Your boat.

Okay, our boat. Brenner wades out to his knees in the dark blue water of the lagoon. He begins casting a gold spoon.

Quinlan says, I'm going out on the bar. Wave your hat if you hit the fish inside.

As Quinlan starts past him, Baker says, Hey, Lee?

What?

Got an extra lure?

Quinlan pulls off his surf helmet and chooses a silver spoon. It has a yellow bucktail and is a longtime favorite. As he tosses the lure to Baker, the surf line is shattered by an explosion of panicked baitfish.

Quinlan begins wading out one leg of the vee toward the far breakers but keeps an eye on Brenner and Baker. They move along the shoreline, casting into the calm water. Baker edges out past the shallow ground until he slips into a deep area that must have chilled him past the chest. He scrambles back to thigh-deep water near Brenner.

Quinlan's bar stays knee-deep shallow as he edges along it, although the current is ripping across. Waves break on the Gulf side, and spindrift blows over him. The wind is much cooler than it has been the last few days, is cold on a wet person's clothes. The sun is well up now, has bled from deepest red to orange to yellow, but is yet to provide any warmth. There is more than a hint of autumn in the air.

Casting downwind toward Brenner and Baker, Quinlan gets long distance with little effort. The spoon lands almost where they are fishing, and Brenner yells something. The words are erased by surf noise. Behind them, coming through a narrow passage in the dunes, Quinlan sees the truck of the Mexican jetty-builders. Quinlan can make out Guillermo at the wheel, and a few of his helpers in the back.

Quinlan whistles, points, yells, Hey, there's Guillermo— but Baker has a fish on now, and Brenner is intent on casting near Baker's fish. Quinlan is near the end of the bar, where gamefish seem to be tearing up the water. He feels the tidal rip tug at his pants legs, urging him deeper along the bar, but making it tough to walk.

Esta no problema he mutters.

He edges forward, feels sand moving under his feet, slips down the outside with cascading sand providing lubrication, loses his balance for a moment. The rush of water is now a river, and a step backward turns into a stumble, then a scramble back and up the bar.

Esta problema.

Brenner is stringing a good fish, and Baker has another on. They aren't far away. Quinlan settles his Styrofoam lure helmet firmly and sticks the butt of the rod behind him in his belt. He can't help shuddering as he moves into the cold blue water and begins side-stroking toward shore.

Guillermo steers around the last of the low dunes, the truck whining in low gear, swaying and bouncing. If he misjudges and goes too fast, the GMC could run up a slope before he could veer, and the truck might roll over. Too slow, and the truck would bog down, requiring time and strain from his six men to get the truck underway again. One of the workers clinging to the stakes in back cries out with falsetto concern. Guillermo nurses the truck down the sloping roadway that leads to the surf, bends to the right and heads on toward Fourth Pass. He is intent on double-clutching and changing gears, and might not have noticed the Gringos, but Anselmo points left, across his face, to the surf.

Guillermo stops the truck while it is still on a downgrade, so he will not have to depend on the battery to start the motor. He offers Anselmo a cigarette and waits for a light. They smoke and watch the Gringos for a time before either speaks.

La Laguna del Tombar, Anselmo says, shaking his head. Netting is good there for red drum, especially in the fall, when the big mamas and papas come in from the open Gulf to spawn.

The Lagoon of Drum was the old name. La Laguna del Muerte, Guillermo replies. Bad business for the Yanquis. His cousin Miguel died right there, near the surf line, trying to take too many fish at one set of his net. Since the jetty was built, a bar has sanded out around the deep place. Surf netters wade the bar and place their Braille pole at the tip, then swim the net across and bag it up, and take everything in the lagoon. One good set can win a thousand kilos of fish. But when the tide is so strong, as it has been for days, the lagoon can take the netter, or a fisherman like the Yanqui he is watching now.

Anselmo says, It is not for us to tell those men where they should or should not fish.

Guillermo nods, lets out the clutch and allows the downgrade to start the motor. The Yanquis can afford to come here for the pleasure of taking a few fish with their expensive rods and reels. Mucho trabajo, poco diñero por el Mexicanos, says Guillermo. At the bottom of the slope, he sees that one Yanqui has started to swim across the Laguna toward the others, who are safe in shallow water. Instead of turning right toward Fourth Pass and his day's work, Guillermo veers toward the fishermen.

Erwin Baker sees a swirl a yard behind his lure as he reels in.

Brenner shouts as his rod dips. Another big trout, yells Brenner, others following it in.

Baker casts near Brenner's fish and has an immediate hookup. He works the fish to his side. Avoiding the treble hook, he seizes it firmly behind the gills. He pulls the fish triumphantly from the water, holding it high as Quinlan had held the big speck two days before, wanting to taunt Quinlan for being in the wrong place.

Baker can't see Quinlan. Then he sees him above the easy part of a wave that has crashed across the distant bar and into the protected area where he and Brenner are fishing. Quinlan's head is above the incoming wave for just a moment, crowned by his white, lure-heavy Styrofoam surf helmet. After a dozen strokes, the helmet floats off Quinlan's head. Baker sees it move away on a wave, watches as Quinlan sidestrokes clumsily after the helmet. The helmet is covered with plugs and spoons, Quinlan's entire tackle box. It is his badge of courage, the insignia of an old salt surf fisherman, and Quinlan is trying to get it back.

Dutch.

Say what, Baker?

Quinlan's in trouble.

He's been in trouble as long as I've known him— Brenner looks up from stringing a large trout. Quinlan's stroke is no more than a splash, and his head is high.

We're gonna have to go and help 'im, Baker says.

And drown all three of us, Brenner says. He's got to get back to that shallow bar.

Baker drops the redfish, throws his rod at Brenner and begins pulling his shirt off. Hold my gear.

Brenner catches the rod, scowls at the younger man, starts to say something, but Baker ducks underwater. Shuddering with the sudden cold, Baker pulls at his shoes. He is aware of shifting patterns of unfocused green and yellow, can vaguely make out the dirty white of his shoes as he pulls each one off. He is up again, blowing salt water, hears Brenner shout.

Forget the hat. Go...back...now! Brenner waves both arms like a football referee signaling an infraction downfield.

Baker can feel that Quinlan is ignoring them. Baker squints against the morning sun and blinks away the salt in his eyes, watching Quinlan. The surf seems to be breaking with new energy on Quinlan's offshore bar. An occasional swell now rolls all the way into their lagoon, finds the shallow edge of their shelf, turns into a breaker and crashes into their chests. The two men watch, wanting Quinlan to show them he can make it.

Quinlan disappears behind a swell, then reappears, his strokes slower, more splash than swimming motion. He has turned away from the surf helmet, is headed in their direction.

He should have stripped down, Brenner says. He's got on long pants and those old high-top desert boots.

Baker pushes through a breaking wave. He's not going to make it. He swims in Quinlan's direction, the Australian crawl, head high and breathing on every other stroke. He swims for what seems a long time, feels himself raised on a breaker, looks for Quinlan nearby, he should be right there, but Baker can't see him.

The current.

Baker is near the opening to the Gulf, is moving perceptibly toward the white water at the end of the bar, although he sidestrokes in the opposite direction. The distance to the shoreline seems immense. A few feet from him, floating jauntily, silver and gold spoons glistening, is Quinlan's surf hat.

He hears Brenner yell something. Baker treads water, waits for a high swell. Kicking, he surges up to look. Brenner has Quinlan, is swimming with him, Quinlan's shirt collar in his hands. Atop another wave, Baker sees that they are now close to the area where the surf breaks. Almost safe, but just where you have to fight through the undertow.

Baker is a long way from the breaking surf and safety. Quinlan's hat. Baker paddles to the foam hat, a dozen feet closer toward the open Gulf. He couldn't help Quinlan, but maybe he can save his hat. Or maybe it'll save him. Baker grabs the chinstrap, and imagines handing the hat full of expensive lures to Quinlan back on the beach. They will all have a good laugh, then shuffle around the shallow portion of the inshore bar and get their fishing gear back.

A massive swell rolls over Baker just as he needs a lungful of air, and he has to swim hard, one-handed, the other hand gripping the surf hat. It offers no real flotation, and the lures grab at his wrist, threatening to attach the hat to his arm. Choking on another swell, he knows the hat will drown him. Baker releases the hat and kicks away, feeling hooks scratch and grab at his bare foot, and glancing backward, sees the hat following in his wake. Then the hat is gone, drifting with the current toward the open Gulf.

He feels the point of the sand bar rake past his foot, and he swims hard back the way he came but he is now in the Gulf, the current moving him out faster than he can swim against it. Raised on a wave for a moment, kicking hard and straining, he can see neither Brenner nor Quinlan. But at the edge of the beach, for just a moment, he can see a truck, and men at the edge of the water.

Erwin Baker swims for his life.

Guillermo and Anselmo jump from the truck before it rolls to a halt. The six laborers in the back vault over the sides and all eight Mexicans race to the aid of the Yanquis.

Guillermo wades into the water waist deep, shading his eyes, looking across the lagoon. Out beyond the bar, he sees one man raised on a wave for a moment. The man is swimming, and may God help him, for Guillermo can't get to him.

Near Guillermo, a few meters past the surfline, he sees a hand below the water. He lunges deeper, pushes away from the shallows, swimming like a dog swims. Anselmo grabs his ankle and follows, and the man behind grabs Anselmo's ankle. They form a human chain, with Guillermo at the point.

2

Morgan is chest deep in the surf. He looks back and sees Weiss gesturing from the edge of the beach. Morgan hacks and coughs. He feels the plug hit the tip of his rod and casts the lure again. Far to his right, near the pass, Morgan sees a tall fisherman—Carmichael? supporting someone; Baker. The pair is trying to hurry. Baker stumbles along in a loose-armed shamble, falls, is helped up.

Morgan starts for the beach. He shuffles past the inner bar, feeling the current tugging at his pants legs, then stumbles up the steep shore. Weiss and Travis watch him as he walks up.

What?

Baker says Quinlan and Brenner got in serious trouble, hell, might both be dead.

Might be dead. Where's Baker?

Changing clothes, vomiting, answers Carmichael. Baker said he couldn't see either one above water. He had to swim with the current and get back to shore on this side of the pass.

Baker walks into the group.

Baker, Morgan says. What the fuck happened?

I went after Quinlan, just couldn't get him before the current got me, pushed me into the open Gulf. I did hear Brenner yell that he had him, but I don't know...I couldn't see either one of them, once I got past the bar.

Shit. Brenner sinks even when he's got on a flotation vest, Carmichael says.

None of us took a vest, Baker says. He looks around the group. The truck and driver we met the other night? I saw that truck on the beach, near where we were.

Morgan looks at Quinlan's battered cooler in the shade of the tarp. 'Stolen from E.L. Quinlan' is scrawled on the near side. Brenner's lawn chair is overturned beside the cooler.

The men look at Morgan. He walks to the tarpaulin and jerks it loose from the boat and truck. He yells, Weiss, Travis, break the trailer hitch free. He jumps into the truck bed, and straining with his big cooler, hoists it over the side of the truck and lets it crash to the sand, spilling ice that minutes earlier had been precious to the fishermen. Travis and Weiss are still fumbling with the trailer hitch. Carmichael and Baker are watching.

Move, Godammit. Morgan has formed a vague plan. There will be no time for discussions, and there will be no bullshit democratic voting on the plan. We're going across that goddamn pass and get Quinlan and Brenner, Morgan yells, and then we're going back to Texas.

Baker says, It's no good, John.

Squatting in the back of the truck, Morgan wipes sweat and beach grit from his face. What?

The tide is higher than it was last night. Baker looks at the pass, then back up at Morgan. It's neck deep now. You can't get across in the truck.

The men stop their work and watch Morgan, waiting for a decision.

Morgan looks toward the pass. The pass would now be a channel, with current surging far into the back bay. But open to the Gulf.

He says, Carmichael, Baker—get everything out of the boat.
Morgan jumps and lands heavily in the sand. At the rear of the truck,
he cranks the trailer tongue back down onto the truck hitch. Morgan
surveys the jumbled mess of equipment.

Weiss—lock the front hubs. He climbs into the cab of the truck.
We'll get everything on the way back, he shouts, cranking the motor.

He slams the truck in gear and slues around a half circle until the
truck and boat are headed toward the pass.

Baker, Weiss and Travis scramble into the bed of the truck as
Morgan stomps the accelerator. The rear wheels throw sand on
Carmichael as he sprints, attempting to climb in the back of the
truck. Running just in front of the bow of the boat, his heel hits the
trailer and he stumbles, but Baker grabs Carmichael's wrist and pulls
him sprawling and cursing into the bed of the truck.

Morgan stops just short of the pass. The current is churning now
in the channel, a narrow El Tigre. He scrambles onto the hood, then
to the top of the cab. The beach mirage shimmers and breaks up any
images at a distance, but he can see a truck and many dark objects.
People.

At the base of the jetties, the sand slopes abruptly into the water
of the pass. It seems a ramp made to order if the sand is firm, and if
the trailer doesn't sink as he starts down.

Everyone out, Morgan yells. But the men are already out of the
truck and Carmichael is alone in the boat, holding the controls.

Travis. Plug in the boat?

Travis nods.

Baker. Check the bow latch.

It's loose.

Carmichael yells, Go for it!

Morgan slams the lever of the transfer case into 4WD-LO. Sand
churning under all four wheels, he backs the boat around in a large
circle and down the slope into the water. The boat slides off the
trailer, floating free in the current. In the rear-view mirror, Morgan
sees blue smoke boiling from the stern as Carmichael tries to crank
the motor. The boat turns slowly, moving without power, drifting
inland with the current.

Shit, Carmichael yells. Son of a bitch is out of gas—the motor
starts.

Morgan shifts to low forward and guns the motor, but the truck doesn't move.

No bueno for the boat trailer, Carmichael shouts from the boat. It's going down in the sand.

Morgan leans out of the truck and looks back. Only the tongue and front bunkers of the trailer are above water and soft sand. The rear wheels of the truck begin to disappear as he watches. Break the trailer loose, Morgan yells. We've got to get the truck up.

Weiss jumps to the hitch and works the latch free. Morgan guns the engine and starts up the slope, tires digging, throwing sand as the men push at the truck. He feels the front wheels grab on firmer ground, and the men yell triumphantly. Morgan rolls out of the truck, falling as he lurches down the slope.

The Mako is now under power, and Carmichael turns the boat back upcurrent for the launching spot. Baker jumps onto the bow and pulls Morgan into the boat.

Morgan takes the controls from Carmichael, more forcefully than Carmichael likes, then jerks a thumb at Baker. Out.

I know the way.

Your choice. If this bitch runs out of gas, you'll be swimming again.

Baker points, Go straight out, then cut way around into the lagoon.

Morgan kicks the boat up to full speed, planing in the water along the outer bar, parallel to the waves.

Bend in here, says Baker as they approach a quiet stretch. This is the opening to the lagoon. They can see figures on shore. Morgan runs the boat aground on the shallow bar within a hundred yards of a knot of men.

It is too deep to run through the water, but Morgan, Carmichael and Baker try, clumsily thrashing and falling before they reach the upward slope of the beach. Eight Mexicans stand in a circle. Guillermo motions to the others, and they step away from two men on the sand. Lee Quinlan looks up, but continues a rhythmical pumping, hands crossed on the middle of Brenner's chest.

You might spell me for a while, Baker.

Morgan looks into Guillermo's eyes. Guillermo shakes his head. Morgan pulls Quinlan to his feet and away and says to Baker, You can try it for a few minutes, but we've got to get him out of here.

Quien es? Carmichael says to Guillermo. The truck driver starts an explanation in Spanish.

C'mon, Quinlan, Morgan says gently, looking over his shoulder at the still form on the beach. As Baker pumps on Brenner's chest, Carmichael checks Brenner for signs of life. Watching, Morgan shrugs out of his shirt and wraps it around Quinlan's shoulders. He's dead, Lee.

I know.

He has to be recovered in Texas waters, the Padre Island surf where he got in trouble and died, Morgan says.

We're going to smuggle a dead American through a Mexican checkpoint and past an American customs checkpoint?

Want him to lay around a morgue in Matamoras, maybe us in jail, while the officials look into a murder charge?

Quinlan looks at the body of his friend, then out where the boat is waiting. Brenner's face is bluish, the bruised eyes half closed, mouth set in a slight frown as though he was considering a rebuke or passing judgment on his handlers. Sand fills the corners of his eyes, and every wrinkle of his clothes. Dark sand, coarse.

Padre Island sand is light, fine-grained.

Morgan looks at Quinlan. The sand has to go, Quinlan.

Quinlan nods. Let's get him to the boat.

The three Anglos gather around Brenner and struggle to lift him. Guillermo and Anselmo join them, then the other men help. The cortege stumbles and lurches as they carry the body of the big man waist deep into the surf. Awash in the waves, the Yanquis and Mexicans are able to support Brenner's body with less effort.

Quinlan, Morgan and Baker gently splash water over Brenner's face and clothes, then grimacing and looking away from one another, submerge him until the Mexican sand is gone.

We can leave the boat at El Tigre, get it later, Carmichael says. Guillermo will take care of it for you.

Baker looks up. The trailer, Morgan.

Yeah, Quinlan. The trailer is gone, sank into the muck at the pass when I launched the boat.

Quinlan shrugs.

The group carries Brenner across the bar to the boat. At the stern of the boat, Quinlan flops a rope ladder down and climbs aboard.

On three, he says from above— three! Straining, they lift the big man by gripping shirt and pants, as Quinlan pulls from above. It takes two clumsy attempts to coordinate the lifting with the waves. Brenner's body rolls over the gunwale and thuds into the boat, one arm bent under, legs akimbo.

Carmichael shakes hands with the Mexicans, one by one. Gracias, amigos.

Guillermo hands Morgan a rod and reel, then the Mexicans move toward the beach, looking back as they go. Carmichael, Morgan and Baker push the bow of the boat off the bar, but sand pulls at the mid-section, refusing to release it. They shove on one side of the boat, rolling it until the suction of the sand is defeated and the boat is free, then hold onto the stern as the boat shudders and moves into the deep gut.

The boat is lifted by a wave and floats free.

Quinlan looks down at the three men as they push the Mako into deeper water.

Dutch would have gone this way, Quinlan says, if he had a choice. I mean, outdoors, fishing with friends. He starts the motor. If the main gas tank was still full, we could try a run across the Gulf. It's smooth empty.

The boat is now in chest-deep water. The three men hold onto the side of the boat, arms extended as a small wave raises the boat, their feet pulled off the sand and swept under the boat.

Back it up, Quinlan, Morgan says, and kill the motor.

Hand up his rod, John.

Morgan squints up at Quinlan. The sun is now behind him. Morgan can see only his eyes and a smile. The boat moves deeper, the bow out over the drop off, the motor idling, blue smoke bubbling up from the exhaust. Morgan looks at the rod and reel, a custom job, For Kurt Brenner, Made by E.L. Quinlan lettered on the butt wrap. He tosses up the rod.

This boat is Brenner's, says Quinlan. And mine. He pushes the throttle down. The boat moves away and gains speed as the men drop off. Quinlan roars away into the Gulf.

3

Three Yanquis are driven by Guillermo over the dunes and along the back-country trail until, two miles back on the far side of the inland bay, he can ford at a wide, shallow stretch, then bring them back to the beach. Standing in the back of the truck, elbows on the cab, they can see the boat out past the far surf line.

Travis and Weiss are waiting at the base of the jetties.

What the hell is going on, Morgan? Weiss yells as Morgan, Baker and Carmichael climb down from the truck.

Baker answers. That's Quinlan in the boat. With Brenner's body.

Holy Mary, Mother of God. Travis says. He limps past the first breakers, into the chest-deep trough. The other men follow. What happened, Baker?

Guillermo pulled Quinlan out, and pulled Brenner to the beach. That's all I know.

The boat drifts a thousand yards offshore. It floats high and brightly visible on big waves, then disappears into troughs. Baker looks at Morgan, but Morgan is still silent. Baker says, It looks like Quinlan's fishing.

Carmichael nods in agreement with Baker. I've been watching Quinlan move around the boat, when it was up on a big swell. He got out a couple of rods and rigged some lures and put 'em out. And he put some life preservers around the gunwales. See the orange color?

No, I can't see a damn thing, says Weiss, blowing water from his glasses. Why doesn't he run it in?

Morgan makes eye-shading circles of his hands and strains to watch the boat. He's out of gas, except for a gallon or so. We siphoned it into the truck at Voss's place.

Behind offshore waves, the boat disappears entirely, then flashes white again, riding high on a wave.

I can swim it, Baker says.

Right. We need another dead guy, Morgan says.

Oh, Jesus. Carmichael squints across the water.

What? yells Weiss.

He's pouring gas from one of the cans around the boat.

Baker lunges into a breaking wave and starts swimming.

No! Weiss shouts. Morgan— but Travis has already grabbed a pants leg, and hauls Baker backward through the water. There is a turbulent struggle, until Carmichael and Weiss help Travis hold Erwin Baker underwater, a bit longer than necessary.

4

As Quinlan pours the remaining gasoline around the deck of the Mako, then over the floatation vests on the gunwales, he can see the men on shore and in the surf, watching. His friends will be concerned for him, but that can't be helped. The jerrycan is almost empty. Gently, he pulls the sleeping bag closed round Brenner's face. Surprise, Dutch. After all these years, it isn't you grieving for me.

He latches the teak doorway, checks to be sure the cap of the gas tank is off. He puts the cap on top of the console, next to the depth flasher where they always put it when they fill the tank. Quinlan finds an old towel, far under the recess of the console, a towel last used to handle a violently-thrashing dorado, blood and stink still a piquant reminder of a day offshore. He stuffs the towel in the gas tank opening and drains the last of the gas from the jerrycan onto the towel.

A wick, leading to a fume-filled bomb.

The empty can goes neatly back in the forward storage area, just the way Brenner would want it. Tidy Dutch, orderly, efficient. Like a hand grenade.

What's left? Check the flare gun. In the chamber is the empty hull Quinlan fired at the gate to Voss's Buena Suerta. There are four cartridges on an attached strap. All look new and shiny and waterproof. Shouldn't need but one.

The boat reeks of gasoline, and it is difficult to see and breathe. Quinlan removes the empty hull, drops one of the cartridges in the chamber and snaps the gun shut. No rain for a funeral? The sky features blueness and puffy clouds and a few birds moving toward shore. Terns or gulls, Dutch?

Quinlan recites the Lord's prayer, stumbling over some of the lines, forgetting exactly how they go, and coughs from gasoline fumes to cover up the lapse. He tries to think of something else to say. Quinlan kneels and places Brenner's rod and reel across the body of his friend. Goodbye, Dutch, he whispers. Wish I had a dog for your feet.

Quinlan pulls the red tab on Brenner's life jacket. The jacket puffs up, pushing his elbows away from his sides. Thanks, Dutch. As an afterthought, he mutters, Thank you, God.

Quinlan rolls over the side of the boat as it moves into a trough. He floats away, kicking, being careful to keep the flare gun above the water. Thirty yards away, leaning backward in the vest, he squints and aims the flare pistol at the gasoline-soaked life vests on the gunwale of the boat. As the boat starts up a large wave, with a feeling beyond conscious timing, Quinlan squeezes the trigger.

Watching the boat intently, five men in the surf and eight men on the beach see the flash and arc of the flare an instant before the first bright flame, then have time to wince at the explosion before the impact of the sound reaches them. Stunned, they watch as an orange fireball blossoms skyward, leaving an intense red smear of flame on the water.

Safe Harbor Sam Caldwell

One afternoon

Damn dog. It's one of the phrases Mae says, sometimes in her sleep, but they are Lee's words from a time back. Affectionate words, really.

She is looking at a stray in the center of the lane, a dog reflecting gray in the puddles of a morning drizzle. A dog with no pedigree, besides being Irish, wiry hair in its hungry eyes, a dog with hope, but no expectations. Maybe a distant relative of a long-gone dog of great expectations that owned them for ten years. And is still missed, twenty years later.

Lee guides Mae a few feet out of their way, closer to the dog. The stray watches them approach, its head cocked, stub tail waving just a bit, wondering if there might be a handout on the way from this old couple, or a sudden kick. Seeing no evidence of food for a dog, it drops tail and moves into an alleyway.

Damn dog, Mae says again and watches the dog trot off. The image finds a place somewhere in her mind that still has visions, memories, sounds, and she smiles and squeezes Quinlan's hand.

Thank you, dog, Lee whispers.

Women pass them, going uphill away from the Irish sea, carrying plastic baskets filled with fish. Wearing shoes that are probably recycled plastic. God, what are you doing to fishwives?

At least, the older ones smile the genuine smile. Auntie Mae, good day, and to you, Father Christmas, one says. Wrinkled, black-garbed from toes to crown in memory of losses. She remembers the Boat Yanks from the early days, before their wrinkles and losses.

2

When Lee and Mae were new in the little village, the Boat Yanks had money. And later, notoriety, after a visit from President Erwin Baker. That was a time of many friends, but the friends aged and are gone, and so has the money gone. Other friends look after them now, just as well as when there was money.

Lee guides Mae carefully through the door of a corner shop. The proprietress is busy behind her high counter, but she brightens as

Lee and Mae move toward her. Lee waves. Breakfast won't be needed, thank you Ness. Tell Liam to look under my pillow, there's an early birthday present for his worthless son. And when was your birthday last year? For you, my dear sweet love, a token of my appreciation for having good tits.

The woman laughs. Your ancient Viagra?

A surprise for you both, and to hell with your ugly old husband, who would need a gallon of Viagra to look at a pretty girl. Tell him I said that.

You're a bad man, Mr. Quinlan.

Mae surprises Lee and Ness. She stammers, A good man.

I know Mae. And he never has seen me tits.

Lee turns Mae and guides her toward the door. Goodbye, Ness. Good day to you, sir.

The Boat Yanks, they are still called from many years ago, when the two fell in love with the people and their village, sold the boat and stayed. Some are Kennedys, and a few are Quinlans, but none are theirs. There was a boy back then...

A boy on a bike, an heirloom of a bicycle, wobbled along beside them in one of the upper villages. Lee and Mae were running a lot, enjoying the sea-coast region and becoming part of it, a place as close as you can get to heaven without dying.

The boy tried to keep up with the Boat Yanks, pedaling just right to keep the chain from jumping missing sprockets, laughing with them as they enjoyed his company until sure enough, the chain found a missing gear tooth and wound around the axle, and the boy waved goodbye. Days later, he showed up at their door, lugging the old bicycle. From the Irish Boy's grapevine, he knew Mr. Boat Yank was a softie who had tools, and was a rich Texan, and might work a miracle with junk.

The boy was just one of the reasons they stayed. He will own their town house. Soon. They miss the boy as much as the damn dog. And the boat, and for Lee, the fishing. If you're careful and stay healthy, you have to bury all your friends. And, get too feeble to reel in a good fish.

As Lee and Mae cross the main avenue, their friend Liam joins them. Huge, ancient, nearly Lee's age. He picked Lee up in his arms on the dock a couple of years ago—was it five years? and carried him to a doctor. Lee limped back into Mae's life two months later, and she did not recognize him.

God bless, Auntie Mae, Liam says, taking her hand and falling in with Lee's direction and walking speed. And your health sir?

Not as good as yesterday. Better than tomorrow. And my Godchild?

The old boatman shakes his head.

He's back in it, is he?

Goddamn the English, and the Irish, too.

Lee takes Mae's arm and turns away, toward the sea. Tell the stupid little fucker we love him. Happy birthday, Liam.

Isn't my birthday.

Happy un-birthday, Liam.

At bayside, the breeze is cold and damp, and reeks of old fish and diesel fuel. Lee moves carefully down a slick stairway to the beginning of the beach, helping Mae a step at a time. She holds his good arm and watches her feet. A bad spot on the right requires care, and they take their time. Dockworkers, fishermen, another basket-carrying young fishwife brush past them, not rudely but in the interest of efficient commerce, ignoring irrelevant old people.

On the upper beach, Lee turns east. Gravel-sand gives way to gravel, then to large and small rocks. With the uncertain footing, his left shoulder becomes Mae's entire universe. Her grasp on his arm trembles, and Lee thinks of a time when she was stronger than him.

3

Lee anchors just off the point, and rows them ashore for a run, and a picnic, and just to get away from one another in close quarters. Mae runs with delight that first day, after being cooped up on a boat for weeks. Her ponytail bounces in front of Lee, and she smiles back at him for being slow. With a stitch in his side, he has to stop and sit on a large stone, a resting place that becomes their Celtic bench.

Mae jogs in place, rubbing it in, saying in her best new brogue, Gettin' a wee bit old, sir?

Cute buns, lady.

Smooth talker.

Got anything on for this evening?

Nothing I can't put off.

4

There is a year without Mae, early on, after they sell the boat. She decides she doesn't like the little townhouse, or the neighbors. Nor him. It is a death time, a time with a dried crab for a heart, until the phone rings one night and Mae says, I could use some company.

How about me and a dog?

You'll do. I miss the dog, too.

Damn dog, Lee says now and glances at Mae. Maybe there's a smile… they walk away from the world and have only the Irish Sea to confine them and the wind to push them about. It's a long, exhausting walk for Mae, and for Lee, as well. They reach the headlands where the hills tumble down into the sea, and they can't go further.

Mae stumbles beside him and they almost fall, then sit on their Celtic bench and lean on one another. Lee feels the wind breezing up. He can feel Mae's hair scatter, brushing his cheek. He closes his eyes. Mae is as lovely as the first time he touched her cheek in a Texas bay.

END

26301608R00140

Made in the USA
Lexington, KY
22 December 2018